WHISPERING HILLS OF LOVE

BOOK THREE

AMERICAN WILDERNESS SERIES ROMANCE

DOROTHY WILEY

WHISPERING HILLS OF LOVE

Dorothy Wiley

ISBN: 1497482917

ISBN-13: 978-1497482913

Cover design by Erin Dameron-Hill

Author website www.dorothywiley.com

Whispering Hills of Love is a fictional novel inspired by history, rather than a precise account of history. Except for historically prominent personages, the characters are fictional and names, places, and incidents either are the product of the author's imagination or are used fictitiously. Any resemblance to actual persons, living or dead, events or locales is entirely coincidental. Each book in the series can be read independently.

For the sake of understanding, the author used language for her characters for the modern reader rather than strictly reflecting the far more formal speech and writing patterns of the 18th century.

Other Titles by Dorothy Wiley

WILDERNESS TRAIL OF LOVE

NEW FRONTIER OF LOVE

Dedication

To my dear sister Maria

PROLOGUE

Just east of the Shenandoah Mountains, northern Virginia, Summer 1797

The western horizon claimed the warmth and light of the sun, leaving Kelly to cry sitting in the darkness, her heart and body aching.

After tapping lightly on the door, William carried a bucket full of water inside and sat it on her table. Grey tendrils of steam curled up off the top of the bucket. He had heated the water. Then she watched as he built a fine fire in her small stone hearth.

She gazed at him for a long moment, then closed her eyes tightly, squeezing out even more tears. She thought her tears might fill another bucket. But she couldn't stop weeping, not yet.

He sighed heavily. "Goodnight," he said simply as he turned to leave. "Stephen and I will sleep outdoors. We're used to it anyway. Don't worry, you'll be safe. I swear."

Her bruised arms and a tattered blanket wrapped tightly against her, and still shaking, she could only nod to thank him.

William responded with a warm smile that lit up his kind face.

After he left, she stared at the wooden plank door to her cabin, wanting to remember the warmth in that smile, the only bright spot in the darkest day of her life. He was already her hero. Not just because he and his younger brother Stephen saved her, but his kindness was something she hadn't felt since her mother died. Someone had actually done something for her. For four years, no one had done even the simplest thing for her.

Kelly needed to wash herself thoroughly in the nearby creek. But for now, the bucket of cistern water William had thoughtfully heated would just have to do. She made herself stand and walk to the door, slid the bolt into place, and removed her ripped and bloodied clothing. She picked up a square of cloth and dipped it into the water. Why was the rag shaking? Rubbing some soap across the cloth, she stared at the terrible rope burns on her wrists and winced when the warm water touched her raw skin. Her ankles burned too.

But her torn raw skin did not hurt nearly as much as the terror branded on her heart.

Kelly closed her eyes to the images—like a mirror in her mind—a special mirror capable of replaying the horror in vivid detail over and over. Seeing it all again made her feel depraved and her body soiled with a filth she would never be able to wash away. She squeezed her eyes as tight as she possibly could but it did not break the mirror. She pounded her fists against her forehead, hating the images.

Feeling vulnerable all over again, she tried to swallow the hot emotions tightening her throat. She wanted to scream, scream, scream, but instead choked back a cry.

Unable to continue standing, she sat down. Shame and anger entwined inside her and wove a heavy dark shroud around her heart. The weight of it threatened to stop her heart completely and she lowered her head to the table top.

Wanting to regain control of herself, Kelly took slow deep breaths until she felt calm enough to at least raise her head. She forced herself to think about something else. She would think about William and his brother. Who were they? Why did they come here, to this remote place? William had said something about being a sheriff in pursuit of murderers.

Oh God, those men could have murdered her! But they hadn't. She was alive. And she would go on living despite everything they did to her. Scrubbing her tears from her face with the back of her hand, she stood and made herself finish washing. Maybe concentrating on that would stop the wave of apprehension beginning to sweep through her, threatening to overcome her mind.

She needed to make sense of it all. Ben Jack and Grover were dead. She clung to that thought for a moment. William and Stephen had killed her rapists. Thank you God for sending help. Just a few minutes ago, they had dragged the two bodies outside. Then William explained that he was in pursuit of the two vile men, and tracked them here because they had killed their friend's husband. They heard Kelly's screams, burst in, and shot Ben Jack and Grover, saving her.

But not from rape. They were too late to save her from that.

Finished with washing and dressing, she turned to the pile of her ripped clothing. She owned only two well-worn gowns, but she never wanted to see the clothes those men had touched ever again even if it meant wearing the same dress for the rest of her life. She flung the garments into the hearth fire and then pitched the wash rag in too. As the wet cloth hit the flames, it sizzled and steamed, matching her growing anger.

She watched her dress burn, wishing the fire could burn her

humiliation away too. Through her tears of shame, the fire's flames sparkled and wavered, blurry and softened. When the tears slid down her bruised cheeks, Kelly turned away from the fire and grabbed her Bible, clutching it to her breast as if it were hugging her, not the other way around. Kelly sat and rocked herself until she could finally open the book.

As she did every night, she read by the warm light of the hearth fire. Her mother's dying wish had been that Kelly read her Bible every day and she had faithfully complied. There were only two other books in the cabin anyway. She'd read them so many times the covers fell off, and the pages came loose. Since her mother died, the three precious books and her animals were the only company she had. She often battled a fierce adversary—lonesomeness. Her trapper father left her alone here for weeks at a time. The isolation and solitude sometimes left her feeling empty, like a bowl with nothing in it.

When he was home, her Papa spent most days drunk and occasionally that made him a little violent. She understood the reason for his fury, but she couldn't understand why he took it out on her. Or why he found showing her affection so difficult. Weren't fathers supposed to love their daughters?

Forcing her thoughts back to her reading, she finished the chapter and put the Bible on the small overturned crate next to her bed. The good book had been right there when Ben Jack attacked her, but the sight of it didn't stop him.

Maybe if she had never let them inside the cabin it wouldn't have happened. Her home seemed changed now. She glanced around the room, remembering happier times when both her parents loved her and each other. That was before all the bad came—her mother's sudden death, her father's drunkenness, and now this.

When Ben Jack and Grover showed up yesterday, she'd been feeling especially lonesome. The big empty spot inside of her had spread and loneliness threatened to consume her entirely. Without a friend in the world, she relished the idea of company, even though her common sense told her to beware of the two strangers. She desperately wanted to just talk to somebody. And they had seemed like such nice young men. Never had she been more wrong.

Remembering the deception of the two wolves in sheep's clothing, her lips twisted in anger and her temper flared. She needed to go to bed before the few shreds of control she'd managed to muster disappeared completely. She said her nightly prayer, quoting a verse from Psalms 103 aloud. "The Lord executeth righteousness and judgment for all that are oppressed." God had seen justice done. She should bury her anger. If only she could.

"Thank you Father for delivering me from evil, for sending two good men to replace two evil ones. Forgive me of my sins as I forgive those who have sinned against me," Kelly prayed, struggling not to cry, and to believe what she was saying.

Can I ever forgive? As she asked herself the question, hatred again welled up inside her like an angry bristling animal. She doubted she would ever be able to feel forgiveness. For now, anger claimed her and it felt right. Better than tears. She wanted to hate those men and her lips pressed together as she thought about how she would punish them if they were still alive.

She heard a soft knock on the door. Not up to talking to them, she ignored it. She would let them think she was asleep.

"Kelly," she heard William call in a gentle voice. "We just

wanted to be sure you were okay. If you need us, or anything at all, we'll be right out here. Try to sleep. Tomorrow will be a better day. I promise."

"How can he promise such a thing?" Kelly whispered to herself. She crawled into bed and clutching the ragged old quilt tightly in both hands, drew it up to her chin. Laying on her side, she stared into the dim light of the waning hearth fire. She again pictured the same vivid images—visions of a nightmare. But you can wake from a nightmare. This time, there would be no waking up to find that everything was the same. Now, everything had changed. Forever.

She wanted to dream now—to escape the oppressive memory if only for a little while. But sleep would not come. Her wrists throbbed and the rawness between her legs remained an incessant stinging reminder. And her mind filled with how it felt when he thrust himself into her, tearing her like a rag.

It felt like what it was—a savage violation—of not just her body, but her soul as well.

She sank into pure misery. She could hear the muffled voices of the two brothers talking outdoors, but she still felt horribly alone. Abandoned. Robbed. Cheated. Damaged.

But most of all, shamed.

She gazed out the small window beside her bed, hoping she could still see the pink and red wildflowers that grew beyond her cabin in peaceful clusters among the rolling verdant hills. But they lay hidden in the darkness waiting for a new day.

"He promised tomorrow would be a better day," she whispered to her beloved hills.

And somehow, she knew he spoke the truth.

CHAPTER 1

Boonesborough, Kentucky, Fall 1797

William Wyllie scanned the fort's largest room once more hoping to set his eyes on Kelly. He was certain she would come. The crowded noisy room, constructed of sturdy pine logs, contained Boonesborough's leading citizens, including its Mayor, director of the land office, members of the militia, Judge Webb, and Kentucky's most famous son Daniel Boone. A number of people stood gathered around Colonel Boone, including William's oldest brother Sam and their adopted Scots brother Bear—by far the largest man in the room.

William's eyes halted, but his heartbeat quickened, when he finally spotted Kelly. She stood frozen in the doorway for a moment, the bright sun behind her outlining her shapely silhouette. Radiant and smiling tentatively, she walked in with stiff dignity, escorted by her employer. William's eyes weren't the only ones taking notice. He saw many of the men in attendance glance toward Kelly—her beauty turning heads all over the room.

The temptation to race over to her before some other man did flew into his head, but he held himself back. He had forced himself to take this one slowly and he would continue to do so. At least until he knew for a certainty that Kelly was prepared for a man's attentions.

Admittedly, he often behaved impulsively—and sometimes he even acted in a ready, fire, aim manner. And he never did anything slowly, especially when it came to relationships with females. He often found himself enamored with a woman on the spur-of-the-moment and then, just as spontaneously, he would become besotted with another. With few exceptions, he found most women charming and many downright bewitching.

But none of them compared favorably to Kelly. This was far too important to rush. He needed to treat Kelly carefully. He had to give her ample time to heal and become the woman he knew she was. In the meantime, he would be certain no one else hurt her ever again.

For weeks, he had left her alone, giving her mind time to mend itself. But with each day that passed, he found that simple task more burdensome. From time to time, he would see her in town for a moment or two and have a chance to exchange a few words. He had savored every minute with her, but those moments were rare and they left him wanting more.

What he wanted to do was wrap his arms around her. To protect her forever. To cover those soft pink lips with his—to cherish her in a way he had never felt toward any woman ever before. He wanted to treat her gently, to show her that what happens between a man and a woman should be soft and tender. And passionate.

Was she ready yet?

He observed her for a few moments before approaching her. She stood off by herself, almost in the corner of the room, twisting her hands and shifting her slight weight from side to side. Her big eyes, so blue they appeared violet, darted from person to person around the room and then widened when she caught sight of him.

Mister Wolfe had told William recently that Kelly worried him because she showed signs of fretfulness and seemed to be growing increasingly ill at ease. Wolfe was hoping that William could help him figure out what might be wrong. William had not revealed the probable reason for her nervousness. Nor would he, ever.

Unable to hold himself back any longer, he swiftly crossed the crowded room to make his way to her. "Thank you for coming to my swearing in ceremony, Kelly," he said when he reached her. He put his hand on her shoulder in a possessive gesture, and let it rest there a moment.

"Mister Wolfe gave me the afternoon off. He knows how close I am to your family," Kelly said, a slight tremor in her voice, "and he escorted me here." Her eyes darted around the room. "There he is over there." She pointed to the portly balding fellow, a land speculator and one of Boonesborough's wealthiest and most respected citizens. William knew him well.

As she pointed, William noticed her hand trembling ever so slightly. He had never seen that before.

"Then I must thank him for that kindness later," he said. "And I hope you will join me afterwards for the cake and coffee social. I'm supposed to meet even more of Boonesborough's fine citizenry. I'll never remember all their names."

"Of course. It's not every day that a man is officially sworn in as the sheriff of a town. Even though you've been serving as sheriff for these past few weeks, this is quite an honor William."

"I am honored. I just hope I'll be able to live up to everyone's expectations, especially those of Judge Webb," he said, raising his brows.

Kelly grinned slightly and it delighted William's heart. He wished he could see her smile more often. It felt like warm sunshine on his face.

"The Judge undoubtedly thinks a lot of you since he appointed you acting sheriff until you could be elected. When you defended your brothers against those vile murderers, you must have impressed him."

"Still, I want to prove he made the right decision," William said. In the short time he'd been in Kentucky, he'd grown fond of the gruff old Judge.

"Judge Webb does seem to be a bit rough around the edges," she said, as they both looked around the room for the Judge. "There he is, standing next to Daniel Boone."

The judge wore a serious grey wool jacket and grey breeches. Both matched his smoke colored hair and his peppery no-nonsense personality. Colonel Boone, however, wore a longer black jacket, accented with gold buttons down the lapels, with black leather breeches and tall boots made of a fine leather. His dark clothing set off his snow white hair.

"Let's join them," William suggested. "Judge Webb, Colonel Boone, may I introduce our family friend Kelly McGuffin."

After both men greeted Kelly, William asked Judge Webb, "What's the secret to how a good sheriff enforces the law."

"It's no damn mystery. It's this," Webb said, holding up his pistol, as if the answer were obvious.

William laughed and said, "And I guess if I asked how a good judge dispenses the law you'd hold up a sturdy noose."

Webb turned to Boone. "The boy learns fast."

"Boonesborough just needs someone with enough strength of character to enforce the laws and take care of the legal business of the county," Boone said, "especially since the militia are often away on duty."

"It's grand that you were able to return to Boonesborough for William's swearing in," Kelly told the Colonel.

"It is my distinct pleasure to be here," Boone said, a glint in his blue-grey eyes, "and it is especially pleasant to be in the presence of such a beautiful woman."

A shadow of alarm touched Kelly's face. She glanced up at Boone, her eyes widened in surprise and her cheeks and neck flushed, then she transferred her gaze to William. His eyes clung to hers, analyzing her reaction. She said nothing and lowered her thick lashes. Clearly, she wasn't used to receiving compliments or attention.

"If you two will excuse us," Webb said, "the Colonel and I have some matters to discuss."

"Certainly," William said, taking Kelly by the arm and guiding her toward a quiet corner of the packed room. William suddenly wondered if living in Boonesborough among so many people might be contributing to her unease. "How are you enjoying living in Boonesborough and your new position as tutor to Mister Wolfe's children?" he asked.

She chewed on her lower lip before answering. "Truthfully, being in town makes me feel like I'm trapped in a cage built for men. I miss the freedom I felt living in the woods. But I love working as a tutor. The children are quite a handful, especially those mischievous boys. But the housekeeper, Mrs. Hudson, keeps them in line. Mister Wolfe's mother Patricia helps a lot too. She's exceedingly strict. I adore the twin girls. I've become like a big sister to all of them. They're like the brothers and sisters I never had."

Well, although she hadn't grown used to living in town, at least the children weren't making her nervous. "What about Mister Wolfe? Is he the gentleman we all thought he would be?"

"Definitely so. He's been quite proper and cordial and he pays me well. And his home is extremely nice, luxurious compared to my old dugout cabin. I have my own bedroom and a four-poster bed upstairs next to the room his girls sleep in."

It appeared all was well with her employment. That left only one thing that he could think of. A far more difficult issue to deal with.

She took a few steps back toward a wall where it was quieter. "Since you asked me a question, may I ask one of you?"

"Of course." William said, trying to flash his most charming smile.

Kelly stared up at him and took a quick breath before she said, "Before your brother Stephen and Jane moved with their girls to live near Sam and Catherine, I asked Jane to tell me what you were like in New Hampshire. She said you've always been a bit of a ladies man. I didn't really know what that meant, but she explained it to me. She said you like many ladies, but never just one. Do..." She hesitated and then swallowed before she asked, "Do you think you could ever like just one?"

So she'd been talking to Jane. He wondered what else Jane had told Kelly. He wasn't exactly proud of the life he'd led back home in New Hampshire. He'd been sheriff of their small town near

Durham. But if he were honest, he took the job for exactly the reasons his brothers all suspected—to keep himself out of jail. Intolerant of ill-bred men and also inclined to drink and gamble on occasion, he'd too often found himself embroiled in a brawl. Ironically, he loved studying law too and someday he would become a lawyer. Until then though, he would serve as sheriff again.

He narrowed his eyes as he regarded Kelly, the most intriguing young woman he had ever known. She tended to be straightforward, often too honest, perhaps because of her youth, or perhaps because of her isolated life away from polite society. But he liked that about her. You always knew what she was thinking. The women in New Hampshire operated under a tight code of conduct that left little room for openness and frankness. Kelly was a refreshing and sometimes startling change.

"Could I ever be happy with just one woman?" Stalling, he repeated her question, both amazed and amused by it. But he could see the earnestness in her face and decided to give her as much of an answer as he was willing to give her now. "I haven't exactly been seeking female companionship lately. I've been so tied up with my new duties and trying to help my brothers get settled. Maybe someday I'll settle down."

A soft curve touched her pink lips before her eyes abruptly glimmered with slight moisture. Then she turned toward the spellbound group still listening to the stories of Daniel Boone. She dabbed a knuckle under her eyes as she ambled closer to where Boone stood.

He folded his arms across his chest, thinking. Were those sudden tears another sign of her concealed trauma? Or was there another reason? And why did she ask that question? Women were always challenging to figure out and Kelly was even more so.

William knew he should return to socializing and make his way around the room again, but he couldn't take his eyes off Kelly, mesmerized by her gentle beauty. Her long blonde hair, the silvery gold color of fresh corn, hung down her back nearly to her waist. Her body was seductive and slender, but not as thin as it was, after living half-starved for so many years. And her pretty face, somehow both wholesome and sensuous, appealed to him as no other woman ever had.

Today she wore the beautiful emerald green gown she'd dressed in when Sam and Catherine married, and a short wool cape. She looked every bit a genteel lady. Catherine, a follower of fashion, had designed and ordered the garment and had it made especially for Kelly. William noticed that the gown showed off her smooth bosom and graceful long arms and the gown's belt accentuated her trim waist.

She was positively perfect.

The first time he'd seen her face though, had been far different. Her tear-reddened eyes, swollen and beaten; her lips cracked and dripping blood; and her ravaged appearance all broke his heart.

Yet, he'd been captivated by her from that very first moment. Despite her injuries, her face remained full of strength and her proud eyes shined with her bold spirit. He saw something special about her beneath her battered and ragged appearance that day. And on their trip here, she never cried or pitied herself and her steadfast courage never faltered. Once she arrived in Boonesborough, determined and indomitable, she set about building a new life for herself.

William was glad he had shot the man who climbed off Kelly's naked body and Stephen had shot the man's brother. They'd caught the despicable men in the act of making a woman bleed as she can only bleed once. And the two rapists had also murdered Mister Adams, Catherine's late husband, just a couple of days before. That's when William's family had first met Catherine. Driving the team of horses pulling her wagon on the Wilderness Trail, they'd found her alone, and looking for help. Sam had ridden up to her first and, after learning of the murder of Catherine's husband, invited her to continue on to Kentucky with all of them. Soon afterwards, William and Stephen set out to track the men who had killed her husband.

The tracks led them directly to Kelly's cabin, hidden in the foothills of the Shenandoah mountains of northern Virginia. The two men, needing to hideout, had convinced her to let them stay a few days in exchange for a horse. Unfortunately, Kelly had agreed.

After finding them violating Kelly, he and Stephen had shot the two murderers, William refused to leave Kelly alone in the desolate hills. For her protection, he brought her back with them to join their family's group, just as Catherine had. From there, she traveled on to Boonesborough with all of them, ready to begin a new life here away from her abusive father.

In this room full of burly, frontier-hardened men and a few stout women, Kelly appeared delicate and vulnerable. But, he believed a woman of great strength lay hidden beneath her slight frame and gentle nature. He vowed to help that woman emerge.

He strolled over and stood next to her. He soon sensed her uneasiness as she listened to Colonel Boone, now in his sixties. Her body became rigid and she clasped her hands tightly in front of her. What was making her so uncomfortable? He had hoped she could relax and enjoy herself.

It was a rare treat to see Kentucky through the aging blue eyes of one of the state's first and bravest citizens. And Boone did not disappoint.

"It took a certain kind of man, and woman, to make it over the Wilderness Trail back then," Boone said. "To quote my friend, that courageous and enterprising founder of our precious Kentucky, Judge Richard Henderson, 'Some to endure, and many to fail, some to conquer, and many to quail, toiling over the Wilderness Trail.'"

William and his brothers had neither quailed nor failed on their long and difficult journey to Kentucky. And he wasn't about to fail as sheriff either.

Remembering that Colonel Boone had been a sheriff once himself, William believed he could learn from those with more time than he in the difficult position. Back home, he had been the sheriff in Barrington for nearly three years, but still had a lot to learn. Things were different here on the frontier. Here, unwritten laws were as important, or more so, than written law. Pioneers were bound by accepted customs and respected rules that centered on hospitality, fair play, loyalty, and respect for the land. And here, a handshake was more binding than a contract.

"Do you have any advice for a brand new sheriff?" William called out, with only a trace of humor in his voice.

Boone chuckled and his clear eyes sparkled. "Good judgment is born of experience, and a lot of that comes from bad judgment."

Everyone laughed including William.

Boone continued, "But if you want a little advice from an old man about life in general, I'd say this. Live a bold and honorable life, then when you think back on it when you're my age, you'll enjoy it all over again."

"Here. Here!" called Judge Webb.

William wondered what kind of life he would lead. He would always be honorable. That's the kind of man he was. Would he be bold too?

Bold enough to love just one woman? Bold enough to marry her?

As he observed Kelly's beautiful profile out of the corner of his eye, he thought that just might be possible.

CHAPTER 2

Kelly felt far more secure when William was nearby. She'd seen firsthand that he possessed great strength beneath his gentleness. Yet, inexplicably, standing near him now also made her uneasy. Keenly aware of his scrutiny, she tried to keep her features deceptively composed. Though he didn't say anything, his countenance spoke for him. His face revealed true concern.

And something more.

She looked up at William, wondering just what she'd seen. An easy smile played on his handsome face, totally disarming her. She thought him easily the most good-looking and well-dressed man in the room, and it gladdened her heart to have him stand next to her. Although he always wore stylish new clothes, he was never especially particular about how he wore them. His cravat, tied at his neck, hung too loosely when compared to the other men in the room. Two waistcoat buttons were still free of their buttonholes and the back of his blue coat suffered from a sprinkling of horse hairs.

She started to reach up and tidy him and then abruptly stilled her hand, unable to touch his person. But she wanted to. Didn't she? She was puzzled and more than a little nervous. What was happening to her? This was William—her hero from the moment he stormed into her cabin. He was the one who had saved her and then looked after her. Before he came into her life, no one ever cared whether she was hungry or lonely.

Later he'd become her closest friend too.

But William had many friends. When they had first arrived in Boonesborough, he seemed to readily make friends even out of perfect strangers. His warm quick smile, dazzling against his tanned skin, endeared everyone he met. And his honest manner made men trust him.

The most handsome of the four brothers, his bright sea blue eyes always seemed to twinkle. Their sparkle reflected his natural ability to entertain others with humor or music. He wore his wavy hair shorter than most men and it was blond, like hers, only a shade or two darker. His well-muscled body moved with an easy grace and a sense of authority. He stood out among other men like a bright vein of gold.

Surprisingly, despite his good looks, he had never married. But she'd seen several unmarried ladies in Boonesborough glancing his way more than a time or two. She couldn't blame them. She turned and glanced up at William. He stood taller than all the other men in the room except his oldest brother Sam and their half-bother Bear. But those two were both giants among men.

Smart, shrewd, and brave, the town nearly unanimously elected William sheriff after he succeeded in revealing the unruly buffalo hunters for the murdering outlaws and traitors they were. An outlet for his tendency to take up for the wronged or the weak, the duties of sheriff seemed to suit him perfectly.

She considered him for a moment then, confused, frowned in bafflement. Never had her emotions been so perplexing. She tried to mull through the haze of her feelings and desires. His nearness to her made her feel strange, but good at the same time. Her mind told her to beware. He was a man after all. But her body was telling her something else entirely. Excitement seemed to make her heart race and a brief shiver rippled through her. She looked at him again. The tremor inside her turned into something far stronger. Just as she was about to figure out what she was feeling, Mister Wolfe strode up beside her.

"Will you be ready to go in a few minutes, Miss Kelly?" Wolfe quietly asked her. "Unfortunately, I need to return to some pressing work matters."

"Certainly, Mister Wolfe," Kelly said. "Just let me say hello to Bear and Captain Sam and bid William goodbye. We've all been occupied with listening to Daniel Boone and I've hardly had a moment to speak with them."

"Of course, take your time," Wolfe responded. "I wanted more coffee and another piece of that apple cake anyway."

She watched him waddle off and wondered if that would be his second or third piece of cake.

She and William ambled over toward Captain Sam and Bear and the two joined them at once.

"I need to leave soon, but I wanted to say hello to both of you before I left. How are Catherine and Little John?" she asked Sam. She looked up to Sam like a big brother and she was happy for him when he'd married Catherine and finally had a chance for real happiness.

"Very well. At the moment, they are enjoying their visit with Stephen, Jane, and their girls. Jane is getting close to her time, and wanted Catherine there for the birth."

"Is Jane still convinced it's going to be a boy?" Kelly asked.

"Aye, she is," Bear answered. "When we left, she was makin' a wee shirt for the lad, no bigger than me hand."

Kelly chuckled. "She must be expecting a big fellow then if the shirt's as big as your hand Bear."

"If he's anything like the other men in our family, he'll be a big boy," Sam said proudly.

"Please tell Catherine and Jane how much I miss both of them," she said. "I hope to be able to visit your new home and see Cumberland Falls someday."

Fond of both women, Kelly genuinely wished Catherine and Jane were still in Boonesborough so she could talk to them about what was happening to her. Whatever it was, it grew worse by the day. She couldn't quite put her finger on what, but something was making her more and more anxious. She just didn't feel like herself. Never one to be easily frightened or fearful, she admitted that lately frightening dreams tormented her sleep and sometimes she felt afraid for no good reason.

"We will look forward to the day you visit us," Sam said.

"Mister Wolfe tells me you are well suited for carin' for his wee children," Bear said, his voice loud even though the gentle giant tried to speak quietly.

"Did he? I am enjoying them, that is once I got used to the constant ruckus. It is quite different than my lonely cabin in the hills." At the mention of her cabin, she caught herself rubbing her wrists again.

"I can only imagine," Sam said, shaking his head.

"I should be going. Please ask Catherine and Jane to write to me because I'll continue to miss all of you. At least I still have William here in Boonesborough, but I haven't seen much of him," she said, looking up at William.

"My list of duties is long and the day is short," William replied. "But, I promise I'll try to be more sociable in the future." He winked at her and gave her another one of his heart-warming grins.

Kelly's heart instantly flittered inside her, but she had little time to enjoy the startling new sensation.

Boone strolled up and joined them. "William, now that you are officially installed as sheriff, do you have a home here?"

"No, Sir," William answered. "I'm afraid my family obligations and duties have kept me from building one and Boonesborough's one inn has remained full with a waiting list since the day of our arrival."

"Where are you staying now?" Boone asked.

"I'm still camping by the river, just west of town, where my entire family camped until they all moved away," he said with a sideways glance and a half-grin at Sam and Bear.

"That won't do much longer with winter just a few weeks off," Sam said, ignoring William's good-humored jab.

"The Kentucky River is getting a bit chilly for bathing," William admitted. "And I sometimes wonder if I can drink enough coffee in the mornings to warm up."

"I have a solution for you," Boone said. "As you know, I am only here in Boonesborough for this ceremony and to attend to some other business matters. I've lost most of my property in Kentucky because of tax laws and disputed land claims. I'll be heading back home soon and then leaving Kentucky for good. My son Daniel Morgan is presently in the Missouri River region of Spanish Louisiana, where he's looking over the land for possible settlement. He met with Don Trudeau, the Lieutenant Governor of the Spanish Territory, and took out a land grant for himself. Trudeau sent an invitation for me to come to settle in Missouri too. I plan to accept his invitation. It's getting too crowded here in Kentucky. But I still have firm legal claim to a cabin and a few acres nestled in a place near here called Whispering Hills. It's about two miles to the northwest and you are welcome to it. At my age, I doubt I will ever need it again. You'd be safe from natives there. They're my blood brothers now and know the cabin is mine, so they leave it alone."

"Your generosity, Sir, is overwhelming. But I must insist on paying you something for it," William protested.

"You can," Boone answered. "And I don't ask this lightly. You can take care of Boonesborough for me. My family's blood, including my dear son and brother's, and the blood of many close friends spilled into Kentucky's soil to claim this spot in the wilderness. It needs a young man of your high character to look out for it. No man in the wrong can stand up against a man defending what's right. Especially a man that won't give up. I think you're the man for the job."

Kelly glanced up, watching William in profile. His strong jaw tightened before he pulled in a deep breath and stood just a little taller.

William had to clear his throat before he could speak. "You honor me, Sir," he replied, with his eyes fixed on Boone. "I pray for the wisdom that comes from God and not from me."

"Everyone," Boone called in a booming voice, "I want you all to know that I hereby place my trust in Sheriff William Wyllie to care for Boonesborough's future. May it always shine brightly under his care. But when she faces the trouble the future always seems to hold, I know he will lead you wisely. As a symbol of my faith in him, I am giving him my land and cabin at Whispering Hills."

The room exploded with the sound of clapping hands and eager cheers.

"And I thank you Colonel Boone. Kentucky claims you among its noblest names. And will forever more," William declared, turning everyone's attention away from himself.

Again, the room erupted in celebration.

Kelly noticed Sam and Bear smiling broadly, their chests swelling, full of pride for their brother and seeming to appreciate the praise and trust Boone had just bestowed on William.

She was proud of William too and a swell of affection filled her. She wanted to give him a hug or at least shake his hand. If only she could. Would she appear too forward? Her stomach fluttered as she decided to reach for his hand.

Without warning, her confidence quaked. Her mind suddenly congested with swirling doubts and churning fears. She quickly pulled back her hand and clutched her skirt tightly with damp fingers. She felt almost sick. A wretchedness filled her that sapped every good feeling she had.

Against her will, she gave in to the tension that had been building since she arrived. Half of her wanted to stay, but the other half demanded that she get away from here. She didn't even know why. But for some reason, she was suddenly frightened—her heart afraid. The harder she tried to deny the feeling, the stronger it grew. She became instantly alert, fully aware of the crowded room, and she wanted nothing more than to get out of there. Jittery and ill at ease, she glanced over her shoulder.

"Excuse me a moment, gentlemen," she muttered uneasily and turned away.

Searching the room, she felt momentary panic until she finally spotted Wolfe, finishing up his cake. She hastened over to him and said she was going outside to wait for him. Even she could hear the nervousness in her voice.

Wolfe nodded and she spun on her heal and fled through the door, gasping in the fresh clean air. Eyes closed, she took several steadying breaths before looking up to locate Wolfe's carriage.

She was losing control and that made her even more uneasy. She hoped William hadn't noticed her hasty departure. And she worried that she had offended his brothers or Colonel Boone by not saying a final goodbye. The thought tore at her insides as she paced up and down in front of her employer's carriage team, trying to catch her breath, and probably making the horses nervous too.

Should she go back inside? Her thoughts scampered around in her head as she tried to compose herself. She would have to do a better job of guarding her emotions or people would start to question her mental stability.

When Wolfe arrived, the concerned look on his face told her the questioning had already started.

As he drove his carriage home, his expression sullen, an uncomfortable silence lay between them.

CHAPTER 3

As soon as the carriage came to a stop in front of Oxmoor House, Kelly jumped off, clutching her cape. Wolfe was from one of the aristocratic families of Virginia, and his home was one of the largest in Boonesborough.

She smelled the smoke rising from the chimney and glanced up to see a pale grey trail climbing into the now cloudy sky. Oxmoor House contained five rooms and a central hall, in which a prettily carved walnut stairway led to the two attic rooms above, one of which was hers.

Not waiting for Mister Wolfe, she bounded up the steps, entered the hall, and after hanging her cape, stood for a moment, listening for the children. She could hear them in the kitchen and started through the parlor toward them. As she passed a gleaming dining table, the crystal oil lamp positioned in the center caught her eye. She stopped and ran her finger across the lamp's carved glistening surface. The home contained so many pretty things and Kelly was still in awe of the luxury found here. Undoubtedly, Mrs. Wolfe, who did not survive the birth of her last child just five years ago, selected most of these beautiful things. Sometimes Kelly felt guilty being in her home, as though her presence was in some way stealing away the life Mrs. Wolfe should have led here.

She noticed a lovely needlepoint pillow, resting in an upholstered chair. She read the words so obviously stitched with love into the fabric. 'Bright be thy path sweet babe.' Kelly suddenly found herself near tears at the simple beauty of a mother's wish for her child.

Instead of joining the children, Wolfe's mother Patricia, and their energetic housekeeper Mrs. Hudson, in the kitchen, Kelly spun around and hurried up the stairs to her room, shutting and locking the door behind her. Now the tears came. Again. She wiped them away, only to have them instantly replaced by more. What was making her so sad? Did the words on the pillow make her miss her mother? Yes, yes, that was it. Her own mother had died five years ago and she not only lost her mother, but her closest friend. Her only friend. Now, William was her only friend.

As much as she missed her mother, it wasn't that.

Whatever it was, it was eating away at her, little by little. Soon there would be little left of her.

Nervously, she bit her lip. Maybe it was all her fault. Did she cause those men to rape her? Was it the way she dressed? Her clothes had been too tight that day, but that was because she hadn't had a new dress in five years, since before her mother died. Even though she was slim, she had filled out between fourteen and eighteen. It wasn't her fault that the dress could no longer hide that she had turned into a woman.

Or maybe those men realized just how lonely she was. Maybe she gave them the impression that she needed attention and affection. But that wasn't affection. Far from it. She curled her fist into a tight ball and pulsed it against her lips. If only she'd been strong enough to fight them. She hadn't been.

"Kelly, dear, are you all right? Come down and join us for some tea and cookies," Patricia called from behind the door.

"No, thank you. I have just had refreshments at Sheriff Wyllie's swearing in ceremony. I'll be down momentarily," Kelly answered, trying to make her voice sound as normal as possible.

"No need, dear. My son and I are taking the children to buy new shoes. Every one of them is wearing shoes too tight. We will see you later this evening. Mrs. Hudson is coming with us. Goodbye."

Kelly heard the click of Mrs. Wolfe's heels as she descended the wooden stairs.

Kelly sat down on her soft feather bed, running her fingers across the smooth surface of her bed covering. She was living in luxury she had never known before. She should be happy.

But she wasn't.

She brought her hand up to her mouth, while the fingers of her other hand slowly encircled her wrist and shame encircled her heart. The weight of it sapped her energy, leaving her feeling leaden and weary. Her eyelids closed as she laid back on her bed. She would sleep for just a little while…

Her struggles only seemed to arouse Ben Jack more. Kelly shrieked and writhed beneath the man's crushing weight. His pounding thrusts against the resistance of her maidenhead became rapid and relentless. He shoved his hips still harder, his breaths hot against her face.

Futilely, she tugged against the taut ropes that tied her hands and feet to her small bed.

It wouldn't take much more and then he would have her virginity.

It wasn't supposed to happen like this.

Kelly screamed louder and then louder still, her voice scraping against her raw tightened throat. She twisted her body away from Ben Jack. He was heavy and his bulk pinned her against her tattered blanket. She had to get away. Frustration swept over her and she flung her head from side to side. But it only allowed her hot tears to wet the feather pillow. Hoping to stop him, she pleaded, "No, please, no."

"Yes," Ben Jack avowed.

Her agony swelled beyond tears and anger trumped her fear. She tried to bite his face, but Ben Jack pulled away with a smirk before her teeth could connect with his skin. Her throat ached with defeat.

He placed his palms against the bed on either side of her head, propping his body up above her like a beast about to devour prey. He leered at her exposed breasts as they rose and fell under her labored breathing.

"No, no, stop!" she yelled, even knowing that her pleas were useless.

Ben Jack's brother Grover put one hand over her mouth, smothering her screams. It didn't matter. Only God could hear her in these lonely hills.

God please help me!

Breathing through her nose, she panted rapid breaths against his dirty hand and shuddered as Grover's other hand roughly mauled one of her breasts. It was the first time a man's hand had touched her breast. It was the first time for all of it.

"You next little brother," Ben Jack said, his breathing hard. "Almost, almost…"

Kelly sobbed, feeling a deep, unaccustomed pain, as her body and heart ripped apart. Her eyes flew open and she howled in impotent anger, impaled by the man's spear, as he shoved deeper into her.

"No!"

Kelly sat straight up in the bed, breathing hard, her lashes wet with tears, still caught between the dream's terror and coming awake. It was only a bad dream.

Yet it wasn't. It happened.

After shaking more hands than William thought a town the size of Boonesborough could contain, he finally allowed himself to leave the fort. Mounting his dappled grey stallion, he had a sudden urge to see Kelly again. The short time they spent together earlier had just stoked his desire to be with her all the more. Sam had a long list of supplies he had to buy and Bear was doing the same for Stephen and Jane. They would both be tied up until later this evening.

Perhaps, since Wolfe had given her the afternoon off, she would have some time to visit with him. Giving Smoke a nudge with his heels, he set off at a trot for Wolfe's home on the other side of town. Greeting the passing horseback men, families in covered wagons, and others driving wagons loaded with skins, lumber, and crops, he found himself tipping his tricorne so many times his elbow was beginning to tire. Becoming sheriff had certainly increased his familiarity with the townspeople.

He was confused about what was happening to Kelly. He grew

more attracted to her by the day, but she seemed to be withdrawing from him in equal measure. More often than not, she was lively, but today she acted more reserved, not nearly as spirited as she normally was. And she also appeared wary, as though she were worried about something. Although she was still just as beautiful as ever, her disposition had changed. The Kelly that had joined his family's group just a few months earlier had been much more comfortable around people. She had never been edgy and uneasy.

He decided to just ask her what was bothering her. No doubt, it was some woman's thing, and he would do his best to understand. Or maybe she just needed to talk to someone. Her life had changed dramatically over the last few months. Perhaps she was finding it difficult to adjust.

Within a few minutes, a dog barked at him as he tied his stallion outside Oxmoor House under a large elm and took the steps up to the porch two at a time. He knocked hard three times, but heard nothing, except the rhythmic panting of the dog, now sprawled out under the front steps. Strange, perhaps the entire family went back to town.

"Kelly!" William called. She had said her bedroom was upstairs, so he took a step back and glanced up. "Kelly," he called again.

This time the window curtains parted and she peeked down.

He soon heard her footsteps coming down a staircase and the door opening.

"What are you doing here William?" she asked. "Mister Wolfe has left with his mother and children to do some shopping." Her hair a little disarrayed and her eyes puffy, she looked like she had just woken from a nap.

William hesitated. Should he tell her the truth? How would she react to the truth? "I…I…well I'm not here to see Mister Wolfe. I just thought that since you had the afternoon off you might come take a look at the cabin Colonel Boone gave me," he finally managed to say.

Kelly stared at him with wide eyes and her mouth hanging slightly open.

It made him want to kiss her and kiss her deeply. "Boone gave me the deed and directions to find it. It's not far. It's a lovely afternoon and I thought you might enjoy the scenery and seeing the old cabin of Boonesborough's most famous citizen."

Kelly's face suddenly brightened. "You know, that does sound like a splendid idea. Will you saddle my mare while I change into my riding clothes and boots? Then I'll pack up a small meal for us."

At the mention of her changing her clothes, William had to fight to keep his imagination from running wild. "I would be delighted to mount your saddle," he said. His eyes widened and his cheeks became warm. With extreme embarrassment, he quickly corrected himself. "I mean saddle your mount."

Thankfully, Kelly appeared not to have noticed his ridiculous blunder and just said, "Thank you," before she turned toward the stairs.

"Bring your cloak. These October evenings can get chilly," he called after her before he closed the door. His cheeks still burned with humiliation. He would have to be more careful and keep his thoughts where they belonged.

He pivoted smartly and headed for the barn behind the house. He knew her horse Ginger well. The beautiful sorrel mare, which had belonged to Sam's wife Catherine before she gave it to Kelly, stood in a pen with her head hanging over a grey wooden fence.

"Hello beautiful!" William said, offering his hand to Ginger to smell.

As he saddled the handsome mare, William thought about Kelly's reaction to his invitation. Her sad eyes had immediately brightened and he could hear eagerness in her voice. Perhaps she shared similar feelings for him as he did for her. He hoped she did.

Kelly soon came bouncing out the home's back door. "I left a note for Mrs. Wolfe, so they won't be worried about me."

"Remember when you left a note for your father—the day you left your cabin and came with us?" he asked as he took the sack of food from her.

"I'll never forget that day," Kelly said, wistfully.

"I'm surprised he has never shown up here in Boonesborough and come after you," William said.

"I'm not. He cared little for me."

William started to help Kelly mount her mare and as he put his hand against her to support her back, he felt her muscles tense beneath her riding habit. With a jerk, she quickly hauled herself into the saddle.

He threw his leg over the saddle and urged Smoke toward the road. Heading away from town, he soon took a trail heading northwest with Kelly riding close beside him. She had learned to ride well on their journey here, often opting to ride horseback instead of in Catherine's wagon. He could tell she enjoyed riding as much as he did and she appeared far more comfortable now than she had at the social earlier that day.

They passed tall stands of loblolly pines and hardwoods shedding their leaves with each rustle of the breeze. The forest glowed with colors of every shade in God's fall palette, including the lively yellow of the beech trees and the crimson red leaves of the maple.

This would be his first winter in Kentucky, but he was sure it would be relatively mild compared to the harsh winters of his native New Hampshire. He would not miss those winds whipping off the White Mountains.

"It's beautiful here, don't you think?" he asked Kelly.

"These woods are lovely. But they are also deep and hide dark things," Kelly said, looking around warily.

That didn't sound at all like the Kelly he knew.

"Sometimes, there's beauty in the darkness too," he said, smiling at her.

CHAPTER 4

In less than thirty minutes, they neared the area Boone had described as Whispering Hills. Rolling tree-covered hills rose on either side of a small valley speckled with a smattering of limestone boulders and rocky outcrops. A small stream flowed through the bottom of the ravine.

"Why do you suppose it's called Whispering Hills?" Kelly asked.

"I asked Boone that very question," Williams answered, "he said that the wind that echoes through this canyon whispers some of the most beautiful melodies and wisest words you will ever hear."

"I'm anxious to hear it," Kelly said, sounding almost excited.

"There it is!" William called out, pointing to the cabin on the top of the next rise.

"What a beautiful spot!" Kelly declared. "Your new home."

"I guess it will be," William said, letting the idea soak in for a moment. "It's time for me to drop anchor somewhere."

"Let's go explore," Kelly said, her face pink with eagerness and their ride. She urged Ginger to gallop toward the cabin and the mare dashed off.

As they rode, William's heart raced with excitement. He didn't know if chasing Kelly up the hill or arriving at his new home for the first time caused the thrill he felt. Either way, it felt good.

They tied Smoke and Ginger and dismounted, taking in the building and surrounding area.

The one and a half story cabin was larger than William expected. Logs ten to fifteen feet long, some of them split, formed the outside walls. William could see small portals for guns on both sides of the front. He peered around a corner and noticed a port-hole on the side as well. The roof was composed of shingles nicely laid on. Tall Sycamores on either side shaded the cabin from the sun. Scanning the area in front of the cabin, he could see a fresh water spring at the bottom of the rise. "It's much nicer than I had imagined," William said.

"It's grand. Look, there's an apple orchard," Kelly said, pointing to a stand of trees laden with apples nearby. "And there's a smokehouse. We had one at my old cabin until it burned down."

"Shall we take a looksee inside?"

Kelly nodded and he opened the heavy door for her. As she passed, William caught a whiff of her scent. He closed his eyes for a second, breathing in the delicious fragrance. She smelled like vanilla. And maybe roses? He couldn't be sure, but the delicate scent made his mouth water and his pulse quicken.

The door was made of broad, heavy, roughly dressed timber puncheons, with one face finished flat and pinned with a two inch pins. The back of the door held a strong bar, so that it could not easily be forced open.

The logs inside the house were hewn down inside and appeared to be tight to the weather. William was surprised to find that it had a planed oak floor. "Colonel Boone clearly had help building a home this snug and some of the men possessed excellent carpentry skills. And that's a well-made stone chimney too, no doubt built by a mason."

"It is a fine home," Kelly agreed.

"I can't believe my good fortune. I think I'm going to be very happy here." He wanted to say we, instead of I, and that surprised him.

"I do hope you are, William."

He stared into her soft violet eyes, framed by long straight strands of blonde locks. The ride here made wisps of hair encircle her head like a golden mist. She appeared more waiflike than ever before.

How he wanted to reach out to her, to kiss her tempting mouth. To show her what a kiss should feel like—tender and meaningful. But if he did, would he frighten her? Maybe for good. Considering what she'd been through, and her current nervousness, it was a real possibility.

He couldn't risk it—not yet.

Kelly rambled around the inside of the cabin picking things up and then setting them down again. She wanted to memorize the cabin's interior so she could clearly picture William in it later. She knew she would lay awake at night imagining him in his new home.

The first thing she noticed was the quilt covered wooden bed. The short bed posters were plain and their dark stain stood out against the dusty wooden floor. At least the flooring wasn't made of packed dirt, as so many were in Boonesborough. A couple of wooden buckets hung to the left of the door and an assortment of pans hung on the wall. A cobweb-covered butter churn hid in the corner along with a rolling pin for pie crust. Both looked like they had gone unused for some time. Two pewter candle holders sat on the hearth's mantle, which was made of a large thick slice of cedar. A good-size wood plank table accompanied by three chairs occupied the center of the large room and another oblong table, with several bowls of different sizes, stood against the wall. Narrow wooden stairs led to what must be a small room for sleeping upstairs.

Yes, William would be happy here. But would he want a wife to join him? Surely, he would. Someone more beautiful than her. She was just as plain as her plain life. He would also need a wife with enough genteel breeding to be an asset to his career. After he became a lawyer, he would eventually become a judge or maybe serve as a legislator in the General Assembly in Frankfort. With William's looks and genial personality, he could have his choice of any of the unwed ladies of Boonesborough. Or all of Kentucky for that matter. Maybe even one of Boone's daughters.

She peered up at him. His eyes instantly locked on hers. They were kind, probing eyes that saw right into her soul. But this time, there was something more there. Something she had not seen before. His eyes seemed to reveal a deeper part of him. Or was he seeing a deeper part of her?

"Kelly," he started and took a step toward her.

She quickly glanced away, her chest tightening with both longing and unease. How could she want to be near him and yet not want to be at the same time? She put a knuckle in her mouth and before she could stop herself, started chewing on it. "I must be hungry," she said to cover herself. "Perhaps it's time to eat the food we brought. I'll need to get back soon, before I'm missed."

William inhaled a breath and then let it out slowly. He hated the idea of taking her back and longed to spend more time alone with her here, but she was right. If they were gone too long, especially after dark, it might harm her reputation. "Yes, I suppose you're right. It will be getting dark soon and I want to get you safely back before the sun fully sets. And I promised Sam and Bear that I would meet them back at my camp. I guess this will be my last night there."

"Your family experienced tragedy while all of us camped there, but we also enjoyed some good times too. Especially Sam and Catherine's wedding. That was the happiest day." Her eyes were misty and wistful.

"That was a night to remember," he agreed, choosing to focus on the joyful event instead of the tragic. "They made a handsome couple. I'm sure those two enjoyed an entertaining and enjoyable honeymoon." He jauntily cocked his head to one side, grinning a bit wickedly at her.

Kelly quickly bent her head and grew quiet. She studied her hands and then ran her fingers across her wrists.

William remembered how her struggles against the ropes, binding her to her bed as she was raped, tore the skin from her thin wrists, leaving them with bleeding deep scrapes. The sight had sickened him.

Something clicked in his mind. That's why she's rubbing her wrists. The thought barely passed through his mind before another followed. Equally disturbing. He couldn't deny the evidence any longer. Time was not easing the pain of her ordeal. It was making it worse. Her misery was growing so acute it had become physical.

He watched, feeling helpless, as she swallowed what must be despair and sat down, her shoulders slumped forward. Torment was eating at her from the inside.

His heart broke for her.

How desperately he wanted to reach out to her, hold her close, and let her cling to him. But he couldn't risk scaring her away. He wanted to help. But he also knew that first she had to help herself. She needed to figure out for herself what was happening to her. How could he make her see that without scaring her further?

"Kelly, I have an idea. Why don't we both agree to something? Let's make this first visit to my cabin special. This will be where and when your healing begins," William said softly. "I know the trauma you suffered is beyond my understanding, and that you are still distressed. But I also know I can help you help yourself heal."

"Heal?"

"When people are hurt, whether it be of the body or the mind, their pain has to heal. Even Sam, as strong as he is, had to heal from the terrible things he experienced during the Revolution. I believe there are two kinds of pain—the kind that makes you stronger and the kind that makes you weaker. You've carried pain around inside of you ever since your attack. And with each day, the weight of that pain is getting heavier, gradually making you weaker. You can't let what happened define who you are."

"I have," she admitted.

"When something bad happens to us, we have two choices. We

can let it break us. Or we can let it strengthen us. I truly believe you can get stronger—by letting go of that burden. Inside you is an exceedingly strong woman. I know it. I saw it on your face and in your eyes the day of your attack."

"If that's true, why am I getting worse with each day instead of better."

"You will have to really think about exactly what's causing you to feel so anxious now. Be honest with yourself. Sometimes the hardest person to be honest with is yourself. Can you do that? Will you let me help you?"

Her chin quivered as the tiniest squeak came out as, "Yes." She covered her face with shaking hands and finally gave vent to her agony. To her loss. To the loss of innocence. Deep honest sobs came up from the depths of her heart, and she wept aloud, for the first time that he knew of, letting her shame come out in tears.

William sat down at the table too and reached across it leaving his hand close to her.

She glanced up, tears glistening on the flawless skin of her face. He could see her mind weighing whether to trust him with just that much of a touch.

She closed her eyes and nearly flung her hand toward him, like a drowning person seizing the hand of a rescuer. William just held her hand and let her cry for several minutes. He knew each tear shed cast off some of the terrible weight she carried.

When her sobs seemed to subside, he squeezed her hand gently and stroked the top of it with his thumb. Anguish burnt his own heart with each stroke. He had broken through her fragile defense and she had let some of her pain out. It was a beginning.

The beginning of healing, he prayed.

Kelly scrubbed the moisture off her face with her fingers. He watched as she got up, grabbed the bundle containing their food, and walked to the door of the cabin, their meal forgotten.

He stood and followed her.

She placed her hand on the door, turned slowly, and looked back over her shoulder glancing around the large cozy room.

William couldn't take his eyes off her.

Then she looked up at his face and smiled tentatively.

When he flashed a wide smile back, she didn't look away. Instead, she smiled back at him in earnest, her beautiful face and dazzling eyes now more alive with what looked like hope.

Good. Hope is stronger than fear.

CHAPTER 5

"Are you sure you'll be all right?" William asked, as he unsaddled her mare, in the dim light of the setting sun.

Kelly could hear true concern in his voice. She shook her head yes, but said nothing. Shedding all those tears back at the cabin made her feel better but she still couldn't find the courage to talk about any of it. William must have sensed that on the ride back because he remained quiet, leaving her to sort out her feelings.

"Just remember what we agreed. Okay? Life is a precious gift. You were given the gift of life because you are strong enough to live it."

Kelly let his words sink in while William plopped the saddle down on the fence and grabbed a handful of straw to wipe the sweat from Ginger's back. Then he let both horses water. Before he finished, he heard the home's back door open and Mrs. Wolfe emerged with a woman Kelly didn't recognize, who carried a lantern.

"Good evening, Mrs. Wolfe. How was your shopping trip?" Kelly asked politely as they walked up. She nodded to the other woman and smiled, glad that in the dim light both women could probably not see her eyes, swollen from crying. "Sheriff Wyllie and I have just returned from viewing the land that Colonel Boone so generously gave him today."

"Kelly," Patricia began without preamble, "we've decided to make a change."

Kelly thought she could hear the girls crying in the nearby kitchen.

"A change in what?" Kelly asked. "Are the girls okay?"

"This is Mrs. Gafford, the girls' new tutor," Patricia said.

Kelly's brows drew together in confusion. She tried to speak, but couldn't.

"I apologize that we couldn't give you more notice, but Mrs. Gafford is in need of employment without delay."

"But what about my employment?" she stammered.

"My dear, after last night, we just had to make a change. You frightened the girls terribly. They think something is wrong with you."

She listened with bewilderment. "But it was just a nightmare, nothing more."

"A horrific nightmare. You were thrashing about and screaming. Dear, I don't know what happened to you, but my granddaughters don't need to know. My son and I are in complete agreement. If you stay, they will soon learn the truth. And we want to spare them that."

"Mrs. Wolfe, Kelly needs your support and Christian love," William said heatedly. "Not this abrupt dismissal simply because she had a nightmare."

"We decided to do this now, while your brothers are in town, Sheriff Wyllie. We thought she should go back with them," she said definitively, as though the decision was hers to make.

Kelly could barely breathe and her heart threatened to jump out of her chest it beat so rapidly. Her fragile world had suddenly shattered like glass.

She glanced over at William, whose reproach filled eyes glared at Mrs. Wolfe. With one final glower at the woman, he turned to Kelly. "Don't worry Kelly. Things like this always work out for the better," William entreated.

Her mind reeled with confusion. But she would not let this woman humiliate her further.

"I hope you'll understand, child," Mrs. Wolfe said, her voice cool and unnatural.

"I'll help your pack your things, dear, and Mister Wyllie can saddle your mount again," Mrs. Gafford suggested.

"Thank you for your kind offer, but I can bloody well pack up my own things," Kelly retorted then looked directly at Mrs. Wolfe. "And I am no child!" She lifted her chin and started for the house.

"We want you to keep all the clothes we bought you," Mrs. Wolfe called after Kelly.

At that, Kelly spun back to face her, fists clenched. "I'll keep only the gowns and things I brought with me. Nothing more." Despite her best efforts not to weep, tears burned her eyes for the second time that night. Not wanting Mrs. Wolfe to see her cry, she turned and sprinted to the back door, flew through the house, and took the stairs two at a time.

After throwing her few things into her bag, she hurried down the stairs. She wanted to say goodbye to the children, but they were nowhere in sight. "Can I at least say goodbye to the children and Mister Wolfe?" she asked when she nearly ran into Mrs. Wolfe in the parlor.

"No, Dear. It's best if you just leave. William has your mare ready for you."

Kelly turned and hurried through the back door, leaving only a part of her heart behind.

❧

"She did what?" Captain Sam asked heatedly.

"The woman's soul is as cold as a frozen pond," William spat.

"Lass, come sit down here with us. Ye look like ye could drop to the ground any second now," Bear said. He gestured toward a nearby log that served as a bench. "Would ye like a wee cup of coffee to bring yer strength back some?"

Kelly nodded and sank down on the log, feeling weak and vulnerable, all her anger spent.

But William's fury rapidly swelled. His nostrils flared as he whirled to stare at her. "Don't let them bring you down. You're too good for them."

She did feel humiliated, deflated. She had tried so hard to excel as a tutor and knew that the children responded well to her lessons. If only she could have controlled her emotions—banished her recurring dream—a frightening red dragon—that wanted to devour her. A fearsome blood chilling beast whose scorching breaths burned her face. The dream had become more frequent in recent weeks and the last time she'd had the dream, she swore she could actually feel the dragon's hot breath on her skin. Then the creature tied her and started to consume her whole. She screamed, but no sound came. She tried again, but her voice remained mute.

Then, just as the beast's jaw, filled with enormous sharp teeth, was about to engulf her, she saw William coming toward her, arms outstretched. She tried to reach out to William but she couldn't move her tied arms. That's when her voice finally came and her own screams woke her up before the dragon could eat her. That was her dream the night her nightmare made the girls cry too.

"Kelly, William is right. You can't let them demean you. They don't understand, that's all. We do," Sam said, in a gentle tone.

"I have no place in the world now. No home. No place where I belong." She felt so alone.

"You are more than welcome to return to Cumberland Falls and live with Catherine, Little John, and me. You're like a sister to all of us now," Sam said.

She peered up at William who stood with his hands on his hips staring at Sam. Did William think of her as a sister too?

"Or Stephen and Jane would welcome ye with open arms," Bear added. "Ye're part of the family now. Just like I am. We willna let any harm come to ye."

Her uncertain future and trampled pride made the blood pound in her head. She could feel her face growing hot with humiliation, conscious of their scrutiny. She wanted to just escape. But where? Against her will, tears began to roll down her cheeks, and she swatted at them, angry at herself.

"Kelly, lass, what's got ye so miserable?" Bear asked. "Are ye worried about leaving Boonesborough?"

Since her attack, shame was her constant burden, sometimes a light burden and sometimes a heavy one. And now, after an abrupt dismissal from her first job she felt an even deeper sense of disgrace.

"She doesn't need to go anywhere," William nearly swore.

She looked up, feeling the blood drain from her face at the adamancy of his tone. What did he mean? Her breaths shuddered. Did he want her to stay?

William eyed first Sam and then Bear. "I think you two should go take a smoke on your pipes down by the riverbank." It was more than a suggestion.

Kelly had often seen the Captain and Bear stroll along amiably together, smoking their pipes, often in a heated conversation about politics, hunting, or Indians. They both grabbed their rifles at once and strolled off into the darkness, leaving Kelly and William alone in the light of the campfire.

William stepped closer, and gazed down at her. For a moment, he studied her intently. Still wearing his best clothes, resolve seemed to heat his handsome face. In the light reflecting from the fire, his profile was sharp and spoke of determination. What was he suddenly so sure of?

She searched anxiously for the meaning behind his look. She sniffled and swallowed the lump that filled her throat.

He handed her a handkerchief and knelt down beside her. His eyes were startlingly beautiful against his tanned skin and light hair. Just looking into his eyes made her chest heat inside her and made her feel a little better. A lock of blonde hair fell onto his forehead and she reached up to push it out of his eyes. Surprised that her hand didn't shake or hesitate, she moved the hairs away from his eye, amazed at the thrill it gave her.

She heard him suck in a breath, but his gleaming eyes never left her face.

Behind William, a tall, dark figure stepped from the dark

shadows of the forest.

Ice spread through her heart and her body stiffened.

Then a terrifying realization made her insides shrivel.

❧

Kelly looked away from him and her expression suddenly darkened. William saw uncertainty and an inexplicable look of withdrawal spread over her face.

The flame of hope in his chest quickly extinguished.

Then her eyes filled with fear and uncertainty.

He swallowed his disappointment. He had been so close to reaching her, to giving her his heart. A mere moment away from letting her know his true feelings. He studied her face with concern, wondering where the Kelly he'd seen just a moment before went. He'd seen desire in her eyes, he was sure of it. But not now. Now all he perceived was fear. It was almost as though she vanished and another woman now sat before him.

A woman silent and defeated.

Then he heard something behind him. He quickly stood, drawing his pistol at the same time, and turned.

A tall man stood near the tree line, feet spread and arms crossed. The man's dark eyes stared at Kelly instead of him. "Hello Kelly," the stranger said. His voice echoed ominously through the forest and darkness beyond.

"Papa," Kelly replied, her voice weak and breaking slightly. She remained seated.

Kelly's father appeared middle-aged, but still robust, although a bit underweight. He was unshaven, but not bearded. His eyes appeared a bit bleary, his face sun dried, and his hands leathery. The man continued to glare at Kelly.

The tension between the father and daughter was immediate and increasing with frightening intensity.

"Sir, I am Sheriff Wyllie," William said extending his hand and taking a few steps forward.

The man didn't move at all and William lowered his hand, but increased his wariness.

Finally, her father's eyes moved away from Kelly and focused on William with a look of suspicion.

"You stole my daughter. I'll have you hung for that!" the man swore.

William heard Kelly gasp.

"Mister McGuffin, you are mistaken. My brother and I rescued your daughter and killed the men who attacked her," William said, his voice harsher than he intended, but this man's attitude was beyond belief. Her father should be grateful instead of accusatory.

Kelly finally stood, and William sensed the apprehension coursing through her.

A flash of protectiveness suddenly filled him. She was afraid of her own father. William wanted to beat the whoreson to a bloody pulp. A child should never have to fear their father. That just wasn't right. He clenched his jaw and fists in an effort to control his rising ire.

"Kelly, gather you things, you'll be coming home with me," McGuffin ordered.

Kelly didn't move, but William did. Incensed, he advanced to stand directly before the man, just inches from his face. "Whether or not Kelly leaves will be her decision—not yours. She's a full grown woman now and can decide for herself where she wants to live."

"Get away from me, you pompous peacock," McGuffin yelled. He put a hand on William's chest and shoved.

"You can shove me but one time. And if you ever lay another hand on her, I'll see that you hang," William spat.

"She's my daughter and I'll decide her fate." His voice hardened ruthlessly. "And she'll learn not to run away again."

"She didn't run away," William insisted, "we invited her to join us for her own protection. What kind of a father would leave a young woman alone in the woods to fend for herself for weeks at a time? You're a worthless excuse for a father."

McGuffin's right fist hit William's jaw before he could dodge away. The blow shook his head, but he still stood firm and erect, ready to return the blow. His lips pursed in anger and he glared at the man. "I don't want to fight you Mister McGuffin. But I won't let you take her either."

"Won't let me?" McGuffin mocked. "Now who is telling her what she has to do?" The man scowled at him, leaned forward, and with narrowed eyes warned, "Don't ever pick a fight with an old man. If he's too old to fight, he'll just kill you."

"Stop!" Kelly screamed. She shot up and marched to her father. "Leave him alone. I owe my life to him."

William was sure she'd yelled it loud enough for Sam and Bear to hear. They would come running back shortly.

"I don't abide a man taking my daughter. Since you're apparently the sheriff here, there's little I can do but punish you myself." McGuffin grabbed Kelly by the wrist and shoved her behind him as he yanked out his skinning knife and glared maliciously at William.

"I don't abide giving men who beat their daughters a chance to take them back," he retorted. "Release her. Now!"

"Or maybe I'll just let everyone know their new sheriff is a kidnapper of young women. What will a charge like that do to your reputation Sheriff Wyllie?"

"I'm not worried about my reputation. I'm worried about Kelly," William snapped.

"Who the hell are you anyway?" McGuffin asked. "And who told you I beat her?"

"I'm justice in these parts, you son of a bitch?"

McGuffin seemed to yield a little to William's authoritative tone. "You say you rescued my daughter. Who did the killing?"

"I did, along with my brother."

"How many of them were there?"

"Two. Both atrocious men. They had already murdered the husband of one of our friends," William begrudgingly explained. He wanted to beat this man, not talk to him.

McGuffin turned his attention to Kelly. "These attackers, what did they do to you?" he asked, his tone expressing more blame than concern.

Kelly just stared at her father, her face bleak, looking like she was holding back tears with great effort. She put the handkerchief to her nose and looked down.

William's heart ached for her. Would she tell her father the truth? She'd already dealt with a lot today and now this. She was actually trembling now, but she took a deep breath, swallowed hard and boldly met her father's reproachful eyes. "Papa, I…."

Without making a sound beforehand, Sam leapt from the trees, and headed straight for McGuffin's back, while Bear charged in from another direction and swept Kelly up in his enormous arms.

Bear stood there, a protective giant, baring his teeth and growling at McGuffin. "Ye're safe now lass. This man will not harm ye."

After relieving the man of his knife, and pinning an arm behind his back, Sam held his own long knife against the whiskers on McGuffin's throat. "What does this mangy fellow want, William?" Sam asked, his tone challenging, as he twisted the arm a little more.

"He wants to take Kelly back to their home in Virginia." William answered. "Although he doesn't deserve the name, this is her father." He spit the word out between his teeth. His eyes met Kelly's intense gaze.

Her eyes clung to his for a moment, then shifted from one person to another, before she said, "Bear, please put me down."

Bear seemed reluctant. "Are ye sure lass?"

Kelly dropped her eyes before saying, "Yes," in a voice that seemed to come from a long way off.

Bear eased her down, but stood within inches of her, a hand on his axe, looking like a real Bear ready to protect its cub.

"Captain Wyllie, release my father."

CHAPTER 6

Sam slowly released McGuffin's arm, but kept the scowl on his face menacing and the grip on his long knife firm.

William studied Kelly's father speculatively. The man's intelligent eyes gleamed, dark and insolent as he glared at Sam. A muscle flicked angrily at his jaw while he rubbed his sore elbow. McGuffin's scruffy appearance matched his surly demeanor.

Would he leave and let his daughter be? Or would the man continue to insist on taking her? One thing he was sure of. He would not let McGuffin take Kelly against her will.

Her father strode up to Kelly and, looking down his long nose, scrutinized her for several uncomfortable moments. Then, with an almost imperceptible note of pleading in his voice, he said, "Gather your things Kelly, it's time to go home."

Suddenly filled with possessiveness, William declared, "Boonesborough is her home."

Kelly took a long deep breath and seemed to force her emotions into order. Without looking at William, she moved toward her bag, still sitting where she'd left it. When she reached for it, he thought his heart might stop.

His anxiety increasing with each second, William gave her a sidelong glance of utter disbelief. "Kelly, surely you don't intend to go with him?"

Her bearing was stiff and proud, but a tremor moved across her lips before she replied. "Yes, I do. It's my home and I have no home and no family here. And now I have no job. Boonesborough is your home, not mine."

"Kelly…" William, Sam, and Bear all started at once.

"Captain, Bear, and William," she said, looking like she was struggling to keep her emotions under tight restraint, "this is my choice. No one else's. I'll thank you to let me go in peace with my father. I appreciate all that your family has done for me."

Her father smirked at them but showed no surprise or gladness that she would leave with him.

"No," William insisted, "he'll mistreat you."

Lips pursed, Kelly faced him. Something flickered far back in her eyes. "Is that why you think I should stay?"

In dazed exasperation, he simply said, "Yes."

Kelly fought to control the mixed feelings surging through her. Masking her inner turmoil with calmness, she peered up at William, unable to turn away. Of all the reasons William could have given her for staying, that was all he had to say? After a moment of silence, she realized she was not going to draw another response from him.

Under his steady scrutiny, she turned away from him and grabbed the reins to her mare.

"Follow me," McGuffin ordered. "My mount is tied nearby."

Her heart clenched and her stomach turned sour as she took her first reluctant step back to her old life. Was this actually happening? She could feel William's eyes boring into her back. Yet he said nothing.

Biting her lip, she refused to look back.

Her father trudged into the forest and she fell in behind him. Her initial shock at seeing him again had evaporated. Now she only felt extreme unhappiness. Her insides were weeping even if her eyes were not. She would not let her father see how this pained her.

She had lost control of her life. Again.

After they mounted, her father said, "We'll camp once we're further down the trail towards the Gap. There's enough moon tonight to see by so we can ride for a while. Then we'll get an early start in the morning."

He sounded almost pleasant, kind even. Had she misjudged him? Then she remembered. He only beat her when he was drinking, and then he turned into another man entirely. A cruel revolting man. Her father's evil twin.

Had he brought alcohol with him? She prayed that he hadn't.

Her father had started drinking in excess right after her mother died. That same night he had gotten so drunk he had slept on the porch, where he had passed out. Kelly had borne her own intense grief all alone, crying herself to sleep for several nights.

That was four years ago. Four long years of extreme loneliness and fending for herself while her father left to tend his traps in the Shenandoah Mountains.

During that time, her animals were her only company and she

had insisted on bringing them to Boonesborough with her when she left with William and Stephen. Now she didn't even have those. Wolfe had refused to keep her cow, chickens and mule and she had been forced to give them to Stephen and Jane before accepting her position in his household. Jane's girls needed the milk and eggs more than she did anyway.

At least she had her memory of William. She could think of him when things with her father got unpleasant. And she would use her remembrance of him to fight the harsh realities of loneliness. She would imagine him performing his duties as sheriff and then returning to his new home. There, he might play his fiddle on the front porch, or enjoy the lovely rolling hills as they whispered to him in the evenings. How she wished she had heard the hills whisper just once.

And oh, how she wished William could have whispered words of love to her.

But clearly, he didn't love her. If he had, he would have said so. That would have been his reason for wanting her to stay.

No, he would want someone far more beautiful than she was. Someone as gorgeous and refined as he was. That wasn't her and she knew it. She was just a simple girl from the mountains. That's where she belonged. It was madness to think she would fit in anywhere else.

She would miss him. Her heart ached for him already and terrible regrets assailed her. She'd almost found a new life. So close.

If she hadn't lost her job, she might have stayed. And maybe, given enough time, William could have grown fond of her. But now, with no source of income and no place to stay, what choice did she have but to return to her home? And she had to admit, she was a little homesick. She missed their cozy little dugout, tucked into the side of a rocky rise and her frequent walks higher in the hills, where she found cascading waterfalls, spectacular vistas, and quiet wooded hollows. Boonesborough was noisy, dirty, and often crowded. She did not enjoy living in town.

"It will be good to have you home again," her father said, "it's been too lonely without you."

She gave a choked, despairing laugh.

"I canna believe ye let her go," Bear said accusingly, his ruddy complexion turning a deeper red.

"Let her? She's a grown woman. I can't force her to stay," William protested. He knew it was a feeble excuse. He should have found a way to make her see reason.

"Can't never could do anything!" Bear declared.

William felt a wretchedness he'd never known before. As if someone just stole a part of him, while he stood by and watched, like some sort of bloody fool.

Sam just stood there glowering. His oldest brother was undoubtedly disappointed in him too. Well it wouldn't be the first time.

He felt guilty and helpless. He rubbed the sore spot on his jaw where McGuffin's fist had landed. The man threw a mean punch. Would he use those beefy hands to hurt Kelly? The thought made him frantic with worry. Unease twisted his gut and the dull ache of foreboding filled his chest.

Why did she leave? Disappointment ripped through him. Despite her nervousness, he had felt an eager affection coming from her all day. Every time her gaze met his, an undeniable sensuous attraction linked him to her. And sometimes, he caught her staring at him with longing. But she would always quickly avert her eyes when his gaze met hers or move away from him. Something was holding her back. It was almost as though she were held against her will, and unable to respond as she wanted.

Not wanting to scare her, he had deliberately held his own affections in check. He'd made it clear, he hoped, that he was fond of her, but he purposely kept his behavior subtle, even when they were alone in his cabin. Now he wished he hadn't been quite so restrained. Perhaps if she'd known how he felt, she would have decided to stay. He'd been a fool to keep his feelings for her hidden. In his endeavor to not scare her, he went too far.

"I vowed to help her. And when she needed me the most, I failed," he admitted. His promise to help her weighed upon him. "Lately, her ordeal has manifested itself in disturbing ways—rubbing her wrists continuously, unsteady hands, and acting wary, especially of men, even me. And terrible nightmares. Thinking it might do her good to get away from the town for a while, I took her to see my new cabin earlier. We talked for a while and for the first time since her attack, she broke down crying."

"That's a good thing. I wondered when she would finally let go of some of her hurt," Sam said.

"I promised to help her! I told her that we would make today the beginning of her healing. Now it won't be. Bloody hell!"

Sam's large forehead wrinkled and Bear's bushy red brows drew together with concern.

"Right after I got her back to Wolfe's home, his mother came out and summarily dismissed her as though she were a worthless animal she was shooing off her property. The woman was just cruel. And now this! That brut of a father intimidated her. That's why she left."

"William," Sam began, a note of censure in his tone, "you told her not to go because her father would abuse her. Then she asked you to give her a reason to stay. But you didn't."

"She did?" He thought back to her exact words. "Oh God, she did! I wasn't thinking clearly," William groaned.

"Settle yerself man. The lass needs ye to think clearly now," Bear said sharply.

"Think clearly? How can I when..." He stopped himself before he could say what he was thinking—the woman he loved had just left. He did love her! He realized that now by how much the possibility of never seeing her again hurt him. If he were honest, love had wrapped around his heart so tightly he was surprised it didn't stop beating. "I'm going after her!" he declared.

"I'll come with ye," Bear offered.

"It's about time you came to your senses," Sam told William. "But we should wait until morning. Give her some time with her father. I have a feeling that the longer she's around that man, the sooner she'll want to leave him. And if you show up now, she'll feel pressured. Better to give her some time to think. Women like to make up their own minds."

"Aye, Sam's right," Bear agreed, "they won't get very far tonight and we'll pick up their trail on the other side of Boonesborough early in the morn."

William didn't like the idea of waiting, but Sam had a point. He didn't want Kelly to feel he was forcing her to choose between her father and him. He rubbed his forehead thinking about it. "All right. But we leave well before dawn.

CHAPTER 7

Kelly and her father headed due south on the Wilderness Trail. Bright moon rays shone through the tall pines and cast jagged shadows on their winding path. The temperature had crept lower over the last two hours and she shivered as she rode. With each step of her horse, her heart sunk lower too. She doubted her heart would be able to feel anything at all by the time they reached her old cabin.

She was doing the right thing, the only thing she could do. Then why did it leave her feeling so bereft? Why did her heart feel so very cold?

"That's a fine-looking mare your riding. How did you come by it?"

"Sam's wife Catherine gave it to me."

"Gave it to you? Now why would she do a thing like that?"

"Because she's a generous and kind woman, and she knew I needed a horse."

Her father snorted and shook his head in disbelief. "I assume you sold the mule, cow, and your chickens, since they weren't with you. What did you do with the money?"

"No, I gave my animals to William's brother Stephen and his wife Jane," Kelly answered reluctantly. "They had done so much for me and I wanted to thank them."

"Gave them away! You stupid little girl. Now how are you going to get eggs and milk? I guess you'll just do without."

"I have a little money. I can buy a cow and chickens," she said.

"No, you'll give it to me when we stop for the night." He gave her a tight-lipped smile. "I'll decide what we buy."

Kelly worried that he would use the money to buy whiskey. Stephen had found the coins when he searched the pockets of her dead rapists and gave them to her, saying the money would be repayment for the food she'd prepared for the two murderers. The coins were the first she'd ever held or owned.

"How did you find me?" she asked.

"Your note explained that you went to Boonesborough with the Wyllies. I just asked a few folks where the Wyllies were camped."

"I had just gotten there. Until tonight, I was working as a tutor and living in a fine home."

"What happened?"

"It didn't work out as I planned."

"Looks like nothing worked out as you planned." With that, her father grew quiet again.

Relieved that he didn't ask any more questions, Kelly's thoughts soon returned to William. She would never see him again, so she should stop thinking about him. But how could she? In her mind, his handsome face gazed back at her and his glorious eyes spoke to her as though he were right there in front of her. What were those eyes saying just before he knelt down next to her back at the camp? He had been about to say something when she caught sight of her father emerging from the woods.

She had simply sat there—too astonished and shaken to move. She couldn't believe he had come for her. It wasn't because he loved her. Her father never showed her much affection or concern. And he rarely needed her to cook and wash clothes for him. He was home for only a few days every other month then he would return to trapping. It must be because she also helped with cleaning and curing his hides and pelts. She'd defleshed and then rubbed salt into so many fresh skins, her own skin grew cracked and dry. She didn't begrudge doing the hard work, but he never thanked her or showed any appreciation. Well, she wasn't about to spend the rest of her life doing a thankless dirty job. So why was she going back to doing just that?

Still stunned by the events of the entire day, she felt like she was in some sort of bizarre dream where nothing was quite right. It was so very late she wished she were dreaming right now. She was so sleepy. She could close her eyes for...

"Kelly!"

She jumped in the saddle at the sound of her father's harsh voice.

"You were nodding off. We better make camp before you fall off your mare," he said, guiding his mount well off the trail and into a small grove surrounded by large boulders. "This spot should provide a little shelter."

They dismounted and unsaddled the horses. Kelly rubbed her lower back, aching from being in the saddle for so long. After relieving herself, she hauled a small blanket out of her bag. Not much of a bed, but it would be better than the damp cold ground.

"It's too late to worry about a fire or a meal," McGuffin said. "Here's a piece of dried meat. Eat and then get some rest. I'm just going to have myself a drink or two and then I'll do the same."

Oh my Lord, no. Not now, not out here in the middle of the night, when they were alone and exposed. She smiled, betraying nothing of her annoyance. "Papa, perhaps you should stay alert in case we're threatened by a wild animal, or outlaws, or Indians. Bear said some of the Indians are stirred up again."

"I'm more alert with a drink or two in me. Don't you worry none. Now eat."

Kelly chewed a couple of bites of the salty meat, but without something to drink, she couldn't force any more down her parched throat. "Did you bring any water?"

"No, I try not to touch the stuff, except now and then from a fast running creek. When I'm in the saddle, I prefer a man's drink—whiskey."

She shook her head and then threw her blanket open and spread it on a smooth spot of pine needles. She stretched out and wrapped a corner of the blanket over her shoulders. At least part of her would be warm. But could she sleep knowing how vulnerable they were? She decided she'd better keep one eye and one ear open. Maybe half of her could rest at least.

"You know," her father began as he leaned his back against a small boulder and then took a swallow of the whiskey, "I was surprised you could run off like that. Leave your poor dead mother all alone. No one to tend her grave."

A soft gasp escaped her. She stared, wordlessly, into the darkness. Had she abandoned her mother? A stab of guilt buried itself in her breast.

When her mother had died, she felt a raw and acute sense of loss. A loss made all the deeper because her mother was her only friend and constant companion. But it had been four years since her passing, and when the Wyllies offered a chance at a new life, she knew in her heart that her mother would approve.

"My mother would want me to be happy," she replied in a low bitter voice.

She heard him guzzling more whiskey, then he said, "And you think I don't want you to be happy. Is that what you think?"

His voice was thick with mockery and derision and the sound of it made her insides twist with misery. She could see her father's face in the moonlight a few feet away, watching her, his expression mean, his eyes squinting.

Crestfallen, she swallowed the sob that rose in her throat as her spirits sank even lower. She closed her eyes, trying to escape her father's terrible glare.

"I miss her. Your mother was the only good thing that ever happened to me."

A suffocating sensation tightened her chest. "I miss her too."

She heard more gulps of whiskey. Good heavens, he'll be drunk soon. That's when he was most likely to beat her. What would she do? She couldn't flee into a dark forest at night. "Papa, please stop drinking."

"Nope." He shot her a defiant look.

His refusal infuriated her. Suddenly overwhelmed by the torment of the past few hours, she stood, tossed the blanket aside, and glared at him. Her fists clenched at her sides, she let her eyes burn with the reproach she felt. She didn't care whether he hurt her or not. "Stop drinking this instant and act like the father you are. If you think so much of my mother, honor her memory by caring for her daughter!" She spat out the words contemptuously, because that's all she felt for the man—contempt.

He glowered at her and then turned away, swallowing even more whiskey.

"If you can't treat me like your daughter, then at least treat me like hers!" she yelled.

She was breathless now with mounting rage. Seething, she drew air through her clenched teeth.

"You left me—just like she did. Left me without so much as a goodbye. You can't imagine how awful I felt coming home to an empty cabin with nothing more than a note left of you." His spiteful voice echoed through the trees.

Kelly drew a breath. "That's what you earned. You reap what you sow. When was the last time you showed me any love? It's been years. The saddest thing is that I remember what you were like before my mother died. You were kind and loving. But you changed. The last few years, every time you came home from one of your hunting trips, I prayed the man that returned would be my old father and that you would love me again. You only want me back now to do your work for you—to prepare the hides for market—so you can buy more liquor. So you can just get drunk all over again. It's an endless and depressing cycle and I swear I'll no longer be a part of it!"

"You're an ungrateful little whelp. You're nothing like your mother."

"Stop! Stop hurting me with your cruel words. You cannot

unsay an unkind word. And, for mercy's sake, stop drinking."

He took another sip of whiskey and plugged the jug. "I'll stop for now."

His words were slow and slurred and in less than a minute, he was asleep. At least she would no longer have to endure the torment of his presence.

She was so furious she would never be able to sleep. She found his rifle and checked the powder, then took his pistol and did the same. She put both across her lap and found a boulder to lean against. Her vision was excellent and she scanned the darkness for any movement and listened to the sounds of the night. There weren't any. She guessed she'd scared off everything including the night critters with her loud outburst.

She wished she had scared off her father.

The only thing darker than her mood was the night. She felt utterly alone despite her father's presence. She should never have gone with him. She should have stayed with William, he would have found her a place to stay. Leaving with her father was beyond foolish, but she felt an obligation to the man. He was her father after all. And she'd desperately hoped that maybe he had overcome his habit of drinking too much. But now, after the way he'd treated her over the last couple of hours, every shred of fondness she'd once held for her father grew as dark as the night.

With the moon casting the eerie forest and shadowy brush in shades of blue, grey, and black, it came as no surprise to Kelly that the night was a long one for her. After thinking about how much she would miss William, losing her position as the children's tutor, and then the sudden appearance of her now soused father, she decided, as William had suggested, to try to figure out what the heck was bothering her even before all that happened.

She recognized that she behaved oddly at William's swearing in ceremony. And her nightmares had been bad for some time. She really couldn't blame Mister Wolfe and his mother for being concerned about Kelly's screams scaring his daughters. The last dream terrified her so much she woke covered in sweat, crying, and shaking.

The root of her nightmares and fear had to be the rape. But why was it getting worse with time instead of better? William had said that pain can make you weaker or stronger. Clearly, she'd been letting the traumatic experience make her weaker, little by little, like a hole in a damn that grew larger as more and more water rushed through it.

But even if the rape was indeed the root of her problem, she still wasn't convinced the assault was the cause of all her fears. There had to be something else. She'd felt more uncomfortable and vulnerable at the swearing in ceremony than she had anywhere else. She should have felt comfortable with William, Sam, and Bear all there. She should have been excited and happy for William. But instead, she'd felt bone-deep panic.

She pondered just what it was that had made her feel so exposed, so much at risk.

At the ceremony, William was the focus of everyone's attention and admiration—even Daniel Boone's. Her memory of him standing next to her, looking so devilishly handsome, was clear and vibrant. He had made her feel what she could only describe as an intense awareness of him. All of him. As she traveled with his family and then camped with them once they'd reached Boonesborough, she'd been around him for months. From the beginning, she'd regarded him as her rescuer and hero, admiring him for his bravery and gallantry. And more than once, she cautiously stole secretive glances at him, appreciating his handsome face and muscular body.

But at the ceremony, she found herself drawn to him in a completely new way. A deeper connection seemed to form between them and it had caused her heart to pound in her chest with the fury of a growing storm. And then, from nowhere, she'd suddenly become frightened. He had given her no reason to fear him. Yet she did. The lightning bolts of desire that had exploded within her had terrified her. Such longings seemed perilous—fraught with hidden danger—and her first impulse was to throttle those strange feelings. Her second instinct was to run from them. And run she did.

But she could not outrun her heart.

Even now, she felt the dull ache of that same desire at the thought of him, but her familiar fears were also there, lurking just below the surface.

Was she feeling fear because she was starting to have real feelings for William? Was that yearning burning inside her because she wanted him? Had she reached the point where she had to admit how she truly felt about him?

She'd recently begun to recognize her own needs and couldn't deny the strong passion within her that called for release. She wanted to love someone. Not just emotionally…but physically.

The notion shocked her. Yet it felt real and honest.

After several hours, her drifting thoughts drew together and something clicked in her mind. The awakening left her reeling. That's what it was. She couldn't deny it any longer. The thought of a man intimately touching her again filled her with overwhelming dread. But, in order to love William, she would have to yield to the passion growing stronger within her. She would have to join with him, and do…that.

It had been easy to deny her fears when there was no reason to confront them. But now, those same fears demanded recognition—acknowledgment that they were real. William was no longer only a hero she admired. No longer just the object of a simple girl's infatuation. Now she wanted him. As a woman.

She felt momentary panic as her mind grasped the realization. But this time, she refused to give in to her anxiety. She forced herself to breathe deeply, to listen to her heart. After considering the thought of making love with him for a few moments, she was more thrilled than frightened at the prospect. She allowed her fear to surface only long enough to recognize the absurdity of it. She had nothing to fear from a man who cared for her! William was nothing like those men—he was far different—and joining with him was bound to be vastly different too.

She saw that clearly now and gave free rein to her feelings for him.

She resolved to never let her fear win again. Without a doubt, it would surface again, but she would never let it win again. She could get stronger now. And she would, by God. Starting tonight. She'd successfully pulled all the pieces together and the relief she felt was intense. She felt more like herself than she had in weeks.

Suddenly, she desperately wanted to get back to William so she could let him know what she finally understood. She wanted to tell him she was no longer afraid. She could now love someone. She hoped it could be him. But she still had serious doubts about whether he would ever consider marrying her. Maybe, just maybe, he would.

She clung to that thought with all her heart.

A deep feeling of peace settled over her as she decided to return to Boonesborough at dawn's first light.

"What's a pretty young woman like you doing awake in the middle of the night out here?" a man asked in a low buttery voice from behind her.

Kelly startled and hit her head against the boulder she leaned on. Alarm entwined with the emotions still smoldering inside her. Frightened, she grabbed for the pistol in her lap.

"Don't wrap your little hand around that handle," the voice said. "I have a gun pointed at your lovely blonde head of hair. Toss that weapon off to your right. The rifle too."

His voice was chilling and dread rose in her chest.

"If you scream for that man over there, I'll shoot him dead."

"He's not my man. He's my father," she replied in a voice made small by fright.

"Then you definitely wouldn't want me to kill him, would you?"

Kelly almost had to think about that.

"Get your horse saddled and be quiet about it. You're coming with me."

"I shall not! I don't even know who you are."

"Very well, the name is Harpes. Now get saddled, and be quick or I might just decide to slit his throat," he said, his calm voice little more than a whisper.

The man soundlessly moved near her father and yanked out his dagger with his free hand. The blade gleamed ominously in the moonlight. He smiled benignly, as if coaxing a hesitant child.

Reluctantly, Kelly stood and started saddling Ginger. Unsettled by the stranger and Kelly's unease, the mare pranced while she tried to attach the saddle leathers. As much for herself as her mare, Kelly whispered, "Whoa now girl, we'll be all right. I promise."

While Kelly saddled Ginger, Harpes gathered her father's weapons and powder horn.

"I smell enough whiskey on him to keep him sleeping till noon tomorrow," Harpes said.

She watched the man move about, catlike quiet, looking for anything of value in her father's things. He was tall, muscular, and beardless. His strong profile, lit by moonlight, was somber and rigid and his black hair was straight and hung loose to his wide shoulders. Dressed simply, but richly, he gave the appearance of someone who demanded instant obedience.

Well, once they were safely away from her father, he would find her anything but obedient.

She shook her head in disbelief. Could this night get any worse? How could this be happening to her? If her father had acted more like William or Captain Sam, always cautious in the wild, he would have stayed alert and been ready for trouble. Instead, he'd been irresponsible and reckless, drinking himself into a stupor.

As a result, she was the one in danger.

And frightened. What did Harpes want with her? What would he do to her? A hard knot formed in her stomach and her heart beat erratically.

When he mounted his horse, she gathered Ginger's reins in her hands and reluctantly leapt up onto the saddle. She had no choice. She wouldn't let this man harm her father.

Kelly glanced back at her father, still dead to the world, as Ginger followed the tall man's horse into the darkness.

CHAPTER 8

William, Sam, and Bear rode through town so early most people were still asleep. Within minutes, they passed through the moonlit Fort's shadow and headed out of town on Boone's Trace, a branch of the Wilderness Road. Through the dark still night, they could hear the Kentucky River flowing on their left. The normally soothing sound of the rushing water did little to calm William's nerves. His mind spun with both hope and fear. Hope that Kelly would agree to return to Boonesborough with them. And fear that she wouldn't.

Or that harm had already befallen her and her father.

Waves of affection swept through him in ways that alternately thrilled and frightened him. He needed to find Kelly and somehow convince her to come back to Boonesborough to marry him. He loved her. He wanted her to be his wife. As he'd lain awake last night unable to sleep, he'd finally understood that she was the first women he ever truly loved and now with a fierce resolve he wanted only her.

The thought of losing her, or never having the chance to show her that love, frightened him as nothing else ever had.

Kelly, stay safe until I reach you.

"Don't worry, we'll find the lass soon," Bear said, almost as though he had read William's thoughts.

"We'd better!" William called back. He muttered an oath beneath his breath, swearing that if Kelly's father had hurt her, the man wouldn't live to regret it.

Because he'd be dead.

"Stay alert," Sam cautioned.

Now William worried in earnest. "I wish we had left last night."

"As I said, she needed some time alone with her father. And if we had followed them last night, and McGuffin had laid a hand on Kelly, you would have been tempted to kill him. I know you, and you would not have let the man get away with hurting her. And if you slayed the girl's father, that would end any chance you have with her. Better to wait until the light of day, when heads are clearer and cooler."

"My head may be clearer, but it's not cooler," William said, his temper heating his words. "You're right. I would kill him if I had too. Especially if he's hurt her."

"Did Boone say when he was leavin' Boonesborough?" Bear asked.

"Today. He'll probably be right behind us," William answered.

"That might come in handy if we encounter Indians," Bear said.

They rode as fast as they dared without wearing the horses out too soon. By sunrise, their mounts covered several miles and they were well south of the fort. Sam and Bear both started looking for the tracks of the two horses and finally Sam spotted Ginger's print in some moist earth.

They followed the tracks for some time and then to William's surprise, they heard McGuffin galloping his mount toward them. Where was Kelly? Was she hurt? God, please no. A deep, unaccustomed fear gripped his heart.

Kelly's father tugged up on his reins as he reached them, his brows drawn and his face twisted in an angry frown. "What did you do with my daughter, you son-of-a-bitch?" he shouted at William.

The man's tone and blasphemous language infuriated William, but he would not release his anger. At least not yet. "Where's Kelly?" he demanded.

"Tell me where she is," McGuffin repeated, his eyes flashing disdain.

"What the hell are you talking about?" Sam barked. "She was with you!"

"She's gone. I know you took her. She wouldn't have taken off in the darkness by herself. Stop this pretense and tell me where she is!" McGuffin looked ready to kill. Bristling with anger, he sat there, tall in the saddle, his expression accusing.

"Mister McGuffin, we were on our way to try to convince Kelly to return with us," William explained, using up what was left of his scant patience entirely. Worry tore at his insides.

"I don't believe you. Where did you hide her?" McGuffin eyed him reprovingly.

"We don't have her! But I do want to know where she is. We need to figure that out right now," William barked, his breath burning hot in his throat.

"Where did ye last see the lass, man?" Bear asked McGuffin.

"We made camp a few miles back. I fell asleep soon afterwards. When I awoke this morning, she was gone, along with her mare and bag," he sputtered, bristling with indignation.

William's eyes narrowed suspiciously. He stared at McGuffin, trying to assess if the man was telling the truth. Had he done something to Kelly to punish her for leaving? Was he doing this to cover up? He wouldn't put it past the miserable man.

"Were there any other tracks?" Sam asked, his voice taut and low.

"I don't know. I didn't look."

That response sent Sam's dander up. "That was nothing short of idiotic," Sam declared. His brother's face hardened with outrage.

McGuffin's black eyes burned with fury as he glared back at Sam. "I was so sure you three took her, I just saddled my horse and took off coming this way," McGuffin answered.

Bear stared at the man, his glower so hot William wouldn't be surprised if McGuffin burst into flames. "Ach man, as ye can plainly see, we didna take her!"

McGuffin's expression grew worried, as though he just now realized Kelly was actually missing.

William's anger, escalating by the second, gave him little tolerance for the man or the situation. "This is getting us nowhere. How far down the road was your campsite?" he demanded.

"Fifteen minutes at a hard ride," McGuffin answered.

"Then ride hard and take us back there. Now!" William ordered.

McGuffin turned his mount south again and took off at a run.

William, Sam, and Bear followed closely behind.

If she wasn't with her father, where was she? Had she set out on her own? Although risky, he actually hoped that was the case. It was better than the alternative—that someone had taken her. Another thought twisted his gut with alarm. Had Indians taken her?

His heart hammered as thunderously as the horses' hooves.

Kelly could barely hang on to the saddle she was so tired. Only mounting fear kept her relatively alert. "Who are you?" she demanded. "And what do you want with me?" She had asked these questions several times, but so far the man refused to answer her. His silence only added to her uneasiness.

Sometime during the night, they had crossed the Kentucky River at a low water crossing, and then Harpes headed northwest. She remembered that Sam had said that the road across the river heading north led to Lexington. Why was Harpes going there?

"I've already given you my name, but my family name is Robinson. And, young lady, I seek only to rescue you from that despicable man you called your father."

"Rescue me?" Kelly asked in stunned disbelief. "I never asked to be rescued!"

"I realize that. But the circumstances made it abundantly clear you needed rescuing. The man is a brut and a drunk."

"How do you know that?" She couldn't deny the truth of his words.

"Because I was camped nearby and heard you yelling. I raced through the woods, thinking you needed help and overhead you arguing with the nasty man."

"That still doesn't give you the right to take me against my will." She was furious, but somewhat relieved. At least the man seemed to have honorable motives.

"Sometimes someone who is abused is unable to free themselves from their tormentor. I sensed that you would be that way."

"You know nothing about me."

"I know that your father said some exceptionally cruel things to you and seemed on the verge of violence. It was all I could do to remain hidden. But I knew he'd pass out soon. When he did, I went back to my camp and tried to sleep for a few hours. But I was so concerned for your safety, I couldn't sleep and decided you needed help. That's when I showed up at your camp."

She gave him a hostile stare. "I demand that we turn back to Boonesborough."

He just smiled back at her. "I think not. If we did, that horrible man would find you again and you'd become his slave. I despise fathers who use their children for nothing more than workhorses. You are too smart and too beautiful a young woman to be yoked to someone as disgusting as your father. What is your name?"

An unwelcome flush crept up her neck and cheeks. He thinks I'm beautiful. She was embarrassed at how much that pleased her. But he was the first man to ever say something like that to her.

"Kelly. Kelly McGuffin," she finally answered. She was proud of her McGuffin name. Although her father definitely had problems because of alcohol, he had once been a good man and her mother told her that he came from an honorable and noble Scottish family.

"Kelly. I have plans for you. You need not worry."

"What plans?" she asked warily. A warning voice whispered inside her head.

"We'll discuss those when we reach Lexington. But to put your mind at ease, I am a man of means and want to provide you with an education."

"I am already well-schooled. I'll have you know I can read and write quite well."

"I am pleased to learn that. However, there's more to an education than reading and writing. Who taught you to read and write?"

"My mother."

"She is an educated woman?"

"Was. She's dead now. She came from a fine northern Virginia family. Her father owned a tobacco plantation."

"Did he? Well, I'm delighted that she taught you to read. And sorry for her that she wound up with such an appalling brut. If she looked anything like you, she could have had her pick of Virginia gentlemen."

If truth be told, she was sorry too. What would her life been like if her mother had married a fine Virginia gentleman? Someone who treated them both well? Kept them both safe in a big fine home. What would it have been like to become a young woman in a home full of life and love? She hadn't felt love from her father in a very long time.

This man seemed more interested in her welfare than her father ever was. But he was a stranger. As he rode beside her, she was conscious of his continued scrutiny. His gaze started to roam freely over her entire body. She became even more uneasy and was suddenly anxious to escape from this mysterious man. As she pondered her situation, Kelly's head ached with worry and her face grew hot.

Growing more and more uncomfortable, she shifted in the saddle and chewed on her bottom lip.

She could not trust this man. Even if she could trust him, did she want to? What she wanted to do was turn her horse and run away, but his more powerful stallion would easily catch up to her mare. And the man looked stout. Any effort to bolt would be wasted.

Besides, alone, deep in the wilds of these hills and woods, there were all sorts of potential dangers. From bears and mountain lions to Indians and outlaws. Leaving might mean jumping from the frying pan into the fire. Logic dampened the last traces of her desire to flee.

She gazed at him in despair. "Please, take me back. I have friends in Boonesborough who will protect me and help me to avoid my father."

"You've already escaped him."

She closed her eyes, her heart aching because he was right. She was glad she was away from her father and did not have to face him this morning. He was probably still asleep, and hadn't even noticed that she was gone.

She tried to hide her inner sadness from Harpes' probing gaze.

But without her father, what would she do? Despite her own attraction to William, he had only acted as a good friend or brother toward her. He obviously didn't intend to court her or to marry her. If he had, wouldn't he have made his intentions known by now? She couldn't blame him for not wanting her. Her mother once told her that gentlemen want to marry unsullied young ladies. And she was far from a pure maiden. William even saw her entirely unclothed with Ben Jack and his brother. The sight probably repulsed him and made it difficult now for him to think of her romantically. She held out little hope that William could ever return her affections.

She looked away from Harpes, off into the darkness of the forest, as she swallowed her disappointment.

Did she have any other options? She didn't want to live with Sam and Catherine, they were newlyweds. And Stephen and Jane already had plenty of responsibilities with two daughters and another child due any day. She didn't want to be a burden to any of them. Even William.

Especially William.

She wished William would want to be with her because he loved and desired her. Because he felt about her as she did him. Not because he pitied her. Her heart tightened with conflicting emotions, some sweet, as she remembered both his gentle promise to help her heal, and her growing attraction to William. And emotions of regret, that he had never shown anything more than brotherly concern for her and she might never know what his love would feel like.

She faced an uncertain future to say the least. Maybe going to Lexington was for the best. She could find another job there and not be dependent on anyone. Maybe there she would have a chance to heal—to rid herself of the incessant shame she felt. She could start a new life, a completely fresh life, in a place where no one would know what had happened to her. The thought gave her a strange numbed comfort.

"All right. I'll agree to continue on with you." But just as soon as she spoke the words aloud, she felt oddly unsettled.

William! A single hot tear slipped down her cheek and she quickly swiped at it with her knuckle.

"You need to rest awhile," he said kindly. "We've been riding for a couple of hours. We'll stop at the next creek and make camp."

She just shook her head, afraid her voice would betray her distress.

They dismounted as soon as they reached a narrow stream and let the horses water. Kelly gulped water down her own parched throat and washed her face and hands. Studying her reflection in the moon-gilded water, she wondered if the man really did find her beautiful. Right now, she felt anything but. Her eyes felt swollen with fatigue, her hair was a frazzled mess, her clothing wrinkled. She dipped her hands into the water again and splashed her face. The cool water felt good against her pounding forehead.

But it would take more than cool water to quench the pain of her aching heart.

CHAPTER 9

His partner Belle would be forever indebted to him. It had been awhile since Harpes had acquired one as innocent and lovely as Kelly. And eventually the young woman would also be grateful to him for rescuing her from the clutches of her father. The man didn't deserve a daughter like Kelly.

He could hardly wait to get her fixed up and have her see her reflection in the beautiful mirror that hung in the home's parlor. The mirror was among the home's many fine furnishings. Belle had insisted on the best of everything for Lexington's most orderly of 'disorderly' houses. Rich velvet drapes, the latest fashionable furniture, cut crystal oil lamps, and, of course, the richest food and finest drinks.

Belle also insisted on the best in female companionship for her clientele—some of the most powerful men in the community and even surrounding states. Her clients often wanted someone new. And he was all too happy to keep Belle supplied with fresh young women and teach the young ladies how to please a man. Almost without exception, they were ignorant of the skills needed for their profession. But he was an excellent teacher.

For his efforts, he got half of Belle's considerable profits and as much time as he desired with his pick of the whores.

Kelly was perfect.

He'd recognized her potential at once. Her beauty was delicate, her lips a rosy flower. They had few blondes at the brothel and none with Kelly's exquisite young figure. She was probably still a virgin too. Yes, he would certainly sample her beauty close up and teach her a few things, just as soon as he could get her into a big luxurious bed. He was not about to soil his fine clothing and pick up ticks and fleas by taking her now. And, he really needed to keep his wits about him in case there were natives roaming about. He'd always managed to trade or talk his way out of Indian problems. In fact, he carried folded silk cloth and pearls in his saddle bags for just that purpose. Fortunately, Indians were honorable and honored their trades.

The sweet thing probably didn't even know what a brothel was. It would be an education all right. For the first few days, Belle clandestinely kept new arrivals drugged with her carefully controlled doses. After that, nearly all of the women he'd cherry-picked for the house chose to stay in order to continue taking the drugs. They enjoyed the fine food and beautiful clothing as well. And for women who were alone in the world or had little family, Belle's home offered some degree of protection.

It was the perfect set-up. In Lexington, the city readily acknowledged the women's work as a profession, alongside physicians and attorneys. Especially accepted, were houses like Belle's, whose clients were among the citizenry's elite.

He could hardly wait to begin Kelly's instruction. With a few drugs in her, just enough to keep her compliant, she would be a willing pupil. He would make sure she learned her lessons well.

❧

After washing up, Kelly returned to where Harpes waited. She approached slowly.

Glancing up from his saddle bag, he openly appraised her. His look was so peculiar it sent a tremor of foreboding through her.

She sat down next to a tree and stretched out her legs while keeping her eyes glued on Harpes. She fought to keep her growing uncertainty from showing.

Harpes offered her a biscuit wrapped in a towel. "Here, you'll enjoy this. You must be famished." His voice was kind, yet edged with something else she didn't recognize.

Ravenous, she quickly gulped the sweet bread down. She would have to sleep soon, her senses felt dulled. She pressed her hands to her burning tired eyes. Her entire body felt heavy with weariness and her heart ached for William. What was she doing here with this man? She began to wonder just what he wanted of her.

"Go ahead, sleep," Harpes suggested. "There's no reason not to rest. We've made excellent progress and it will be dawn in a couple of hours. I'll keep a watch out."

She gave a forced smile and a slight nod of consent. "Maybe just a few minutes. Do you promise to stay over there?"

Amusement flickered in his eyes. "Indeed, I'll just be taking a short nap myself, right here." He tapped the ground beside him as he too sat down and leaned back against a large pine tree.

"First, give me back my father's weapons." Kelly tried to sound demanding, but to her dismay, her voice broke slightly.

He frowned and shook his head decisively. "No my dear. I

might need them in case we're attacked." He sat there, blatantly intimidating.

That set alarms ringing in her heard. "If we're attacked, it would be better if we were both armed." She drew a settling breath and forbade herself to tremble, but her hands, hidden in the folds of her dress, twisted nervously.

He seemed to enjoy her struggle to maintain her dwindling composure.

She lifted her chin, boldly meeting his eyes, and fought for self-control. "I insist that you give me the weapons. They belong to my father, not you."

His expression darkened and something disturbing revealed itself far back in his eyes.

Kelly's guard was fully up now. Her heart thudded within her chest. They stared at each other across an uncomfortable silence. She swallowed and found her voice again. "I am a competent shooter, I assure you. I had to hunt my own food where I liv...." She couldn't finish the sentence. She gasped, realizing something was not right with her. A warm pressure filled her head and then all of a sudden she felt like she was laying in quiet field in the sun. All her confusion, all her loneliness, all her shame, gone. She felt so good...

She struggled to open her eyes, but they refused to stay open. Before her lids closed again, she saw Harpes mouth spread into a thin-lipped smile.

Harpes wasn't surprised that the drug affected Kelly so rapidly. The poor girl was exhausted. But the drug would make her sleep deeply. He would let her rest for an hour or so and then tie her on her horse. It would be late in the morning before the drug wore off, but by then he would have her safely hidden away at Belle's house.

He studied her. He'd seen strength of character on that delicate face and a strong mind in her intelligent eyes. This one might not be as easy as most to bend to Belle's iron will. He felt sure there would be an interesting skirmish between the two until he got Kelly under his control. In fact, he rather looked forward to her resistance. It would make taking her all the more exhilarating.

He decided to catch a few winks himself. He covered his face with his tricorne and crossed his legs and arms, a smile of satisfaction tipping the corners of his mouth.

The instant they reached McGuffin's campsite from the night before, William leapt off his stallion. Sam and Bear did the same and right away started searching the area. Most of it was covered in pine needles or rocks and finding a good track was going to be a challenge. But, as their father taught them, Sam could track a butterfly flying over solid rock. And Bear was nearly that good too.

Sam and Bear spread out looking for tracks leading away from the campsite. William focused on finding any clue that would tell them what happened to Kelly.

"Where did you see Kelly last?" he asked McGuffin.

"Over there, leaning against that boulder. I slept here." He pointed to the spot. William studied the area and found a man's boot print. The boot sole was quite large, larger than McGuffin's or his. Her abductor had big feet. Likely a tall man. At least Indians hadn't captured her.

"Was anything of yours missing?" William asked.

"Yes, my pistol, my rifle, my lead, and powder horn. The only other thing of value was my whiskey. That was untouched," McGuffin answered. "Glad of it too, because I'm parched."

Kelly's father reached into his saddle bag.

"Don't you even think about drinking," William hissed. "At a time like this, all you should be thinking about is your daughter."

"My guess is she's all you're thinking about," McGuffin countered with an air of defiance as he uncorked the jug. "I'll leave the worrying to you while I take a quick sip or two."

It was all he was thinking about, but William found a perverse pleasure in the challenge. He placed his hands on his hips. "If you even breathe the fumes from that jug, you'll feel my fist going down your jaw instead of the whiskey."

McGuffin tossed his head and eyed him, a melancholy frown darkening his features.

William boldly met his eyes. Kelly was not going back to Virginia with this bastard. But first, he had to find her. Tension coiled within him, hardening the muscles in his arms and making his fists clench.

"William, over here," Sam yelled.

William quickly raced over to where Sam stood, and Bear joined them at once. McGuffin moved without haste, ambling up to them as Sam was explaining what he'd found.

"This hoof print is from a much larger horse than Ginger. Probably a stallion. A man mounted here. See the mark of his boot there. And then, over here, you see Kelly's mare follows behind it."

"I found the print of a man's boot heel close to where Kelly rested," William said.

"Where do the prints lead? Back to the road?" McGuffin asked Sam.

"That's safe to assume, but I'll confirm that. Get mounted and bring my gelding. I'll follow the tracks for a bit on foot."

They followed behind Sam at a safe distance, careful not to damage any of the tracks he followed. As expected, they led back to the road, and then headed north. "If they went north and we've just come south, they must have passed by the road to Boonesborough before us and took the fork north toward Lexington."

"Let's get going, we'll catch up to them soon. Whoever he is, he'll pay for taking her," William swore. "And if he's hurt her, I may only be sheriff for a day, because I'll have to strangle the man with my bare hands." That was a very real possibility. The thought of another man attacking Kelly made his teeth grind together in anger. He would not let being a sheriff stop him from killing the man.

Sam remounted and took off first, keeping his eagle eyes on the tracks. William and the other two men followed behind. Sam was able to keep them at a steady trot and still follow the tracks, but their slow pace grated on William's nerves.

They followed the trail left by the two horses for several miles and then across the Kentucky River, where the tracks disappeared. William waited, thumping his fingers on his saddle, for several minutes on the north bank until Sam picked up the hoof prints again. Whoever abducted Kelly was smart enough to walk their mounts upstream through the low water and rocks to hide their tracks.

But the man was not clever enough to elude Sam. After walking his horse upstream, his brother picked up the tracks again about a hundred yards west. Sam yelled, "I've got it." The three of them rode along the river's north bank in Sam's direction and then followed him into the woods. The tracks, still heading north, ran parallel to the main road.

All of a sudden, Sam stilled his mount and held his hand up. William scanned the thicket ahead, and realized they'd come face to face with a party of Shawnee. A small band of about ten, probably hunters, slowly moved in their direction. They were outnumbered more than two to one, and every one of the muscular braves held a bow in his hand. Those odds did not overly concern William because Sam and Bear were both experienced and formidable Indian fighters, and he could hold his own too. But he had no idea what kind of a fighter McGuffin might be. He put his hand to his pistol, but did not pull it for fear of setting off a fight. He did not want Kelly's father killed in an Indian skirmish. She didn't need any more grief in her life.

At once, Sam started using sign language to communicate with the Indians. His oldest brother was the only one in the family who knew how to sign. To use the ancient language of the natives, understood by many tribes, was a sign of respect. William hoped it would help them to avoid a battle with the Shawnee. His belly tightened. They did not need this delay.

"We seek only peace on this beautiful morning," Sam translated for their benefit as he signed.

William urged his mount alongside of Sam. If there was going to be trouble he didn't want Sam to be out in front alone.

The warrior who seemed to be the group's leader positioned his horse in front of the other braves and stared back at Sam and William. He was a large, lean man with muscles that rippled across his chest and stomach. His long, sinewy legs were bare. Three rows of paint striped his cheeks, and his smooth gold skin stretched over high cheekbones. What looked like eagle feathers entwined with his long black hair. He held his bow, notched with an arrow, at the ready, as he appraised Sam through squinted dark eyes.

"His name is Strong Eagle and he asks why we are north of the Kentucky River, off the trail, in their hunting ground," Sam said.

Then Sam answered, "We search for one of our women, who was taken by a big man on a large horse. Have you seen such a man with a woman whose hair is the color of the sun when it is high in the sky?"

Sam translated the brave's answer. "He says, 'I see not'."

"Ask if we can continue to search if we promise not to hunt in this area," William said.

After Sam signed the question, Strong Eagle responded, "My people are the friends of the birds, the animals, the trees, and the flowers. We respect all living creatures. Leave the woods and the fields as you find them. Go, and find woman you seek."

Sam answered, "We will try to leave this forest as we found it, so that it may be enjoyed by all and all those who come after us."

"And, ask if they will try to steal her if they find her with the white man before we do," William urged.

Sam regarded him uncertainly, but then translated William's question.

Strong Eagle responded without hesitation. "Shawnee promise Big Turtle not to take any more women from whites. Will take woman not."

William knew that 'Big Turtle' was the name the Shawnee had given Boone when they made him a blood brother.

"We are friends of Big Turtle and will tell him of your loyalty to your promise," Sam said.

"Tell him I will remember his cooperation on this day," William said.

William glanced back at McGuffin, who thrust out his jaw and then said, "Captain Sam, how do we know they haven't already taken her? I say we give them a fight."

William shot him a burning look. "Shut the hell up," he shushed through stiff narrowed lips, "before you cause problems."

McGuffin's face went livid. "How dare you speak to me with that tone, you insolent cur."

"Time to leave," Sam said to them in a voice of authority. Then Sam turned to Big Eagle. "May your hunt be successful and your bellies full tonight."

As soon as Sam finished his sentence, his brother took off and William trailed behind him. He earnestly hoped that McGuffin would be smart enough to follow peacefully with Bear in the rear.

As soon as they were well away from the braves, Sam's eyes drew downward in a frown and he turned to McGuffin. "You, Sir, are as dumb as a rock. It's always easier to go around a mountain than over it. You almost provoked a nasty fight back there and one or more of us could have been killed. Maybe even all of us. That would have left no one to rescue Kelly. Don't question me in front of natives or anyone else ever again."

"My apologies, Sir, I'm just so worried. I thought that maybe whoever stole her might have traded her to those Indians."

"I could see the truth in Strong Eagle's words, even if you could not," Sam said. He spat out the words contemptuously.

William could tell his brother thought little of McGuffin. He had to agree with Sam's assessment.

"We all know what that man could be doing to my sweet Kelly," McGuffin said, pitifully.

The man sounded to William as if he were on the verge of tears and, for the first time, truly concerned about his daughter. Maybe the danger she was in finally sunk in to his thick head. McGuffin was right. They were all well aware of what Kelly could be enduring, and it made his stomach clench with impotent rage.

He was also mindful of how much she had already suffered. His mind burned with the terrible memory. But her clueless father remained ignorant of her rape.

William's mouth twisted. Should he tell the man? He clamped his jaw tight and quickly banished the thought.

Bear pulled alongside him. "Steady man, we'll find the lass. Then we'll kill the bloody bastard."

CHAPTER 10

Harpes carried Kelly to her horse, admiring her slender white neck and full bosom, and carefully placed her in the saddle. He tied her to the mare with her chest leaning over the mare's neck, her long blonde hair mixing with the horse's flaxen mane. Her wrists were delicate. He hoped the ropes didn't burn them, but scars already ringed her wrists anyway. He tied her ankles to the stirrups then looped a rope around her waist that he tied to the saddle. Where had the scars had come from? One of these days, when he had a moment alone with her, he would ask.

For now, she slept like an angelic baby. But she sure didn't look like a baby. Unable to resist touching her seductive young body, he stroked her arm sensuously. Beneath the fabric of her riding habit, he felt firm muscles. Yet she was also slim and elegant. His gaze traveled slowly over her voluptuous figure. His curiosity as well as his body aroused, he ran his fingers through her yellow hair. Her tresses felt like silk. His gaze slid rapidly from her beautiful hair to her breasts. Unable to resist, he let his hand wander down and under her to cup her bosom. So soft and full, a perfect fit in his large hand. Then he considered her narrow waist and shapely thighs. He slid his hand under her gown and up her thigh to feel the smooth skin there. Soft as a rose petal. He let his fingers linger there. She reminded him of a white rose, delicate and enchanting. He clutched her bottom and laid his face on her thigh, then closed his eyes and inhaled her scent.

A fire kindled in his loins. Sorely tempted, he considered untying her.

But, he had already tied her securely to the mare and taking a drugged woman who could not respond to his skilled seduction would be a lukewarm experience at best, even with one as enthralling as Kelly.

He would begin her lessons and sample her charms soon enough. They were no more than an hour or two from Lexington. Then this lovely rose would be his. Wholly his.

Forcing himself to stop his sweet exploration, he climbed onto his mount and hauled Kelly's horse beside him by the reins. He would have to take it slow. He did not want to risk her falling out of the saddle. That could be disastrous. She was a far too valuable asset to damage with scratches and bruises.

The crisp air cooled his face, but the sun shone through the trees in brilliant crystal rays that promised a warmer day. The beautiful morning and the prospect of bedding Kelly soon, boosted his spirits and he inhaled the sweet scent of pine deeply into his lungs.

He wasn't worried about Kelly's father following. They'd come out upstream of the Kentucky River and made their tracks disappear into the woods, and they had a significant lead on the man. Even if her father did catch up to them, he could easily handle the miserable drunk. In fact, he hoped McGuffin would show up. If he could dispatch the man and send him to hell, he would never have to worry about her father attempting to find her in Lexington. He tried to avoid murder anywhere near a town. That only drew trouble, but out here in the middle of nowhere, he could dispose of the body somewhere where only the wolves would find it.

And Kelly would sleep through it all, unaware that her father was dead.

&

After some time, Sam picked up Kelly's trail again and within a half hour located their campsite. "They camped here for part of the night," Sam said, dismounting. He peered around the area.

"That bastard better not have laid a hand on Kelly," McGuffin swore.

It was the first thing the man had said that William entirely agreed with.

"There's no sign of a struggle," Sam said.

"Let's see how long ago they were here," Bear suggested. He dismounted and strode over to a fresh pile of horse manure. His expression grew serious as he studied the dung, moving the round clumps on the top aside until his fingers were in the middle of the pile. A half smile crossed his face. "They just left, judgin' by the freshness of these droppings. They're still a wee bit warm," he said and then stood, grabbing a handful of leaves to wipe his fingers on.

Still mounted on Smoke, William spun the stallion around and took off at a gallop up the trail. He soon heard the other three men following close behind him.

His determination to reach Kelly before her captor could harm her surged though him with the force of a tidal wave. Even running at his fastest, Smoke could not gallop fast enough to suit him.

If the bastard had hurt her, he would soon be a dead man.

William clung to the belief that she would be unharmed—that he would reach her in time. But even if she was unharmed, this ordeal was the last thing Kelly needed. How far would this second trial set her back?

McGuffin trailed behind William and his brothers, struggling to keep up with their superior mounts. His old horse couldn't stand this pace for long, and would start slowing soon. But he wanted to be there when they caught up to Kelly. He had to be there. As her father, it was his duty to protect her and by God, he would from now on. He'd done a lousy job of it so far. He knew that now. The prospect of losing Kelly for good had woke him up. He couldn't stand even the thought of her dying too.

Losing her mother changed his life in ways he just now understood. Kelly looked so much like her mother, he could hardly stand to look at his daughter. She remained a constant painful reminder of his loss. He'd loved Kelly's mother with his entire soul and when she died, his soul seemed to die too. Only one thing kept him alive at all—whiskey. It fueled his sorrow just enough to keep his soul from dying.

Kelly was right. His life spun around in a negative cycle, again and again. Could he break the pattern? Could he become a real father again? Affection for his daughter gripped his heart. He loved Kelly, he knew that, but could he accept her as a loving father should? Could he put aside how she not only looked just like her mother, but sounded and acted like her too? Their voices were identical—soothing and infinitely compassionate. When Kelly spoke, the gentle softness in her voice only hardened his heart. The only thing he wanted to hear were words of love from his beloved wife. But death silenced her lovely voice forever.

And Kelly's eyes, serenely wise and beautiful, gazed back at him just like her mother used to. Their soft violet color gleamed with intelligence and a proud spirit. But in Kelly's eyes, he also often glimpsed pity and a burning faraway look. Her generous nature pitied him. But he had provided her with only hard disappointments. He didn't deserve her. He couldn't blame her for wanting to get far away from him. No wonder she had left.

It made his heart clench.

And now, he had also caught a glimpse of pain and fear in her eyes. What had happened to her at the cabin? He'd been so concerned about getting her to leave with him, that he never gave her a chance to answer his question.

McGuffin suddenly realized that during his musing, he'd fallen even further behind. He could barely see them in the distance and as his horse slowed to a walk, they disappeared completely from view.

His eyes clouded with visions of the past and he found himself speaking aloud to the love of his life, his head bowed. "Oh my darling, please forgive me. I've treated our daughter miserably. I can only pray for God's mercy on my miserable remorseful soul. And I pray for Kelly now. That whoever took her will inflict no harm and that William and his brothers will indeed rescue her. I also pray that she will someday understand why I shunned her. Why…."

His words trailed off when his heavy tears slipped down his cheeks and his blurred eyes cleared.

Indians surrounded him. They were not the same natives they'd encountered earlier. These appeared to be Cherokee.

Dear God, help me…please. Help me live to see my daughter again.

His heart nearly stopped in his chest as their sharp eyes bored into him.

☙

William glanced back over his shoulder. Sam and Bear rode just behind him, their mounts maintaining his thunderous pace. But where was McGuffin? He peered down the trail and saw nothing. "What happened to Kelly's father?" he yelled.

"He fell further and further behind us. His mount couldn't keep up," Sam shouted back.

William turned his attention back to the trail and studied it as far as he could see, fervently hoping to spot something. But as yet, he'd seen no sign of Kelly or her abductor. They could not afford to go back for Kelly's father or slow their pace. He wouldn't stop until he caught up to Kelly. McGuffin would just have to fend for himself.

"Ye need to slow down a wee bit, man," Bear yelled. "Let the horses rest. They're tiring and we willna catch the lass if we kill them."

"No!" William called back. "She's just ahead. I can feel her."

And his instinct proved true. There they were.

☙

McGuffin's stomach knotted with fear. He struggled not to let his panic show. His pulse beat erratically as a quick and disturbing thought entered his head. If he died now, he would never have a chance to ask Kelly's forgiveness or to be the father he could be. The misgivings shattered his heart. He wanted to cry. Not from fear. From regret.

One of the Indians moved out in front of the others. A large man, he carried a Kentucky rifle and a knife hung from his neck in a beaded sheath. A straight red pin about four inches across pierced his nose and numerous earrings hung from both ears. His polished shaved head gleamed in the morning light under a cluster of bright feathers perched on the top of his head. The native's manner, cool and aloof, chilled his blood as the Indian moved his horse closer.

As a trapper in Virginia, he often traded with natives for his safety. But here in Kentucky, the Indians didn't know him and they were far more unpredictable. Paralyzing apprehension coursed through him as he remembered the horrifying stories about what happened to some white men on this trail. All these natives would leave would be his mutilated smoldering body.

McGuffin felt impaled by the brave's penetrating steady gaze.

A painful silence loomed between them.

If only he knew sign language, like Sam. Terror made his chest tighten as he tried to speak. "I…I…am here in peace," he began. With his weapons stolen, he had to be.

At his words, the one in front held up his hand, silencing him. He felt as if that hand had closed around his throat. The air grew tight with tension and his escalating terror.

The contemptuous look in the leader's eyes told him the Indian knew of his fear. Then the brave's eyes hardened and something disturbing replaced his smoldering look. He gestured to two of the other natives. They dismounted and yanked him from his lathered mount, their grips around his arms tight and forceful. The horse trotted off as the two pushed him toward a nearby tree that stood off by itself. The strong scent of the braves burned the inside of his nose and throat.

But that was the least of his worries.

He breathed in shallow, rapid gasps, certain he was about to die, as the two braves tied first his hands behind him and then his chest and feet to the tree with rawhide. Panic rioted through him, making him tremble. He stood there, knees shaking, powerless to stop this. What could he do? What could he say? They wouldn't understand him even if he could come up with something to tell them. Never had he felt so helpless, so alone.

The large group of Cherokee, at least twenty in number, all dismounted and began yelping.

Their shrill primitive yaps stabbed at his heart, each chilling cry more horrifying than the last. The sound was so dreadful, so alarming, he almost wished they would kill him and be done with it. They seemed to be celebrating. Why? Oh dear God, they were reveling his impending death. Horror gripped him, stronger than ever. He squeezed his eyes shut, unable to watch them any longer.

"Little Turkey, First Beloved Man of the Cherokee," a man bellowed.

McGuffin opened his eyes and turned toward the deep voice.

The magnificently dressed older man, with thick snowy white hair, astride his tall horse, held himself with an air of distinction and pride. He rode right into the group of natives. Was the man daft? They would kill him too.

"Why do the Chickamauga Cherokee tie this man?" the man asked the native's leader, at the same time translating in sign language.

McGuffin thought he detected a note of censure in the man's voice and eyes. Whoever he was, he had guts or he was just plain crazy.

The native, who must be Little Turkey, spoke up, answering in a clipped voice.

McGuffin recognized only one word. Boone. Could this be Daniel Boone?

"Beloved Man of the Cherokee, you know that killing this man would be an unwise violation of our treaty. He is but one man. Is killing him worth risking raising the anger of all the whites?" His voice was calm, his hands unwaveringly steady as he signed the words.

Little Turkey's lips puckered with what seemed like annoyance.

The white-haired man turned to McGuffin. "Sir who are you and what are you doing here?" His tone was deadly serious.

"My companions and I are desperately trying to reach my daughter Kelly who was abducted last night. Sheriff Wyllie and his two brothers are in pursuit of her captor now. I fell behind because my horse is old," McGuffin explained rapidly, struggling to keep his voice from shaking. "Please help me. I believe they intend to kill me."

"Indeed they do, Sir. You were mere minutes from having your scalp and manhood lifted. I know what it is like to have a daughter abducted. A Cherokee-Shawnee raiding party captured my daughter Jemima and her friends, the Callaway girls, but we succeeded in rescuing them. I will do my best to help you. But say nothing and at least try to appear brave. A white man's fear is incendiary to the native man."

The Colonel dismounted and approached Little Turkey and then seemed to explain what McGuffin had just told Boone. Little Turkey's dark eyes widened as Boone spoke. Then for a moment, the Indian leader looked over at him quizzically. Would the brave believe Boone?

McGuffin could tell that these Indians held a high opinion of the Colonel by the way they regarded the aging frontier fighter and Kentucky hero. Boone first entered Kentucky about three decades ago. It was common knowledge that in that time, he'd earned the respect of not just the early pioneers, but the natives as well. He couldn't believe his good fortune that Boone had come along when he did. Perhaps God had heard his prayer and sent Boone to his rescue.

To his astonishment, Little Turkey motioned for the other Indians to mount up, then the brave grasped Boone's arm and held it for a few seconds before releasing it and smoothly swinging up onto his own horse.

After the Indians left, Boone turned to him and plucked his knife from its leather sheath. "God must have some reason to let you live, Sir. If I hadn't come along when I did, you would now be turning to ash."

As soon as the ropes fell away, McGuffin sank to his knees, unable to stand, his throat still feeling choked. "Thank you, Sir, for your timely assistance," he managed to croak. "Do I have the honor of addressing Daniel Boone?"

"I am Colonel Boone."

"I thought as much. Only you could command that much respect from the natives with no more than your presence."

"That respect took an exceedingly long time to earn," Boone

replied, with a deep sigh.

"Colonel, I must get going. My daughter needs me. I believe that is why God allowed me live." He tried to stand, but his legs were still unsteady.

"Your mount has had a chance to rest. He's over yonder grazing," Boone said pointing about a hundred yards away. "Have a rest yourself while I retrieve him."

When Boone returned with his horse, McGuffin took a few deeps breaths and then managed to stand again. Anxious to be on his way, he said, "I must get going, but I thank you again for your timely assistance. How can I ever repay you?"

"You said your daughter's name was Kelly." Recognition shown in Boone's eyes. "I met her, at Sheriff Wyllie's swearing in ceremony."

"My apologies. My name is Rory McGuffin. Yes, Kelly is my only child."

"At his swearing in ceremony, William seemed quite taken with your daughter. I could see it in the way he looked at her. And if my old eyes didn't fail me, I'm sure I noticed a fondness for William in those bright eyes of hers too."

Boone seemed to think for a moment. "My dear wife Rebecca is always warning me not to interfere in the personal affairs of others, but I find that sometimes frontier love needs a bit of encouragement," he said with a laugh. "And I can never resist an opportunity to play the match maker."

McGuffin was surprised to hear this battle-hardened soldier express a softer side.

"You can repay me by encouraging your daughter to marry William. He's one of the finest young men I have ever had the pleasure of meeting and he has already proven his bravery and integrity to the people of Boonesborough. Judge Webb and Colonel Byrd both speak extremely highly of him and his family. Before I left, for his service to the citizens of Boonesborough, I gave William the deed to my old cabin. It has fresh water, a nice orchard, and a smokehouse. So he'll have a comfortable home for your daughter. I don't know much about her, but she's a lovely young woman and William would be lucky to have her."

McGuffin stared, amazed that this man's insight recognized all that and that he had missed it all. Whiskey must have dulled his mind. But Boone's perceptions rang true to him. William was clearly taken with Kelly, his concern for her amply evident. The Colonel was right. The two seemed meant for each other. "Sir, you have my word, I will not interfere if William should ask her to marry him."

"No, I want your word that not only will you not interfere, you will encourage your daughter to consider William favorably," Boone retorted.

McGuffin had to admire Boone's negotiating acumen. "I'll agree, but why do you care so much?"

"For two reasons. First, Sir, because young people like them are Boonesborough's only hope. I have a large number of friends and family resting eternally on the other side of the sod. All of them sacrificed for Kentucky. Both my mind and my heart want to be certain Kentucky has a bright future. Without brave men like William, and spirited women like Kelly, Boonesborough will vanish like mist in the morning, and the fort will become only a perch for the owl and a hiding place for the fox."

McGuffin's mouth hung open at the simple eloquence in Boone's words. He could see now how the natural leader had inspired men by the thousands to answer the call of destiny and migrate to Kentucky.

"In addition," Boone continued, "it has been my own personal experience, and I have observed in others, that behind every successful man is a woman who inspired and buoyed that success through her own strengths and capabilities. Men often underestimate the impact a woman can have on a man's life. My impression of Kelly is that she is a woman who will inspire William to greatness here in Kentucky."

"She is indeed," he said proudly. "You have my word, Sir. I was quite impressed with William myself." In truth he was. He just had not let William know it. They had gotten off on the wrong foot. In fact, he had to admit he'd acted like an ass to William and his brothers.

"Good, then we are in agreement," Boone stated with finality.

"Are you headed north? If so, I surely hope you will join me. I'd hate to run into Indians again without you."

"Indeed I am. I have business in Lexington," Boone replied. "Then I am headed home, to the mouth of the Little Sandy River in northeastern Kentucky. Although I suspect Providence may soon call me elsewhere."

With that, they both mounted and urged their horses to a fast trot.

Thank you, Lord. Now just let William reach her in time.

CHAPTER 11

William urged his stallion to run with all that was left in the weary animal. He needed to reach Kelly. He could see her slumped over Ginger's neck, her head bobbing and hair flopping with each step the mare took. Was she hurt? Dear God, please no.

He searched his mind for an explanation. Who was that tall man who led her mare? She sure as hell better be all right or he would be a tall corpse in mere minutes. He swallowed hard, trying to hold his raw emotions in check.

He would be there in seconds.

As Smoke drew close, he saw the man gawk back toward him with first surprise and then alarm. The fellow seemed to hesitate for a moment or two and then dropped the reins to Kelly's horse, before spurring his sizable stallion to a full bounding run.

Confused, Ginger started to run after the stallion. William could see Kelly's body beginning to slip to the mare's left side, just seconds away from being tangled in the horse's galloping legs.

"Oh God, no!"

Swiftly closing the short gap between them, William pulled alongside the frightened mare's right side and reached down for the bridle with one hand, while trying to support Kelly's drooping body with his other hand. He couldn't let her slip further. "Whoa girl, whoa. I've got you now. Whoa."

Ginger and Smoke both slowed and then finally came to a full stop. William stepped off his stallion and grabbed Kelly, supporting her limp body in his shaking arms. "Kelly. Kelly. My God, what has he done to you?" Worry and fear crowded his mind. "I'm here Kelly. I'm here for you."

Seconds later, Sam and Bear tugged their mounts to an abrupt halt beside him and instantly dismounted.

"She won't wake up," he told them, feeling a wave of panic sweep through him.

"Let's get her off her horse," Sam said.

Bear held the horses and Sam held Kelly, while William untied the ropes binding her to the mare. He couldn't believe this was the second time he'd had to remove ropes from her wrists and ankles. As before, her skin was an angry red and raw in places.

As he gently lowered her to the ground, he swore he would use these very same ropes on the man who had tied them on Kelly.

Both of his brothers knelt next to Kelly, examining her. "No head wounds," Sam said.

"It appears she has na broken bones," Bear stated.

"Thank God for that at least," William said, "but why doesn't she wake?" His heart thumped madly as he held her hand in his.

"Let me smell her breath," Bear urged and nudged Sam aside. "Drugged. The poor wee thing has been drugged."

Sam smelled her breath as well. “I agree,” he said. “Opium. Her breath has the sickly sweet smell of the poppy flower. During the war, surgeons gave it to those with the worst injuries. If the bugger didn’t overdose her, she’ll come around eventually.”

“And if he did?” William asked, a pulsing knot forming in his stomach, because he already knew the answer.

Sam didn’t respond.

William stood as icy fear wrapped around his heart. “I’ll kill him!” he swore. If Kelly died, nothing would do any good but a first-class killing and he was the man that would give it to the bastard. He tucked the ropes into his saddle bag. Then he bent a knee and lowered his lips to hers, sealing his vow with a gentle kiss. He never envisioned that this would be the way he would kiss Kelly for the first time, but his heart leapt at the feel of his lips brushing against hers.

He would see the end of this nightmare for her. He stood and vaulted onto his horse. “Both of you stay with her. Take her to my new cabin. Whispering Hills is north and west of Boonesborough, no more than thirty minutes. But first be sure the doctor checks her over. And keep her miserable father away from her.”

Before they could respond, he took off. With a snap of his reins, he urged Smoke to a hard gallop. He prayed his stallion would be as fast as the abductor’s stallion was. Even if it was, though, his mount had been running at a steady pace for some time. But the man could be no more than a quarter mile or so ahead of him. All he needed was a bit of luck and he’d soon catch up with him. And there it was. A clearing in the forest provided a gap through which he could ride, cutting a shorter path. He took it, weaving around the few trees in the glade and angling so that he would intercept the man.

A few seconds later, he charged out onto the trail and skid to a halt, his stallion angled to block the road. "Get off your mount you son-of-a-bitch," William ordered.

"Sir, I beg you to wait just a minute and listen to reason," the man said in a smooth voice.

"Get off of your mount. I won't ask again."

As soon as the man dismounted, William did as well, keeping a watchful eye on the man's every move.

"Sir…" the man began.

But William's fist whacked the man's jaw before the next word came out.

The man doubled over to his left side but did not go down.

William kept his fists clenched. "What is your name?"

The man lifted his chin and responded, "Harpes."

"Harpes what?" William demanded, his tone nearly as hot as his anger.

"Harpes Robinson."

"Mister Robinson, why did you abduct Miss McGuffin?"

"I rescued her!" the man replied abruptly. He stood there, looking indignant and offended.

William got the sense the man was a braggart—all gurgle and no guts. "Rescued her from what?"

"From her brut of a father."

William couldn't quarrel with the man's description, but he still wanted to punch the man's haughty face again. "Did Miss McGuffin ask to be rescued and how was she endangered by her father? Did he hit her?" He would do his best to wait for the answer, but it took all his self-control not to hit Harpes again. His distrust grew stronger by the minute.

"No, he did not hit her. And she did not ask for my help," he admitted. "But her father was drunk and acted like a boar towards her. I waited, hidden in the woods, until he fell asleep to be sure he didn't hurt her. Later, I came to her and she subsequently agreed to go with me to Lexington."

William found that hard to believe. But Kelly was in a precarious and fragile state of mind. Maybe she thought she could escape her problems by going with this man. With narrowed eyes, William regarded Harpes for a moment. He stared unflinching into the man's stony eyes.

"Her father was treating her pitifully," the stranger explained. "I heard their argument from some distance away and came to her assistance. I felt sorry for her. If you had heard the hurtful things the bully said to her, you would have wanted to rescue her too. Once you crush a beautiful rose, it cannot be uncrushed."

William bristled at the man calling Kelly a beautiful rose, but he couldn't disagree with his logic. Had Kelly's father crushed her beautiful spirit? William sincerely hoped she'd found the strength to stand up to her father's verbal assault.

But for now, his primary concern was this vexing man. "Is that why you drugged her? Because you felt sorry for her?" William questioned, squinting his eyes again.

Harpes' left eyebrow rose. "No, I…." he stammered, and lowered his head.

William's jaw clenched. "What did you do to her, you filthy bastard?"

"Nothing, I assure you."

"Did…you…touch…her?" William enunciated each word with a snarl.

"She is untouched. I was taking her to Lexington to provide her with an education. I am a man of means and property and can provide her with all she needs."

"I can just imagine what kind of education you had in mind," William seethed, feeling like a volcano on the verge of erupting. "And as for providing for her, that is none of your concern. I'll ask you one last time. And I warn you a poor answer will have equally poor consequences. Why did you drug her?"

The color drained from Harpes' face and his eyes darted to the ground as he struggled to rationalize what he'd done. He gave an anxious little cough before finally answering. "Opium can take a person to great heights of extraordinary pleasure. There's nothing quite like it. I wanted to give the young woman some pleasure, that's all. May I offer you some?" His lips curled slowly into a cloying smile.

William's fist slammed into the man's jaw again. This time, knocking Harpes to the ground. "I should just hang your sorry soul. Right here. Right now." He glowered at the bastard, letting his eyes convey the fury within him.

"On whose authority?" the pompous man asked as he regained his feet.

"On my authority," William snapped. "I'm Sheriff Wyllie of Boonesborough. And you, Sir, are under arrest for abduction and assault of a woman."

For the first time, the man looked worried. "I did not assault her!" Harpes insisted. "I helped her." A shadow of doubt swept across his face.

"Drugging a person to the point of rendering them unconscious is assault."

Harpes stiffened and haughtily tossed his head. "Says who?"

The abductor's contemptuous expression sent William's temper soaring. "Says the law. And that's me. Turn around and put your hands behind your back."

"Perhaps you are in need of a few extra gold coins sheriff?"

"Keep your coins in your pocket you weasel. Now, turn around."

"I am a man of considerable means. I'm sure I can find an amount that will persuade you."

"No amount of money is worth a man's honor," William replied, making his voice lashing. "I swore an oath to uphold the law. Right now, though, I wish I hadn't. Because then I could just kill you for what you did to Kelly."

Harpes took a step forward, but did not turn. "Just how do you intend to dispense this law? It's just the two of us. Out here in the middle of nowhere." He raised his chin with a cool stare in William's direction.

William pulled his pistol. "With this. And if Kelly says you harmed her, a sturdy rope. For the third, and final time, turn around."

Harpes hardened his features and slowly turned.

William reached into his saddlebag for the ropes Harpes used on Kelly.

Harpes spun, and teeth bared, charged, shoving his head and

shoulder into William's stomach.

The impact sent them both flying to the ground.

CHAPTER 12

Kelly drifted in and out, her hazy mind refusing to come awake despite how hard she tried. Why was she sleeping? She continued to struggle toward wakefulness, but it was like trudging uphill through a murky gloom. Finally, she managed to wake enough to open her eyes. Her muddled wits strained to make sense of where she was. Where was William? She could hear Sam and Bear's voices, sounding muffled and distant, but not William's.

She also smelled coffee brewing. Her sense of smell seemed heightened and the aroma wafting through the air was marvelous, like sugar browning or nuts roasting.

"I made this coffee strong enough to float horseshoes," Bear told Sam. "and I let it cool a wee bit."

"Let's see if she'll drink any," Sam said.

She felt one of them lift her neck and she tried to open her eyes again but her heavy eyelids wouldn't stay open. Her breaths were shallow, her awareness coming and going.

Bear dribbled the lukewarm brew into her mouth and she swallowed. Never had coffee tasted so good. It was strong, but its warmth soothed her thirst and the brew took the feel of cotton off her tongue.

Sam and Bear made her drink several more times until she finally sputtered some of the coffee out.

"Kelly, can you sit up? We need to be on our way," Sam said, tossing the rest of the coffee.

Kelly pushed herself up and leaned on Bear's big arm for support until her head cleared. "I feel well rested," she said after a few moments, "like I've slept for a week. Just how long was I asleep? And why, for heaven's sake, was I asleep at all?"

"We'll explain later, after we are on our way," Sam said.

"I'll carry her first," Bear volunteered. He mounted and Sam gently lifted her up into Bear's arms.

Kelly settled herself against Bear's massive chest, but resisted the temptation to go to sleep again. "Where's William?" she asked, still somewhat groggy after a few minutes. "I thought I heard his voice too."

"Perhaps in your dreams," Sam replied smiling.

"He'll be happier than a butcher's dog to know ye've come around," Bear said, sounding pretty happy himself.

"Come around?" Kelly asked, the coffee finally starting to wake her up.

"Ye were drugged Miss Kelly," Bear said, "by that evil man who stole you away."

"Drugged. That's why I feel so...so strangely."

"Yes, Kelly," Sam said, "but you'll be fine. You're safe now."

"Where are we? Bear, turn me around so I can see where I'm

going," she said.

"All right, lass," Bear said. He lifted and turned her so her legs hung off the horse to his right and she could face forward.

"Who was that man and why did that man take you?" Sam asked.

"His name is Harpes and he said he wanted to give me an education," Kelly answered, trying to remember more of what exactly had happened to her.

Bear and Sam exchanged a meaningful look. What it meant eluded her, but she felt sure they didn't trust the stranger. Neither did she. Why did the man drug her? She'd been cooperative. She had agreed to go with him to Lexington. He had no reason to drug her. Unless...unless he meant to do her harm. Numb with shock, and increasing rage, she started to rub her sore wrist, but then stopped. Her chest swelled with her determination. No, she told herself. No fear. No more fear.

And no more shame.

She straightened herself and held her head a little higher. From now on, she would not let herself feel anything other than self-respect. No longer would she question her worth. She felt as if her dormant dignity had renewed itself while she was sleeping. With a sense of strength filling her, she came fully awake. With abrupt clarity, she immediately thought of William. "Where's your brother?" she asked.

"He's gone after the bastard. Oh, excuse me, lass. He's gone after your captor," Bear corrected.

"Gone where?" she demanded.

"When we finally caught up to you, your abductor let go of your mare and took off like a lightning bolt," Sam answered.

"After William determined that you were all right and told us to escort you back to Boonesborough, he took off after the man. By now, your abductor is probably experiencing the fullest extent of the law."

Kelly wasn't sure what Sam meant, but she was concerned for William. "Will he be all right? What if that man hurts him?"

"Nay, tis far more likely it will be yer abductor who will be feeling the hurtin'," Bear said.

"Stop these horses. Right now!" Kelly ordered.

After they both slowed their mounts, Sam asked, "Why Kelly? What's wrong?"

"We are not leaving William to fend for himself against that horrible man. If he drugged me, he might do the same to William, or worse. Turn these horses around this minute!"

"Kelly, William is quite capable of taking care of himself. He's been dealing with outlaws for years," Sam said.

"Aye, he's been known to deal with several at a time. One will na be a problem for William," Bear agreed.

"I would not leave him if I thought he was in serious danger," Sam said. "William possesses considerable skills with weapons. And he's shrewd and brave. Rest assured, he can handle this Harpes."

"You cannot be certain of that. I spent time with that man. He's slick as an egg white and I don't trust him. You have to go help your brother and you have to do it now!" She felt a curious pull toward William and she was growing more ill at ease by the minute as her concern for him grew. An uncomfortable shudder passed through her.

She peered at Sam, imploring him with her eyes.

"Kelly, we can't risk letting you get hurt again. William would never forgive us if something happened to you. We need to get you safely back to Boonesborough. It's what William wanted," Sam argued.

"But William didn't know what I want," she said determinedly, "and I want you two to go help him." Her emotions swelled with a driving need to be with William. Now, not later. She had to be sure he was all right. With pulse-pounding certainty, she wanted to be near him. Just his presence brought her joy, but now she could no longer deny herself his touch, his affection, too. Her heart thudded within her and her breaths quickened. "Put me down, Bear. I can ride my own horse now." Sam had been pulling her mare behind him.

"Nay, Miss Kelly. You may be awake now, but the drugs may make you fall asleep again soon and we do na want ye to fall off yer mare, now do we lass?"

"Certainly not, however, I am well awake now."

"Kelly, Bear's right. You should stay put for a couple more hours, till we know the drugs have fully worn off," Sam said.

"All right, I'll agree, but only if you go back to find William," she said, meeting Sam's disapproving eyes without flinching.

Although she thought of both Sam and Bear as brothers, it wasn't easy standing up to the two enormous, equally obstinate, warriors. But she had to convince them to go to William. She glanced uneasily over her shoulder, back in the direction they'd come from. Her confidence that she was right spiraled upward. With desperate firmness, she said, "If you don't turn these horses around, I will jump down from here and go myself. And if I break a leg or my foot when I jump, it will be your fault."

"Och, but the woman can be stubborn," Bear complained to Sam.

"Indeed," Sam said, with a smile.

Powerful relief filled her when Sam turned his mount.

☙

McGuffin peered ahead, anxious to catch his first glimpse of William and his brothers. He prayed they would have already caught up to Kelly and that she would be all right.

"Don't worry, Sir, your daughter will be located. With William, Captain Sam, and Bear after her abductor, he stands little chance of success," Boone offered.

"I pray you are correct, Sir," McGuffin answered. "I have much to say to my daughter. And much time to make up for. I had just come to collect her and take her home when she was abducted."

"Can I ask how Kelly came to be in Boonesborough and why you are just now coming to claim her?" Boone asked.

McGuffin told Boone what he knew of the events that led up to Kelly being in Boonesborough. He was ashamed that he didn't fully understand what happened himself. He should have had the good sense and patience to question her further and listen to what William had been trying to explain.

"I sense you are struggling with other problems as well," Boone said.

"The last few years, ever since my beloved wife passed, I have cultivated a regrettable habit of drinking whiskey too often and too much. It's caused problems between me and my daughter."

For a moment, Boone didn't say anything. He seemed pensive, not judgmental or angry. "Fine whiskey is one of Kentucky's proudest achievements and we've developed a reputation for our distillers' skills, especially Bourbon County, just north a short distance from where we are now. They're blessed with the right assets —a steady good crop of corn, sweet water, and abundant hardwoods for making barrels. But, the brew can be a powerful temptress if one does not possess the ability to know when to put the cork back in the bottle. I've known others who have had the same problem. Some overcame it and some didn't. Only the strongest of men win that difficult battle. What kind of man are you? Strong or weak? Are you prepared to lose someone you can't bear to lose—someone you love more than your own life?" Boone's blue eyes pierced the distance between them.

McGuffin stared squarely back at Boone, asking himself the same questions. The day of reckoning has come, he thought with fearful clarity. He drew his lips in thoughtfully. A few moments ago, his life nearly came to a horrifying end. Was this a chance to start a brand new life? As a man and as a father? With a startling realization, he decided that it was. If he didn't take this chance now, he might never have another one. He could lose the only person he loved in the world—his beautiful daughter.

"I'm going to stop drinking. I swear to God and to you, I am. Right now." He halted his horse and reached behind him and into his saddle bag. He wrenched out his jug, and with his heart beating rapidly in his chest, he let the contents escape to the earth below. It pained him, like pouring out his own blood.

"Emptying that jug out won't banish the desire for it from your body," Boone said, looking down at the puddle of wet earth. "There's only one thing that can."

"What's that?" McGuffin asked, anxious to hear the answer.

"Love is the only answer. Love for, and from, your maker. And love for your daughter. As far as love for God, as scripture says, it has to be with your heart, soul, and mind. All three. And as for God's love for you, if you let it fill you, strengthen you, there's little room left for temptation or evil."

In that moment, McGuffin recognized that Boone, considered a formidable Kentucky warrior, was a kinder, gentler, spirit than most people knew.

Perhaps God would be too.

CHAPTER 13

They both fell backwards, tumbling against William's squealing stallion. Smoke side-stepped as the two men plummeted underneath the horse. With Harpes weight on him, William's back slammed into the hard ground. He caught glimpses of Smoke's hooves stomping around their heads, dangerously close, as the stallion tried to get out of the way. His breath deserted him and his mouth gaped open, but he couldn't let the lack of air in his lungs stop him. He thrust his knee into Harpes' stomach and tossed the man off to his left.

Quickly searching for his weapon, knocked out of his hand as they both crashed against his startled mount, he spotted the pistol to his right and darted over to it. William snatched up his flintlock and straightened while sucking in much needed air.

Harpes scrambled upward and drew his own weapon.

In the next instant, they both held pistols aimed at each other's heaving chests.

He stared into the man's malicious grey eyes, flashing like silver lightning, knowing Harpes could kill him in the next instant. Any chance of a future with Kelly could vanish with a single tiny lead ball fired from Harpes' flintlock. He couldn't let that happen.

"Drop your weapon," William ordered, narrowing his eyes. "I caution you to give up now."

"Drop your weapon," Harpes countered, his face a frozen smile. "Unless you're prepared to die today."

William scowled at the vile man. "Harpes, you are in enough trouble without killing a sheriff too."

"I'm not going to kill you," Harpes said. "I'm an excellent man with a firearm. I'll just geld you."

The repugnant threat fueled William's anger even further. He would have a hard time not killing this disgusting man. His chest heaving, he gripped the gun's handle even harder. "You can't make a threat like that without expecting dire consequences."

Cool as ice, Harpes posture was relaxed, his face calm. "Do not corner something that you know is meaner than you." The man took a deep, satisfied breath and straightened his waistcoat. William half expected the dandy to start whistling.

He had to make himself just as composed. He needed his wits about him if he was going to beat this devil. Then, he would release his fury on Kelly's abductor like the wrath of God.

"I'm warning you Harpes, give up you weapon, now. I won't ask this a third time."

"No," Harpes answered simply.

It was time to end this. Taking a few slow breaths, William regarded Harpes with somber interest. He needed to find a way to distract the loathsome man.

He started to walk unhurriedly in a wide circle, his footsteps sure, his gaze unrelenting.

His movement forced Harpes to pivot to keep William in sight.

His steps easy and unrushed, William continued to breathe slowly.

Harpes looked as if he were weighing whether he was faster with a pistol than William was. William had half a mind to make that clear to the contemptible man.

When he'd taken Harpes through a half circle, William abruptly glanced up and let his face brighten. "Ah, at last, my brothers are catching up to us," he said eagerly.

Harpes' started to turn and then, as he recognized William's attempt to distract him, he swore under his breath, narrowed his flinty eyes, and fired his weapon.

In one fluid motion, William spun to his side and discharged his own pistol.

The lead from Harpes' weapon hit the ground just past William and kicked brown dust up to mingle with the smoky cloud of the black powder from both their weapons. Through the haze, he saw Harpes clutch his chest.

"You son of a..." Harpes began, before he fell forward on his knees, grabbing at his wound.

"I warned you more than once to give up," William said, wishing the fellow had listened.

A moment later, Robinson crumpled over, unconscious.

William rushed over to Harpes. Already, bright red blood stretched outward across the front of what was an exceptionally white shirt. But he hadn't hit the heart. The abductor might live.

He retrieved the rope that Harpes had used on Kelly and quickly tied the man's hands in front of him. He wasn't taking any chances.

Then he searched Harpes and found not one, but two daggers, hidden in his jacket and boot, and an exceptionally small pistol in his waistcoat.

He used Harpes' handkerchief, also amazingly white, to apply pressure to the wound. He'd rather let the swine bleed to death, but it wasn't in him to just let a man die.

Within a minute or so, the man regained consciousness. "Am I done for?" Harpes asked, his voice weak.

"If we can get that bullet out of you, you stand a chance. But, I'm not inclined to dig around on you much myself. Hopefully, you'll make it back to Boonesborough. Then the doc can take a look at you."

"We both know I won't make it that far," Harpes said, his voice husky with emotion.

"I'm inclined to agree with you."

"We're a lot closer to Lexington. You can take me there."

"I have no business in Lexington. My duties require me to return to Boonesborough, and that's where you're going."

"But I don't want to go to Boonesborough," Harpes whined.

"You should have thought of that before you abducted Miss McGuffin."

"Are your brothers really coming?"

William gave him a half smile. "No. Not yet." He didn't want to reveal that the two had already returned to Boonesborough with Kelly. "They'll be along soon enough."

"What did you do with the young lady?" Harpes asked.

"She's with my brothers," William answered. "She's no longer your concern. She never was."

"If I tell you why I was really taking her to Lexington, will you promise to dig this bullet out of me?" Harpes entreated.

"How do I know you'll tell the truth? You haven't so far."

His voice rose an octave as he said, "Because I want to live."

That, at least, William believed. He said the words with the certainty of a man who knew he would die without help. His eyes caught and held Harpes' stare. "I'll not help you unless I'm absolutely convinced you're telling the truth."

Harpes coughed and a little blood splattered onto his shirt. That wasn't a good sign. Watching a man die, even a despicable one, was a grim prospect.

William sighed with exasperation. He decided to try to get the truth out of Harpes before it was too late. "All right, I promise to try to get the bullet out, if you are strong enough, and if you tell me the truth."

His tone cold and exact, Harpes began. "I am a partner in a bordello. The finest one in Lexington. My partner's name is Belle. I acquire young women for the house. Usually women with little or no family and poor prospects. We drug them for the first few days, until they settle in. Then I teach them what they need to know to pleasure a man. I was taking Kelly there."

William's scant pity for the man evaporated entirely. He shot him a withering glance. "You vulgar bastard. Again, I should just hang you right here. Right now."

"Sir, I may be a bastard, in fact, I think I am. But I am certainly not vulgar. Nor should you hang me. I fear it will be unnecessary."

"Civility and fine clothing do not make a man decent or a gentleman," William hissed. "You, Sir, are as vulgar and loutish as they come."

"If you will cease throwing stones at me for the moment and start digging this bullet out of my chest, it would be much appreciated."

"All right. Do you have any whiskey? You're going to need it."

"No, but I have opium. It's in my saddle bag on my horse's left side." Harpes coughed again. He sounded weaker.

William considered Harpes speculatively. Should he risk trying to get the bullet out? The man would probably bleed to death. He decided he had to try. He located the package of opium. "How do I give it to you?" he asked.

"The best way would be to make some tea, but I can't wait that long. Put some on one of the biscuits in my other bag," he said, closing his eyes, and biting his lip.

After he gave Harpes the biscuit, he opened the blood soaked shirt with his knife and lifted the handkerchief. Blood still spilled out of the hideous wound just above his right nipple. William quickly replaced the cloth and applied as much pressure as Harpes could tolerate.

He had no idea how deep the bullet might have penetrated or if it would even be possible to get to it. He decided to use one of Harpes' daggers. They were probably cleaner than his own knife. He pulled one. The blade sparkled in the light, needlepoint sharp, and spotless.

Harpes watched him with a critical squint. "Have you ever removed a bullet before?"

"Yes, but not from a man's chest." William didn't want to do this, but he'd promised he would and he meant to keep his word. He sighed, then gave a resigned shrug. "Are you ready?"

Harpes blinked and his face grew even paler. "I feel lightheaded. Sir, if I don't make it, will you tell Miss McGuffin something for me?" His imploring eyes searched William's face.

"That depends."

"Tell her I'm sorry. That's all, just, I'm sorry." Harpes eyes examined William.

"Sorry you took her or sorry you got caught."

"I'm just sorry…"

"I'll tell her."

As his labored breaths faded to a hushed stillness, pleasure briefly lit the abductor's face.

In the next twinkling, death abducted pleasure from Harpes' eyes forever.

William stood and looked down at the lifeless body, a heavy feeling in his stomach. "I'm sorry too."

And he was—sorry that Harpes forced him to take a life. Sorry the evil man doubtless just arrived in hell. Sorry for the trauma Harpes inflicted on Kelly.

What emotional havoc had Harpes caused Kelly?

His mind feared for her.

His heart ached for her.

His soul needed her.

CHAPTER 14

At the sound of horses approaching, William glanced over his shoulder. This time it really was his brothers—and Kelly. She was sitting in front of Bear, fully awake and Sam had her mare in tow.

A powerful cry of relief broke from his lips. He was amazed how much the sight of her cheered him.

Suddenly anxious to be away from Harpes and with Kelly, he started running toward them. Toward her. His body nearly vibrated with excitement. He couldn't wait to see her beautiful eyes shining back at him. He leapt over a log and lengthened his stride. It felt good to run. To feel alive when he could so easily have died back there.

He kept his eyes on her as he ran, waiting expectantly for her to hear or see him coming.

She soon peered ahead and caught sight of him. Her somber face lit up with a bright smile, like the sun coming out from behind a dark cloud. "William," she called.

He was just moments away from her! His heart beat faster with the tick of each second.

Bear stopped his horse Camel, and with just one of his powerful arms, lowered Kelly down from his saddle. She grabbed her skirt and starting running too.

William caught a glimpse of the huge smiles on both Bear and Sam's faces. He was going to have to give the two of them a piece of his mind. They were supposed to take Kelly back.

But right now, though, as she leapt into his arms, he was enormously grateful they hadn't.

"Kelly! How I've prayed for this moment," he whispered into her ear as she hugged him fiercely, and without any hesitation.

He embraced her so tightly, glee bubbled out of her in a laugh. She drew back a little and gazed up into his eyes, happiness radiating from deep within her. She had changed. That much was clear. But how? Why? He had expected her to be worse off, not better—not this euphoric bundle of joy.

"I had to come to you. I did it William. I did it!"

"Did what Kelly?" he asked, putting his hands on her arms and searching her face.

"I realized why I've been afraid. And I won't tell you all about it now, but you were right, fear was making me weak. And afraid. I'm not afraid anymore. Or ashamed. In fact, I feel stronger than ever before. You helped me kill the dragon. I had a dream while I was drugged, and we slayed the dragon together."

William had no idea what she was talking about, but he was delighted by the confidence he heard underlying her words. "Kelly, you can't imagine how happy it makes me to hear you say that. But first things first. Did Harpes hurt you?"

"He drugged me, but that's all. He said he wanted to take me to Lexington to give me an education."

William had to bite down on his tongue to keep his angry words in his mouth. Any remorse he felt for killing Harpes vanished.

"I made Sam and Bear bring me back to you. They didn't want to, but I had to be sure you were all right," she said, running her fingers affectionately over his coat and chest. "Dear God William, there's blood on you. Are you hurt?"

Her touch sent wonderful shivers up and down his spine. "No, not me." He gestured for Sam and Bear to join them. "It's Harpes' blood."

"I was a fool to go with him. I was just desperate and..."

Sam and Bear pulled alongside them, interrupting her. "Where's Harpes?" Sam asked.

"Over there," he pointed, "dead."

Kelly gasped and her heavy lashes flew up. "You killed him?" She bit her lip and seemed to stifle an outcry.

"It was either kill him or be killed. He would not yield peacefully, despite my repeated requests. Then he pulled his pistol on me," William said. "And, of course, he forcibly abducted and drugged you. For that, I wanted to hang him. Nevertheless, I was going to take him back to Boonesborough for trial, but he refused to surrender to me."

Once the shock of what he'd said wore off, she threw her head back and with her hands on her hips said, "If he tried to kill you, the man deserved what he got." She boldly met his eyes. "He was a bad man William. Why on earth did he drug me?"

"I know he was Kelly," William said, relieved that she didn't appear too startled by the news of Harpes' death. "He had his reasons for drugging you, and they weren't good." There was no reason to burden her with the details.

"I'm so glad he didn't hurt you," she said.

"He wanted me to tell you something," William said.

"What?" Kelly asked without flinching.

"That he was sorry."

"Well, at least the man repented," Bear said.

William wondered about that.

"Did he tell you why he drugged me?" Kelly asked again.

William's body stiffened at the question. Should he tell her? He took hold of Kelly's waist and lifted her up to Bear again. "Bear take Kelly off a ways to rest while Sam and I bury Harpes."

"No Sir! William Wyllie I have waited long enough to be with you," Kelly said, with defiance in her tone. "Put me down. I can ride my own mount. I am perfectly fine, now that we are all together again."

He sat her back on her feet and stared in astonishment, momentarily speechless. There was more than a subtle change in Kelly. Every curve of her body seemed stronger, more resilient. Her spirit was more vibrant, more alive. He'd been worried sick that this experience with her father and the trial of her abduction would set her back, but it was just the opposite. Somehow, she had dug down inside of her and found the courage and strength she needed to deal with it all and come out stronger than before.

Kelly turned, marched to her mare, and then climbed up into the saddle.

"No sense arguing with the lass," Bear said, smiling. "We learned tis as useless as a one-legged man in an arse-kicking contest."

Kelly chuckled and the delightful sound of it warmed William's heart.

Then she looked around. "Where is my father?" Kelly asked, as she settled into the saddle and gathered the reins in her hands. "Did he not come with you?"

William eyed his brothers for an answer.

"Yes, he was with us, but the last time we saw him, he was at least a half mile behind us," Sam said. "Then we lost sight of him. His older horse was unable to keep up the pace William was setting trying to reach you."

"Well, where is he now?" she asked, her voice heavy with concern. "He should have caught up to you by now." She waited for an answer, her vexation evident. He couldn't tell if she was mad at her father or at all of them for letting him go missing.

"She's right," William said. He gritted his teeth. One of them would have to go back for the useless man. It needed to be him. "Kelly and I will go back and check on him. Can you two stay and dig a grave for Harpes? And when you're done, bring Harpes' stallion and catch up to us as quick as you can in case there's any other bands of Indians out there."

Sam raised his chin and eyed him pointedly.

William was sure Sam thought they should wait for him and Bear in case of Indian trouble. But he wanted, no he needed, time alone with Kelly. And Sam and Bear wouldn't be far behind in case they ran into trouble. He gave a slight negative shake to his head and Sam nodded his understanding.

"Aye," Bear said, "we've both dug many a grave with just our knives. We can dig one more. But we'll na be burying the scoundrel very deep."

❧

After he retrieved Smoke, William and Kelly took off riding south, side by side, back toward Boonesborough. An undeniable and utterly sensuous aura passed between them for the first time. But as they glanced back and forth at one another, there was a definite significance to the visual exchange beyond their physical attraction for one another. Finally, they had set their feelings for each other free. He no longer had to worry about scaring Kelly if he showed her that he cared for her. And his love for her palpably leapt at the chance to be unfettered. And she no longer had to fear him. Or feel shame for what happened to her.

She had set herself free from her past.

At the same moment, they both grasped the significance of what had happened between them. Their eyes locked in understanding. Her smile broadened and her eyes sang with happiness.

His own freed feelings soared, higher than he ever dreamed possible. Just watching her brought so much joy to his heart. Even with her hair tousled and her gown dirty and wrinkled, she was stunning. When he'd first spotted her with Bear and Sam, his primary emotion had been relief. But now, his heart swelled with much more. As the bright rays of the morning sun lit up her hair, he could swear an angel rode beside him. He thanked the Lord for protecting this particular angel, because he loved her. Deeply.

Almost losing her made him realize that even more.

He made no attempt to hide the fact that he couldn't keep his eyes off her. Totally entranced, his gaze traveled over her face and searched her eyes. She gazed back at him with soul rendering tenderness. He could get lost in the loving way she regarded him. A knot rose in his throat. "Kelly, I came so close to losing you."

"And I came so close to making the worst decision of my life," she answered. "How could I have been so foolish?"

"Did Harpes threaten you? Force you to go with him?"

"Yes, he threatened to kill my father. But, I'm not talking about going with him. I had no choice really. Papa was passed out and couldn't defend himself and Harpes would have slit his throat if I hadn't agreed to go with him. What I was talking about was leaving Boonesborough to begin with—with Papa. Almost immediately, I knew I had made a terrible mistake. I missed you. During the night, I made myself stay awake because Papa had left us defenseless. I was afraid Indians might come or worse, a man like Harpes. I had Papa's weapons in my lap, but Harpes snuck up behind me."

"I'm so sorry I wasn't there," William said. "I should have followed you immediately."

"But it gave me time to consider things. I mulled over everything that happened to me yesterday—your ceremony, what you said to me at the cabin, losing my position, my father's sudden reappearance. For several long hours, I did nothing but think about why I was fearful—why I seemed to be retreating inside myself. Why I felt I had to get away. Then, I realized I was afraid of you."

"You never need to fear me," William said, disappointment flooding him.

"I wasn't really afraid of you. I was afraid of what loving you would mean. It meant being…well…doing that." She looked down demurely. "It would mean yielding to the feelings that were growing inside of me. Those feelings were at war with my feelings for men in general. Men like the two that attacked me. Then I realized the absolute absurdity of those fears. I have nothing to fear from you. You're nothing like them. Being with you could never be frightening."

"Your feelings weren't absurd, Kelly. They were completely understandable. You experienced something extremely traumatic."

"Your understanding that means a great deal to me. You told me that I could let fear make me stronger. It has, I promise. Now, I realize that I no longer need to fear your touch or the feelings growing inside of me. In fact..." she hesitated and then finished, "if I am not being too bold, your nearness brings me comfort. And I also feel a strange inner...I'm not sure how to describe it. Thrill might be a good word. But it's more than that. "

Her confession made him want to deliver his own passionate message. But not with words. His mouth throbbed with an overwhelming need to kiss her. Yielding to his intense craving for her lips, he dismounted, went to her, and reached up.

She nearly leapt into his waiting arms and he pulled her roughly to him.

"Oh Kelly, I love you so. I think I always have." He lowered his lips to hers and, remembering that she might still be anxious, cautiously gave her a soft, tender kiss. The kiss sent spirals of pleasure and desire twirling through his body. Then, at her own eager response to the light touch of his lips, she shocked and thrilled him, when she deepened the kiss and held on to the muscles of his arms.

William wanted to keep kissing her, even make love to her, right here. He wanted to show her what it was supposed to be like between a man and a woman. And he wanted them both to experience passion—the passion ignited by love—the only true passion.

"I love you too William," she breathed. Her lips brushed against his cheek as she spoke. "I think I've loved you from the moment you burst through my cabin door."

"I want to go on kissing you more than I want to breathe, but we need to find your father," William managed to say as his lips brushed against her brow and then her forehead.

"Yes, I'm worried about him. There will be time for us. Time to share our love." She caressed the length of his back with both of her hands and then released him. "But, for now, we must be on our way."

He gave her one last kiss that quietly promised of more.

CHAPTER 15

Kelly's lips still tingled from the thrilling kiss. And her insides jangled with excitement and something else she couldn't quite understand. His kiss touched a part of her she didn't recognize and his arms wrapped her in a pleasurable warmth she had never experienced before. It was almost as though his kiss wakened a long-slumbering part of her.

He loves me!

She still couldn't believe William said he loved her. Up until now, he kept his feelings for her hidden. And she'd kept her feelings obscured beneath a veil of fear. A veil that grew heavier and darker with each passing day until it became impossible to see clearly. But now, with William's help, she had lifted that veil.

Now she could see him clearly for what he was—utterly entrancing—handsome, smart, brave, kind. All the things she could ever hope for in a man. And he made her smile. She loved his quick wit and the gentle teasing tone he often used with her.

Despite his profession of love, a lingering doubt raised a question in her head, hurtling her back to reality. Did he love her enough to marry her? She was a simple, country girl, with no sophistication. Even if he could disregard that, he could never overlook the fact that she was no longer a virgin. That was not something a man could just put out of mind.

It would break her heart if he didn't want to marry her because she was no longer pure. She could think of no place she would rather be than in his arms. But not merely as his lover. She would rather never feel his touch again. Oh God, how could she possibly live without him?

Was she thinking clearly? Or letting fear trudge uninvited through her head once more? With sudden clarity, she realized how foolish and rash such notions were. She'd stepped into the mud of self-doubt and self-loathing yet again, and she needed to cleanse her mind of it once and for all.

William said he loved her. She let that thought wash over her.

And she loved him. She let that feeling bathe her soul.

Their love was pure, untainted, and strong. That was all that mattered. With her mind and heart cleansed of doubt, she realized they would love each other forever.

He was the only man she would ever want. She was certain no man could ever measure up to William. She could never love another. He must feel the same way.

She glanced over at him, and immediately felt better because she saw love looking back at her. Just the sight of him made her feel secure, made the world a safer place. When he was around, everything around them took on a pure brightness. Not only was the world a safer place, it was a prettier, happier place.

Her feelings for William wrapped around her like an invisible warm blanket, banishing all her cold disconcerting doubts.

But her feelings for her father remained cold. He had treated her so cruelly, said such terrible things. And then he'd drunk whiskey to the point of intoxication. His intemperance with alcohol was a burden she no longer wanted to carry.

But she loved her father, despite all of it. He was the only family she had. He'd once been a loving father. Could he not be one again?

"You're thinking about your father, aren't you?" William asked.

"Yes, I need to send him home, alone," she said. "I can't bear to be around him anymore."

"Then that's what will happen. We should catch up to him soon. I'll leave it to you to say what you will to him, but if you need me, just look in my direction and nod."

The sound of William's voice and his reassurance affected her deeply, cheering her again. "I'm so grateful to have your support, William. Saying goodbye to my father forever will be hard, even if he is a drunk."

"Maybe it won't be forever. People can change."

"There he is," William said, pointing far down the trail. "And that man with him looks like it might be Daniel Boone based on that abundant white hair."

Kelly took off, running her mare at a fast gallop and William followed closely behind her.

"Papa," she yelled, even before she reached him.

McGuffin tugged his horse to an abrupt halt and bounded off his mount faster than William thought the older man would be capable of moving. "Kelly, come here my daughter. I'm so relieved you are safe. What happened to you?" he asked, reaching out to her.

Kelly grasped her father's hands, but did not hug him, William noticed.

William tipped his hat to the Colonel and Kelly said hello before she turned her attention back to her father. "A man stole me away. He threatened to kill you if I didn't go with him," she explained.

"The devil is raging in wicked men," Boone said, shaking his head in dismay.

"Later, he drugged me," Kelly continued, "but William found and dispatched him to hell—where men like him deserve to go when they die."

"You're safe now. That's what matters," McGuffin said.

William noticed that Kelly's father seemed more alert and less antagonistic, and he still gripped her hands in his.

"Kelly, I have some apologizing to do, girl. I never should have said those things to you last night. I'm ashamed of my hurtful words and for leaving you all alone in the dark when I succumbed to my whiskey. As Franklin said, 'nothing is more like a fool than a drunken man,' and I was a fool. I'm going to stop drinking. I promised that to Colonel Boone earlier and now I'm promising you."

"He poured out his jug a few miles back," Boone confirmed.

"You did?" Kelly asked. Intense astonishment touched her soft pink face.

"And, I'm going to start being a better father to you. I've been a lousy one the last few years. I admit that, much to my shame. But it's never too late to start loving someone again. If you'll let me," he said, his voice a little unsteady.

"You are?" she said, surprised again by the changes in her father.

"I am," he declared.

"And Sheriff Wyllie, I have something to say to you," McGuffin said.

William stepped down from his stallion and approached McGuffin, unsure of what was coming.

McGuffin released Kelly's hands and turned toward William, looking at him intently. "Sir, I am indebted to you and your brothers for going after my daughter and for her rescue. If you hadn't pursued that evil man, well, let's just say this could have ended much differently. I'm sorry my old horse couldn't keep up, but I guess God had his reasons. I came terribly close to dying a horrible death in the hands of the Cherokee. Colonel Boone showed up just in time to save me. Nearly dying made me realize what a fool I've been—how much I had to live for. That's when I decided I needed to beat the whiskey temptress and I intend to do just that."

"I'm sorry to hear of your ordeal, but I am delighted to learn of your change of heart," William said.

"I have more to say," McGuffin said in a firm voice.

"Continue, Sir," William replied deferentially.

"You seem to have some affection toward my daughter," McGuffin said.

William was momentarily speechless in his surprise, but then managed to say, "I do not have affection for your daughter."

He heard a soft gasp escape Kelly, before he could go on.

"I love your daughter with all that is within me."

"Well then," McGuffin said, "you have my permission to court Kelly."

"But I don't want to court Kelly," William said.

"What?" Boone, McGuffin, and Kelly all said at once.

"I want to marry her," William announced. "Do I have your permission to ask your daughter for her hand in marriage?"

Kelly's beautiful eyes widened in astonishment as they awaited her father's answer.

William took hold of her hand, but his gaze returned to her father.

"You most certainly do, son," McGuffin said, his voice quavering.

William knelt to one knee and peered up into the face of his angel. "Kelly, you are everything I could ever want in a wife and I think I can be the kind of husband that will make you happy and keep you safe. Will you consent to marry me?"

Too stunned to speak, Kelly's chest tightened with overwhelming emotions. Her eyes misted over and she swallowed the lump in her throat. She must be dreaming. Maybe the drugs were still affecting her, making her hear things. All she could do was stare at him, tongue-tied.

"Will you marry me right now?" he asked, his voice vibrant.

At his words, she took a sharp intake of breath, surprised again. He really was asking her to marry him, right here in front of her father and Daniel Boone. She froze, her mind and body numb with shock.

"Kelly?" William asked, as he stood.

Still astounded, her mind became instantly alert. Her head filled with questions. "You want to marry me? Now? Here, in the middle of nowhere? How?"

"It's not the middle of nowhere," Boone proclaimed. "It's the middle of the proud new state of Kentucky. May God bless her and keep her."

"The Colonel can marry us. He's a Justice of the Peace and can perform marriages," William stated.

"It would be my privilege and my great honor to perform the rites of matrimony for you two," Boone said.

She turned to William. "Truly, you want to get married right now, right here?"

"I do," William replied without hesitating.

"You want to marry me?" She drew a step nearer to him. "Even though…but what about…" she asked faintly.

William interrupted before she could finish. "That doesn't matter to me, it never did. What matters is that I love you."

His tender words healed her soul as nothing else could have. It didn't matter to him, she repeated to himself. She was so relieved she wanted to cry. She covered her mouth with a trembling hand. Her other palm pressed to her gladdened heart.

She still couldn't believe this might be possible. No, it couldn't be. She backed away a step. She struggled to speak, to find the right words. "I love you too, William, with all my heart. But I'm just a simple, ordinary, plain girl from the mountains of Virginia. You should have a wife more suitable to your station. You have a bright future ahead of you. You need a wife who can help your status. I would only hold you back."

"You are none of those things. You are extraordinary. Marry me and I will tell you all that you are, every night, for the rest of your life." He peered at her intently. "Kelly, I don't give a damn about station. And even if I did, you are in a class above all others. You make all those genteel girls back in New Hampshire look like coddled silly dimwits."

She heard both the Colonel and her father chuckle.

"I want my future to be with you and no one else," he said, reaching out for her. "I love you for all that you have been, all you are now, and all you are yet to be."

His words made her suddenly breathless and her body light, weightless. Joyful tears filled her eyes. She stepped to him, her hands grasping for his. "Every night?" she teased, finally letting this miracle sink in to her heart.

Fervor lit William's face, framed with sunny wavy locks of hair. His tanned skin was smooth across his cheekbones, except for a hint of whiskers that covered his strong jaw. His lips parted in a dazzling smile, displaying straight, white teeth. She saw hope in his kind eyes. He was so handsome a dizzying surge of desire flared within her.

"Kelly, will you do me this great honor?" he pressed, enjoyment in his crystal blue eyes.

In a choked voice she managed to say, "You've just made me happier than I ever thought possible. Yes, my dear William, yes!" Her heart quivered in her chest. Her stomach tumbled. Her feet wanted to dance a jig. Shaking with excitement, she spun in a circle, arms outstretched, looking up. She couldn't believe she could feel this blissfully happy. She clasped her hands to her chest.

She studied William's eager smiling face, glanced at her expectant father and then Boone, and scanned around her, savoring the glorious beauty of the woods and the clean smell of the tall pines. A mockingbird sang in a nearby tree, its tune perfect for the happy moment. She wanted to keep this memory tucked away in her heart forever, and be able to remember every wonderful small detail. Smiling, she reveled briefly in the momentous moment and then turned to Boone.

"Colonel Boone, Sir, if you would be so kind as to marry William and me, right here in the middle of the great state of Kentucky," Kelly said. Tears of joy filled her eyes and her chest and stomach felt like a thousand butterflies had just escaped their cocoons to fly, set free at last. She turned to William, nearly breathless, and said, "The honor is all mine."

He reached out and pulled her to his side.

Tonight there would be no fear in her heart she promised herself.

CHAPTER 16

"Are you ready to be married Sheriff Wyllie?" Boone asked.

William turned to Kelly. "Do you think we should wait for Sam and Bear?"

"Of course we should!" she answered.

"It would mean a lot to me to have them here," William said, "especially since Stephen, Jane, and Catherine won't be here. Jane will never forgive us, you know."

"Do you want to wait until the whole family can be with us?" she asked.

"Absolutely not. I don't want to wait another second, but I will agree to wait a few more minutes for Sam and Bear to arrive. Tonight, this very night, you will be my wife," William declared with a broad smile.

"William, I must look a fright. Could you grab my bag off my mare?" Kelly asked. "I need a comb and a wash rag to dust off my clothing."

"Indeed," William answered, and reached for her bag.

"Although a bride of your beauty needn't concern herself with primping."

"You flatter me," Kelly said, a blush creeping up her neck and into her cheeks.

"While we wait, let's make some coffee and warm up some of my dried meat," McGuffin suggested. "That is if you brought along any water Colonel."

"Outstanding idea," Boone said, "and yes, I have water and some corncakes too."

"I have some water too and jerky. We nearly have a feast," William said, happily.

While Boone and McGuffin busied themselves with starting a cook fire, Kelly sat on a nearby log and began combing through her long hair. William kept an eye on her, not wanting to let her out of his sights, and soon became completely entranced. Her large oval eyes glittered with happiness and excitement made her complexion glow. He saw both strength and intelligence on her proud face. He couldn't believe how lucky he was.

Kelly raised her long lashes and found him watching her. Her rosy lips parted slightly and then the corners of her mouth curved into an impish smile.

She drew a rag from her bag. "William, could I have a bit of water?" she asked, breaking into his reverie.

"I wish I could bring you a gilded tub full of clear warm water," he answered, "but this will have to do for now." He poured a little water onto her rag from his white oak wood canteen. Then he leaned over to whisper in her ear. "I can hardly wait to see your beautiful naked body floating in the clear water of that stream by my cabin. I'll be enchanted forever, you are so lovely."

Kelly gaped up at him, eyes widened, her temptingly curved lips open. Color like a rising sunrise bloomed on her cheekbones. "William! Is that something a husband and wife do—see each other—completely unclothed?" She sounded shocked and slightly appalled.

William searched for a plausible explanation. Had he sliced open a recently healed wound? He could kick himself for his brashness. A warning voice chastised him in his head. He needed to remember that she was new to the idea of intimacy. "Well," he swallowed, trying to manage an answer.

"I would love to see all of you," she whispered, secretively, her voice full of longing. She licked her parted lips.

His eyes widened and overpowering desire flared through him with the speed of an unleashed arrow. William was glad he held the water bag in front of him. Entranced by her young innocence and unworldliness, he wanted nothing more than to see all of her beautiful body as well. His pulse quickened at the captivating speculation. He suspected she could see his swift desire flare in his eyes, but he couldn't help himself. He cleared his throat and tried to regain control of his body.

"Kelly, I can't wait to have you alone and in my arms. I promise you, I will be gentle and slow and teach you what you will need to know. Don't worry about anything that will happen between us. Just take comfort in the wonderful things that await you."

☙

His words did give her comfort. She stood and tried to ignore the strange aching in her limbs and the tingle in her breasts. She moved toward him, compelled by a need to touch him. She wrapped her arms around his neck. A pleasant shiver ran through her. His nearness made her heart hammer with pleasure. "William, you make me so happy my heart is smiling for the first time. I never realized what love was until now. I'm not worried. I trust you. There will be no fear."

"Promise me that if ever you are afraid, you'll let me know," William said, running his fingers through the hair she had just straightened, and twisting the locks in both his hands.

"I promise." Soon, it would be time to make another promise. She heard Sam and Bear galloping toward them.

"Here they come," William said, looking up.

She turned and squealed in delight. Reluctantly, she released William's neck, and quickly returned to her grooming, trying to comb the new tangles William just created, out of her hair. If only she had Catherine and Jane here to help make her look presentable. Catherine was the most beautiful woman she'd ever seen the night she married Captain Sam. And red-headed Jane was stunning as well. Oh well. She was getting married. Nothing else mattered. She tucked her comb back into her canvas bag and ran the cloth over her face and hands one more time. At least she would look clean.

As William strode over to greet his brothers, she found her father, hoping to have a few private words with him. "Papa, I can't tell you what it meant to me to hear you say what you did. I'm so glad you've given up whiskey and want to be my father again." Her heart filled with hope.

"I do, Kelly girl. I always was your Papa, but when I drink, I forget that for some reason. I don't even feel like the same person. I feel rotten and wretched. And I know I don't act like myself. Something happens to my mind and it lets out all the bad in me."

His words echoed her own thoughts. "I know. I hardly recognized the man you became."

"You're all that I have left in the world and you mean everything to me. Forgive me, forgive me for all the wrongs I've done to you. Can you?" He stared at her, imploring her absolution.

"I'll forgive you, Papa, but I won't be able to forget. I wish I could." A cold shiver spread over her as she recalled some of his recent stays in their home—the days when he turned into another man. She regarded him somberly. "However, I understand now how losing my mother could have changed you so much. I realize you loved her deeply. I don't know what I would do if I ever lost William, and we're not even married yet." The thought made her shudder. "But William taught me something important. When bad things happen to us, we have two choices. We can let it break us or we can let it make us stronger. We both need to try hard to be stronger."

"He's a wise man. He'll make you a fine husband, my girl."

"Will you move to Boonesborough?" she asked, wanting to keep an eye on him.

Colonel Boone ambled over and overhead her question. "You could have a productive farm near Boonesborough. A man can grow a hundred bushels of corn an acre with good care. Seventy-five with middling care, and fifty if you don't plant at all."

McGuffin laughed. "Could it be that you are exaggerating just a bit Colonel?"

"I guess that's possible," Boone acknowledged with a wink at Kelly.

"I've spent my life in the wild maneuvering around tree

stumps," McGuffin said, "I guess I'm too old now to start plowing them up."

"Life is simpler when you plow around the stump," Boone said. "But I understand."

"Kelly, lass" Bear shouted in his booming voice, as he hurried over to her, leading both Camel and Harpes' stallion. "I hear ye are going to be our sister."

"Is that all right with you my wee little friend?" she asked, reaching up to place a hand on the giant's broad shoulder.

"Aye. And it's about time. I don't know what took William so long to ask ye." With one of his enormous hands, he affectionately disheveled the hair she had just finally got straight.

"Bear!"

"I'll second that," Sam added with enthusiasm, and reached over with one of his big hands, patted her head, and scrunched up her hair too! "Welcome to our family, Kelly."

Good heavens. Did all three brothers have something against straight hair? She had probably never looked worse. She quickly retrieved her comb yet again while Sam and Bear both shook her father's outstretched hand and returned his stolen weapons to him. Soon, she heard them exchanging words of congratulations and saying cheers with coffee cups in hand.

"I believe we all have a wedding to attend," Boone said after a few minutes, drawing a Bible out of his saddle bag. Then he showed Kelly and William where to stand. Her father took her arm and stood before the Colonel. Sam and Bear stood on either side of William, who beamed back at her with a smile as bright as the morning sun.

With her heart shaking within her breast, Kelly listened

intently, as Boone began.

"Marriage as an institution, is appointed by God, honored by Jesus, and declared to be desirable by the sainted apostle Paul.

"Yet this honorable institution requires grace and understanding for one another to prevail over the often wayward ways of fate and life. The prevailing winds of love are sometimes a hearty gale, now and then a steady gust, at times a gentle wind, and even on occasion, a whispered breeze.

But you must respect all of these times, for the gift that they are.

"And do not fail to listen to one another and to God. As the natives so beautifully say, 'Listen to the wind—it talks. Listen to the silence—it understands. Listen to your heart—it knows.'

"From the first book of this Bible, we read, 'Therefore shall a man leave his father and his mother, and shall cleave unto his wife: and they shall be one flesh.'"

Kelly remembered the next verse. 'And they were both naked, the man and his wife, and were not ashamed.' She had forgotten it earlier when William mentioned seeing her unclothed. He was right. It would be perfectly natural. And she did want to see all of William and love all of him.

As her mind drifted to that tantalizing image, Boone continued, and before she realized what was happening, she found herself saying, "I do."

CHAPTER 17

"I must be on my way," Boone said. "I need to reach Lexington before dark and these fall days are growing short."

"We understand, Colonel," William replied. "You have our gratitude for so much—for the cabin, for saving Kelly's father, and now for marrying us. What a great honor it was to have you be the one to marry us."

"The honor is all mine," Boone said, with a kind smile. With that, he shook the hands of all the men and gave Kelly a quick kiss on her hand.

"Before you leave," Sam said, "I just want to say, I will remember with grateful emotions the day you pitched your tent and identified yourself with the wilderness of Kentucky."

"Aye," Bear agreed.

Boone nodded to them both, acknowledging their expressions of gratitude.

"Enjoy your ride home Colonel Boone," Kelly said.

"Indeed I will," Boone said. "I believe heaven must be a

Kentucky kind of place."

William watched as Boone rode away, hoping the aging hero would arrive safely at his final destination. Then William decided that for men like Daniel Boone, there was no final destination, just the next starting point.

"Shall we get packed up and head home?" he asked his new bride.

"Yes, husband," Kelly answered jauntily, a breeze fluffing her blonde locks.

"Catherine and I will give you two a special wedding present. She'll want to have a say as to what," Sam said after they had mounted and were on the trail to Boonesborough again, "but how about this for a start. I would like to offer you a job Mister McGuffin. I can pay you well and provide food and a tent. We need another hand to help with the building of our new home near Cumberland Falls. The architect has finalized the plans and yesterday I bought the remaining tools and supplies we will need. Bear has agreed to help as well. With three men, we can make rapid progress."

"Oh Papa, what a generous offer," Kelly exclaimed. "Now you won't have to spend the winter trapping in those hills."

"I thank you for your offer, Captain Sam, and now that we're family, please call me Rory," McGuffin said. "I built our cabin myself, so I do possess some carpentry skills. It will be hard to miss the trapping season, but it would be nice to have a change of scenery. All right, I accept," McGuffin said.

"There will be only one caveat," William said, interjecting. "You cannot bring any whiskey with you or consume any while employed by my brother."

"To do so, will result in your dismissal," Sam added, his tone leaving no doubt that he meant it.

"And one more," Kelly said, "you must accompany Captain Sam to Boonesborough every time he makes a trip there, so I can see you often."

"Agreed," McGuffin said, "no more drinking and a lot more visiting."

William watched Kelly study her father as though she were trying to decide if he could keep his promise. He sincerely hoped the man would. If her father ever gave Sam any trouble or caused Kelly any more grief, McGuffin would answer to him.

"Was that thunder?" Kelly asked, her long hair blown into disarray by a sudden wind.

William and Sam both stopped and turned their horses back toward the north. Clouds were quickly enveloping the horizon. The upper part of the cloud mass was the shape of an anvil and below it, the sky was an eerie blue-black color. A rapidly moving autumnal cold front could drop the temperature twenty or thirty degrees in a few minutes.

"It's a blue-tailed norther," Sam declared.

"In Virginia, we call those a winter whistler," McGuffin said. "The wind just whistles through the trees and sets the stage for the first frost."

The wind, stiffer now, brushed against William's cheeks. "It's moving our way fast. We'd best pick up our pace. Mister McGuffin, ride Harpes' stallion. Carrying you, your horse won't be able to keep up."

"But I'm fond of old Alexander the Great," McGuffin said. "Alex and I have been through a lot together, me and him."

"Well it's time to give the old boy a rest," William said. "Switch horses and be quick about it, Sir."

For some time, they rode at a fast gallop, McGuffin's older mount tied to the back of the handsome stallion Kelly's father now rode.

Before long, the gentle wind turned to determined gusts from the north, carrying drops of rain that slapped at the backs of their necks.

Sam shouted to William. "The temperature will soon drop like a rock."

"The front of our mounts will be lathered from heat and their arses frozen," Bear said.

Bear was right. The sudden change in the temperature was not only hard on people it was especially bad for horses.

The drops of rain turned to squalls and within minutes, they were all soaked to their skin. He wished he could do something to make it easier on Kelly. He measured her with an appraising look, wondering if she was up to coping with the storm. She seemed to be holding up all right, but he detected a slight quiver in her hands and the heavy rain forced her to keep her uncovered head facing the saddle. "Here, wear my hat," he shouted, handing his tricorne to her.

"It's too big, I'm sure it will just blow off," she yelled. "but, I'll try." She placed the hat on her head and it seemed to fit snugly. She managed a smile at him and a shrug. "I guess I have a big head."

William thought she looked charming in his hat, her long wet hair hanging down both sides. The sight of her warmed his insides as no fire could, but the outside of him continued to grow unpleasantly chilled.

The rain continued to pelt them, with the drops getting colder by the minute. William held one arm across his forehead and tried to shield his eyes in the crux of his elbow from the deluge's constant barrage. His wool coat grew heavy on his back and his wet shirt felt like an icy second skin. Kelly didn't even have a coat on. "Where's your coat," he called to her.

She was actually trembling now. "In my bag, but it's not really a coat. Just a jacket."

It had been so warm when they'd left, he hadn't even thought about bringing his wool cloak. But he sincerely wished he could offer it to Kelly now. Before he could retrieve the jacket from her bag, the rain turned to hail and they rushed to find a bit of cover under the trees. But the wind was so high it whipped pieces of branches and leaves at them with nearly as much force as the hail. Kelly tried to cover her face with her bent arm.

"We have to find shelter," William yelled.

"This squall will blow through soon. Then our real worries begin," Sam replied.

"Why?" Kelly asked, sounding worried.

"Because that's when the wind becomes even colder," her father answered.

Being wet was bad, but being cold and wet was serious, and combined with a strong wind, even dangerous. William twisted the reins in his hands nervously, worried Kelly would get sick and catch a fever. He glanced at her uneasily and his mind clouded with fear when he noticed her teeth chattering and her body trembling. He would do anything, fight anyone, to keep her safe, but how could he get her out of this weather? It's impossible to fight the wind.

Sam seemed to sense his disquiet. "Let's head toward those boulders. Perhaps we can find a dry cave or at least a shelter against the wind. I'll scout ahead," he offered and took off.

The rain was so heavy, William had a hard time keeping Sam in sight and the four of them struggled to keep up with his brother.

Sam led them down a deer trail and then they crossed a gulley and started climbing upwards. The thick trees in the ravine offered some measure of shelter, but water was pouring through the layer of fall leaves covering the ground, making the surface slick. The higher they climbed, the more treacherous it became. Where was Sam taking them? Having spent so much time in the backwoods, his brother seemed to have a sixth sense in the wild. He would trust in Sam.

To the sound of thunder, they wove their way through sandstone outcrops, which opened into a natural enclosure. The blustery wind instantly died down, blocked by the limestone cliffs surrounding them. But the icy rain continued unabated.

Sam pressed on, searching to the left, and Bear joined him and began searching to the right. The three of them held back, waiting to see what the two men found, if anything. He was about to reach over and pull Kelly in front of him, to let his body warm her, when Bear finally waved and shouted. He'd located an opening at the bottom of the cliff on the right. It looked like a cave entrance—wider at the top, narrower at the bottom, and large enough for a man to step through.

Sam and Bear dismounted, and as soon as the three of them reached his brothers, they stepped off their horses as well. Sam tied his gelding to a tree limb, and then unsheathed his huge knife. He cut four branches from a small tree, sheltered from the rain under a nearby limestone outcrop. In the same spot, Bear collected a few old vines and McGuffin used a square of oiled canvas to gather up some dry leaves and tinder from under the overhang.

William tied the other horses and then took Kelly's arm and guided her out of the storm and into the cave opening, to wait for the others. He put his arm around her shoulder and drew her into his side.

"What are they doing?" she asked, snuggling against his shoulder.

The vigorous wind and cold had whipped color into her cheeks and her beauty made him just stare at her for a moment before he could answer. "They are gathering what we will need to make torches and a fire," William finally answered. He wanted to kiss her, deep and long, and hold her soft curves against him, as he explored her luscious mouth. But with her father and his brothers just a few feet away, he had to be satisfied with just a look at her.

"You're ogling me like a fox looks at a chicken," she teased.

"Well I have been called a Wyllie fox and I would like to taste..."

Bear crowded under the opening with them. "Is it tall enough for a giant like me to enter?"

"I believe so," William said, grinning, "if you duck about a foot."

"We need to be sure there are no wolves or something else in there," Sam said, joining them. "Animals will have sought escape from this storm too."

"Aye. And the Black Bear's color makes it easy for them to hide in dark spaces," Bear warned.

McGuffin strode up and crammed into the opening as well. "I'll go in first in case there's a people eating varmint in there," he volunteered.

"Papa, no, there could be a Bear in there," Kelly protested.

"I'm the oldest and I'll take the risk. I've dealt with many a Bear in my day," McGuffin said with just a hint of boastfulness. "If it's clear, I'll use my flint and this tinder and get a fire going quicker than you can spit. You men make up the torches in the meantime." With that, Kelly's father disappeared.

"He's got courage," Sam said. "I'll give him that much. William keep your pistol trained on the opening in case he comes running out with something chasing him."

William quickly grabbed his pistol and put fresh dry powder in the flintlock's pan. Then he kept an eye on the opening while Kelly watched his brother and Bear make torches by tightly winding the dry vines around the top of the tree branches Sam had cut.

"Where did you learn to make those?" Kelly asked, rubbing her arms to stay warm.

"From my father," Sam answered.

They had all learned a lot from their father. And from the way their father loved and honored their mother, they even learned how to treat a woman. William wanted to love and honor Kelly in the same way. He couldn't resist a quick glance at her, marveling that she was now his wife.

"I'm worried about my father," Kelly told William after several minutes.

"I'll go in to check on him." He quickly stepped toward the cave entrance, keeping his eyes pinned on the opening.

Just as William was about to step inside the hollow entrance, McGuffin yelled, "All clear in here. But you're not going to believe what is in here."

❧

After the men lit the torches with the small fire her father had just built toward the entrance, they entered the gloomy cavern. The top of the cave was just above her head. All the men stooped to keep from hitting their heads. Bear had to bend over at the waist.

It smelled damp, earthy, and old. Exceedingly old. A tremor passed down her spine. It almost seemed like they were walking back in time.

Kelly's breathing quickened. She'd never been in a cave before and the thought of being under tons and tons of rock was terrifying. And their torches cast eerie black shadows on the rock walls. But William held her hand and it gave her the courage she needed.

Whatever they faced, she could do it with him by her side.

All of a sudden, the narrow tunnel widened and the men all straightened their backs. Then, after a few more yards, it opened upward. They found themselves standing in an enormous chamber and Kelly's heart nearly stopped when she peeked up.

Intricate draping deposits lined the walls in colorful cascades. Thousands of exceptionally beautiful rod-shaped formations, moist with the cave's humidity, sparkled under the light of their torches.

Kelly could barely breathe and her eyes widened in absolute

soul-stunning awe.

Some of the formations hung like glittering icicles, downward from the ceiling, while others appeared more like pillars growing from the floor. Several joined together to form complete columns. All the multi-colored formations shimmered and some were even luminous. It was a mystical ancient wonderland, hidden from people. It seemed magical and she almost expected fairies to come dancing out to greet them. Or angels spreading their wings in welcome.

Her mouth hung open and she let go of William's hand and stepped forward.

A nearly spiritual aura surrounded them.

Surely, this place was divine. Otherworldly. Ageless. Sacred.

She could see a labyrinth of openings throughout the vast chamber, no doubt leading to more rooms filled with these amazing formations. One wall twinkled like a frozen silver waterfall, while another seemed to be nothing but clusters of little rocks that resembled shiny white pearls. And on one more, the rock unfurled gracefully, like spooled gold ribbon. She glanced back at William. He stood like a statue, motionless, his face frozen in wonder. Sam, Bear, and her father seemed equally amazed.

"What is this?" she breathed. Her voice echoed in the hushed stillness.

"Astonishing," William said, holding his torch higher.

"I heard Kentucky has beautiful caves like this all over the state," Sam said. "I was hoping I could find one, but this greatly exceeds my expectations."

"This might exceed even God's expectations," Bear said. He let out a long audible breath.

"We best be getting back to the fire before these torches give out," McGuffin suggested.

"He's right," Sam said, already turning back toward the entrance.

"Oh, William, I wish we could stay," Kelly said. Reverently, she surveyed the dazzling chamber, one last time.

"We'll come back, just the two of us," William promised. "For now, we need to get you dry."

That reminded her how cold and damp she was. She'd totally forgotten the storm in the excitement of entering the cave and seeing this breathtaking cavern.

When they reached the cave entrance, her father volunteered to go get more firewood. They would need a bigger fire to dry out their clothing.

"I'll fetch your bag. You can change into another gown," William suggested.

Kelly gave William's tricorne back to him. "You'll need this."

After William returned and the other men got the fire burning brightly near the cave opening, she dug around in her bag, and hauled out a gown and jacket. The gown was an old one that Jane had given her, but at least it was dry. "All right, I'm going to change now," she said, shivering. "You men turn your backs."

When William didn't move and just stood there, arms crossed, she had to laugh. "Not yet, William Wyllie. You turn around this very minute."

William frowned and then obeyed her command. "Married and still denied," he complained.

"Stop yer whining," Bear said, "there will be plenty of time for that when we get you newlyweds back to Boonesborough."

As soon as she finished changing, she spread her wet gown out to dry on the rocky ground. Keeping only their breeches on, the men began removing their accoutrements and most of their clothing. Sam's shirt was made of fringed buckskin, while her father and Bear both wore sturdy hunting frocks. The linen fabric was heavy and durable, but unfortunately held onto water. William, however, still wore the fine clothing he'd worn to his swearing in ceremony—a white linen shirt, with a lace cravat, a silver silk waistcoat with a dark blue wool coat trimmed with pewter buttons. She was amazed that the ceremony was just a day ago. So much had happened, it felt more like a month. Most important, she and William were now married. It seemed almost too good to be true. Yet it was true.

As the men spread their garments out on the rocks to dry, she stood by the fire and turned her head over, letting her long hair tumble down. As she finger combed her hair trying to get it to dry, she couldn't resist a peek at William's bare broad chest and tight abdomen. He didn't have even a hint of fat. Feeling quite naughty, she wished she could run her fingertips across his well-muscled body.

"How long do you think it will rain," Kelly asked, suddenly anxious to be on their way. After all, it was her wedding night and she wanted to be alone with William.

They could hear the rain still falling like a waterfall outside the cave opening

"No telling," Sam answered. "It doesn't appear to be letting up."

"Then let's make a wee batch of coffee," Bear suggested. "It will help warm us all."

"I'm not going out there again," Sam said. "Cold and me stopped being agreeable years ago. I'm just starting to warm up."

"I'll go," McGuffin volunteered again. "I've got coffee and a small pot in my saddle bag."

When her father came back, they quickly made coffee with the rainwater he had collected in his pot before coming back inside the cave.

Kelly went over to her father and sat down next to him, holding a rag she had pulled from her bag. She started wiping the rain from his dripping hair, but he nearly swatted her hand away.

"No. I thank you, but I'll dry off quick enough," he said tersely. Then he sighed, stood, and moved away from her.

"You've been drinking whiskey!" Her bitter voice echoed down the cold edges of the cave walls.

CHAPTER 18

McGuffin stared down at the damp ground and nodded, his shoulders pulled low. "I took just a swallow to warm me up," he said. "No more than a small sip. I swear it."

"I thought you poured out all your whiskey," William said, his voice accusing.

"No, I poured out one jug, but I kept a second," McGuffin confessed. "Just for medicinal purposes. Nothing like it to warm a man's insides or clean a wound to keep it from festering."

"Sit down," Sam ordered.

Her father sat down, looking cowed by the Captain's tone and commanding presence.

Sam sat down next to him. "Sir, I'd enjoy a swallow myself right now and I'm sure Bear and William would too. But we'll not tempt you by having it, until we're sure you're strong enough to see it and not have an uncontrollable craving for it. That's called respect. And you'll not lie to us about stopping your drinking. That's called honesty. I expect you to be honest and you can expect us to be respectful of your weakness. Because that's just what it is—a weakness—not a flaw or fault. It's just a weakness in your body. For some reason, you lack the ability to stop. To overcome your weakness, your mind will have to grow stronger. Frankly, it's the only defense you have."

Sam's words, though wise, embarrassed Kelly. This was her father and she was ashamed of him—mortified that he had lied to all of them. Frustrated too, because he was weak and his abstinence so short lived. Would he become the mean, intimidating, spiteful man he'd been before? His evil twin? Her belly knotted as the thought filled her with regret and worry.

She felt betrayed. A cold numbness unrelated to the weather crept through her. She'd held such hopes for her father. All her bitter disappointment in him seemed to return at once. Her eyes narrowed with her wrath. "You lied. You said you'd given up whiskey. You said you would be a better father." She had managed to stop loathing him, but now, those negative feelings were returning full force and she hated that. She didn't want to detest her father. She wanted to love him! Tears started to slip out of her burning eyes.

McGuffin scrubbed a hand over his face, then looked up at Kelly. "As God is my witness, I shall make it up to you," he swore. "I will be a better father. A better man. Captain Sam is right. I have to make my mind stronger than my body's weakness." He knelt down, and held his head in his hands.

William sat down next to her father. In a gruff challenging voice Kelly had not heard him use before, he said, "You just told God and all of us what kind of man you want to be. If you go back on your word one more time and hurt Kelly again, you'll have me to answer to, not God, and I won't be as merciful."

Kelly swallowed the knot in her throat and swiped the tears off her cheeks. She hated that her father had dampened—far more than the rain ever could—what should be the happiest day of her life.

Her father stood and moved closer to her. Kelly backed up a step. She had no desire to be near him.

"Kelly, please girl. I know you are saddened by this. I've let you down again. But give me one more chance to earn back your love. I won't disappoint you again. It hurts me too much." He laid a hand against his chest.

Kelly looked to William but he gave no indication about what she should say. He knew it was her decision and she appreciated that he recognized it. She studied her father's imploring face. He appeared sincere, but could she trust him? It saddened her that she even had to ask herself the question. "All right, one more chance Papa. No more."

"You won't regret it Kelly girl. I can promise you that," he said.

He could promise her, but would he keep his word?

The couple strolled away from the others, into the cavern, taking a log with a flaming tip as a torch and staying within the fire's dim light.

"I have a feeling he means it this time," William said. For most people, giving them a second chance was like giving them another loaded weapon because they missed you the first time. But he had a good feeling about Kelly's father. McGuffin seemed to have a good heart beneath his roughhewn exterior.

Kelly's features remained scrunched up in a serious scowl and her whole body appeared rigid, her disenchantment palpable.

"I think you could level an entire English regiment with that glower," he teased.

"Well, I'm still upset with him," she answered grumpily. "I need time to get over my disappointment. And I'm not sure I can trust him."

"You told him you would give him one more chance. Give the man the benefit of the doubt until he proves otherwise. He loves you Kelly. I think his love for you is strong enough to help him win this." He held the burning log higher as they entered the cavern's interior.

"I surely hope you're right." She let out a long sigh, then glanced up and stared into the cavern.

William noticed her eyes brighten immediately. He turned to look too and the cave's astounding splendor awed him again. The dim light only seemed to make the cavern walls and oddly-shaped cylinders shimmer even more. "The only thing comparable to this beauty is you," he whispered.

She turned her face upward, toward him, and grinned.

Relief filled him. Her anger had subsided.

"Sit with me," he coaxed. "Over here." He took her hand in his. A few moments ago, he'd spotted the fairly flat rock that appeared nice and dry. William intended to take full advantage of it. They couldn't make love, not with her father no more than thirty feet away, but he could teach her a thing or two about kissing. He couldn't wait to taste those luscious lips. "Kelly, let me show you just a little bit of how much I love you."

"I would truly like that William," she said softly.

He sat first, balanced the flaming log on nearby rocks, and drew her into his lap. He left his hands around her tiny waist. She was so petite, the top of her head reached only to his chin. He reminded himself to take even this slow, so he kissed her forehead, then her ear, before trailing soft kisses down her neck and up again to her chin. "Can I kiss you Kelly?" he breathed.

"Kiss me," she murmured in a low sensuous voice. "I've wanted more of your kisses ever since you kissed me for the first time on the trail."

William thought about the first feathery kiss he'd given her, just before he left to chase after Harpes, when she was still unconscious from the drug. But he didn't want to remember that one. He would remember the same one she did—the first time they had shared a soul reaching kiss that changed their lives forever.

Hungry for this gorgeous woman who was now his wife, he lowered his lips to hers. The warmth of her lips surprised him. The taste thrilled him. Their softness made his body throb. He deepened the kiss, wanting to convey all the love he felt within him, as he leaned her back into his arm. His hand moved to cup her breast and he could feel her heart beating wildly beneath her gown. She started to moan softly, and William smothered her mouth with his to quiet her. He wanted to groan himself with his own dizzying desire when she ran her hand gently across his bare chest. Her tentative innocent touch was enough to send rippling tremors through his entire body.

He drew his lips away, just long enough to let her breathe, and then kissed her again, possessively, claiming her as his own, his love, his wife.

She started to moan again and William forced himself to pull away from her sweet lips. "Hush, my love. They'll hear you," he whispered into her ear.

His senses spun with the scent of her rain-washed body. He breathed in deeply. She smelled like raindrops, clean and pure, and he wanted to drink her in. But they needed to end this while they could both still stop.

"William, your kisses do something odd to my insides. And the feel of your bare skin on my hands, it…" Her lips quivered with unspoken desire. "I'm tingling everywhere, and my legs feel like limp ropes. I don't even know if I can walk."

"Then, I'll carry you," he said, sweeping her into his arms and standing. He looked into her eyes savoring the desire he had aroused in her.

She placed her palm against his jaw. "Let me behold this wondrous place one more time."

As her widened eyes roamed the cavern, their violet color glistening with flecks of silver and gold, William decided he was the luckiest man alive.

As the five of them mounted their horses, Kelly felt the shock of the dry bitter wind. If it was this chilly in the ravine, she did not look forward to the rest of their journey back to Boonesborough. But Sam said they weren't far away now. They should be back in Boonesborough in another hour or two.

But even as chilly as it was, William's kisses left her blazing on the inside. If what he did to her in the cavern was a taste of what he had in store for her tonight, her curiosity was aroused along with the rest of her. Her reaction to him had been swift and nearly overwhelming. What would it be like in private, in his bed?

And now, as they rode back toward the trail, every time his crystal blue eyes met hers, she felt her pulse leap. And each time his eyes raked boldly over her body, he stoked a growing fire within her. He had unshackled her heart and now he was freeing her body. Under the beauty of the glorious cavern, he deftly brought her untried sensuality to sparkling life. For the first time, she felt like a desirable woman.

His eagerness toward her was evident, yet she could tell he was deliberately making an effort not to scare her or rush her. What he didn't know was that now, after tasting the passion in his kisses, and after touching his broad bare chest, she ached for the fulfillment of lovemaking. She was certain she wouldn't be afraid.

She could already sense a tangible bond—both emotional and physical—between them. She needed his nearness and he seemed to feel the same way. As he kissed her, his heartbeat thudded against her own and she cherished the intimate sensation. And his hands had felt so warm, so gentle.

Kelly also felt secure in his arms. She trusted William as she had never trusted anyone, except her mother. She smiled at the memory of her mother and wished she could have met her new husband. Maybe mother can see him from heaven, she thought. Her mother would think him handsome, but most of all, she would appreciate his kindness toward her daughter.

She closed her eyes, imagining her mother's face, her smile, her voice, the gentle touch of her hand. And she heard the voice say, "Bright be thy path sweet babe."

Her mother's blessing.

Her eyes misted beneath her eyelids.

This was a magical place.

When she opened her eyes, she heard a gurgling creek teeming with rain water descending the craggy hill. Sometimes hidden by dense stands of woods, it came into view again from time to time, the water tumbling languidly down limestone rocks and colorful boulders.

As they passed one particularly beautiful spot, Bear commented, “Water is sacred. It is the lifeblood of the earth.”

The brook’s peaceful sound added to her sense that God meant for them to find the remarkable cave. The profound place seemed to change her. Not only did she experience passion there for the first time in her life, she experienced what it felt like to be loved, cherished even. And it happened in an enchanted place she would never forget.

“Are you warm enough?” William asked, observing her as he rode. “If not, you can come sit on my horse in front of me. I can warm you up.” He had the same hungry fox look on his face.

“If I did, you’d wind up having to take me off in the forest somewhere,” Kelly whispered over to him.

“I don’t see the disadvantage there,” William said, with a sensuous grin and twinkling affectionate eyes.

She met his smile, shyly, the thought of going off into the woods with him sending tiny sumptuous quivers down her spine.

Then a softer and more loving look touched his eyes. It seemed with every hour his love deepened and intensified.

Catherine had told her some time ago that a man who loved her would be gentle and make lovemaking something she could look forward to. She was pleased with their initial intimacy—more than pleased—thrilled even, and powerless to resist him. Her flesh tingled at just his touch. But she worried if tonight she could respond as he would like her to. She had no idea what to do or even what to expect. She didn’t want to disappoint him.

She supposed that when the time came she'd figure it all out—with William's help, of course.

CHAPTER 19

They reached Boonesborough sooner than William expected and as they made their way into town, he noticed people out and about as usual, despite the chilly wind. Settlers were hardy souls and their abundant courage and tenacity impressed William. Some men on the frontier were adventurers, seeking their fortune, but most were just hardworking ordinary people in search of a decent life in the newborn state of Kentucky.

As they passed a lumber mill, he observed a man using a broad ax to hew timbers for floors, tables, and benches. Another labored making shingles out of chestnut wood for roofs to cover cabins and barns. He'd learned chestnut bark was useful for tanning and dyeing and to make medicine. And farmers used the tree's nuts to fatten hogs. Further down the main road, he smelled hog fat boiling over an open fire and nearby a lady stirred a pot of steaming wood ashes to create lye. The woman would use both to make soap. Pioneer people were nothing if not resourceful.

"Sheriff Wyllie!"

It was Colonel Daniel Byrd who'd yelled out and was riding up to them. The Colonel, in charge of the local militia at Fort Boonesborough, was a man William highly respected. Byrd's light red hair and freckled fair complexion made him appear younger than his forty years.

"A good day to you, Sir," William replied as Byrd urged his mount up next to them.

The militia were vital to Boonesborough's safety. For the last ten years, Kentucky law required most men to keep ready a good musket or rifle, half a pound of good powder, and a pound of lead, and to respond to their commanding officer whenever called upon or pay a fine of ten shillings. Byrd ensured men complied with the act, including paupers, for whom he supplied arms and ammunition at public expense. But the ever-present peril of Indian raids, more often spurred men to duty than the threat of fines.

William introduced Kelly's father to the Colonel.

Byrd exchanged greetings with McGuffin and the others and then said, "Glad you're back sheriff. We had an incident while you were away. A group of men was gathered around at the blacksmith's while he was attending to one of their horses. An argument developed. A man named Helms attacked one of the men with a knife. Someone hollered, 'Just shoot the scoundrel.' So Helms did, even though the man had no weapon and had left his firearm at the boarding house."

"Did he kill him?" William asked, concerned.

"No, the doctor thinks he'll be just fine, but it will take some time for him to completely recover," Byrd answered.

"Where is Helms now?" William asked.

"In your jail at the Fort. Deputy Mitchell is keeping an eye on him," Byrd answered. "I'm afraid you will have your hands full as Boonesborough's sheriff. Before you became sheriff, our town suffered from a lack of enforcement, and without law men tend toward anarchy."

"Not only will we have law and order in Boonesborough," William declared, "we will have justice." He glanced over at Kelly. "And we will also not tolerate any kind of violence against women in Boonesborough. Only the lowest of men hurt women." He would enlist the help of Judge Webb to be sure men who assaulted women received just punishment.

"I believe you're the man who can ensure it," Byrd said.

"Aye, he is," Bear agreed. "The best way to stop a bad man with a gun is a good man with a gun."

"And the plumb line of justice," William added.

"Colonel, the sheriff and Miss McGuffin were married earlier today by Colonel Boone," Sam said. "We met up with him on our way back to Boonesborough." Sam wisely left unsaid what took them away from town to begin with. The Colonel would likely assume they had just gone out to look at a potential land claim.

"My congratulations to you both," Byrd said and smiled warmly at Kelly. "I guess it is fortuitous Colonel Boone gave you his cozy cabin." Byrd regarded William with a good-humored look in his lively ice blue eyes.

"Indeed," William replied, keeping a straight face with some difficulty.

"Well, I certainly think we can let Helms wait one more day before you question him," Byrd said.

"Agreed, I believe I shall let the hot-headed man stew a while," William said. "We're all starving. It has been some time since we've eaten. Would you join us at the inn for a meal?"

"Thank you, Sir, I believe I could use a good meal myself," Byrd said.

William turned to Kelly. Her eyes appeared weary. It was no wonder, considering what she had been through in the last twenty-four hours. "I know you're exhausted and have had little sleep," he told Kelly. "But a good meal can do wonders. Do you think you can eat before we go home?"

Home. He liked the sound of that and he couldn't wait to get her there. Just looking at her sent hot gusts of desire through him. He'd always wondered what it would be like to have a house with a wife to come home to.

Maybe someday, even a family.

"I would love a hot meal and an even hotter cup of coffee," she answered. "What's more, I'd truly love to get out of this chilly wind."

"Well then, let's go fill you up and warm you up," he said. Later, he would cradle her in his arms and warm her from top to bottom.

Kelly's body shivered with chill and fatigue, yet excitement and trepidation engulfed her mind. Her thoughts kept returning to what it felt like to be in William's arms and she hungered for the taste of his mouth on hers. His kisses left a burning imprint on her. Yet, her own insecurity and inexperience made her anxious about the evening to come.

As they dismounted and entered the inn, William held her elbow and guided her through the door. It felt good to have him next to her, and her unease seemed to subside somewhat.

The dining area of the inn's parlor was noisy with the hum of conversation and nearly full, but a round table in the corner by a blazing hearth was open and William and the others quickly moved toward it. The smell of fresh bread, roasting meat, and pies baking made her stomach growl. She'd been too preoccupied to think about food, but now she was suddenly ravenous. And the welcome heat from the hearth penetrated all the way to her chilled bones.

They sat down and ordered food and coffee and then Kelly glanced around the room. She was glad she didn't recognize anyone because she was in no shape to be sociable. She needed a bath, fresh clothes, and a good night's sleep.

Pensively, as the men discussed local politics, she wondered just how much sleep she would be getting tonight. The thought was another of the ceaseless, endless questions chipping away at her confidence. She began to wonder if she should feign not feeling well and put the inevitable off.

But she couldn't start their marriage being dishonest with William. She never wanted to lie to him or deceive him. Her thoughts drifted back to the day she'd met him. As she looked back, she recognized it for what it was—both the worst and best day of her life. She doubted she would ever have another experience as bad as the rape. And meeting William, who immediately became a caring friend, was the best thing that ever happened to her.

"Mrs. Wyllie," Colonel Byrd said. "Could you please pass the bread?"

"Kelly, he's speaking to you," William said gently.

"Oh, my pardons," she said quickly, "I guess I'm not used to being called Mrs. Wyllie."

"You're a Wyllie now," Sam said. His expression was inscrutable, but his keen probing eyes revealed he'd seen more. Sam was a well-honed observer of human behavior.

She always thought she was as well. She seemed to be able to figure out everyone but herself. But then, she had figured it all out sometime during last night. She needed to remember what she'd decided. She'd chosen to be strong.

She had no reason to fear. None.

William reached under the table and took her hand. His secret contact rekindled the desire simmering slowly within her. She wondered if she should feel guilty for the extreme pleasure those feelings brought her. Then he rubbed one of her fingertips with his thumb. The small quick movements sent extraordinary sensations through her entire body. How did he do this to her?

"Would you like dessert?" a young lady asked them.

William eyed Kelly and smiled roguishly. It was the hungry fox again. Plainly, the fox craved dessert. She could feel a hot flush creeping up her neck.

"Aye, Miss," Bear answered for them. "We'll have one of everything ye have."

The young woman snickered and winked at Bear, then said, "I'll be right back with those, Sir."

Kelly had to laugh too. She adored Bear. His protective spirit was generously applied to her as well as all the Wyllies. She could well imagine him thinking of all of them as his clan. He'd left his own Scottish clan as a young lad and was orphaned on the long sea voyage to the colonies. William's parents later adopted Bear, treating him like one of their own. Stephen was the closest in age to Bear and the two were nearly inseparable until Stephen married

Jane.

Now, Bear lent a hand to whatever Wyllie needed helping or defending. A formidable hunter and fighter, much like Sam, she knew Bear would defend any member of his family to the death.

"And a round of ales to toast to the bride and groom!" Colonel Byrd ordered as the woman turned away to retrieve the desserts.

All of them, except Byrd, looked at her father.

"Excellent idea. After all it is a wedding feast," McGuffin said. "But I'll be toasting with my coffee. Give my ale to my new son." He sounded resolute and sure of himself, and enormously proud of William.

Kelly nodded her head in approval and smiled at her father.

When the desserts arrived, carried by three women each bearing two or three plates, Kelly's eyes widened. She'd never seen so many sweets in one place. In fact, she couldn't remember the last time she'd eaten anything sweet. But now, the table nearly overflowed with luscious temptations—apple and chess pies, bread pudding, apple tansey, gingerbread, custard, and apple dumplings. The smell of nutmeg, ginger, and cinnamon, along with the tantalizing aroma of fresh pie crust, made her mouth water.

"Ladies first," Bear said, "as long as ye don't pick the apple dumplings."

"I won't, Bear," Kelly reassured, "but I simply can't choose. They all look delicious. Why don't you gentlemen take your pick and I'll just take what's left."

"Good heaven's no. You'll have first pick, my bride, including the apple dumplings," William said, giving Bear a reproving glance.

With a mischievous grin at Bear, she reached for the apple dumplings, then at the last second, moved her hand to pick up the gingerbread.

"Ye had me frettin' there lass," Bear teased.

The men all found something they couldn't resist and when he quickly finished off the apple dumplings, Bear took a second, and then a third dessert. It seemed as though the giant's belly was bottomless. William only ate a small custard sprinkled with nutmeg, but seemed to relish each spoonful.

"Kelly, do you know how to make custard?" he asked after finishing the last bite.

Kelly swallowed a mouthful of gingerbread. "Well no, but I can learn easily enough. But you need to have chickens to have eggs and a milk cow."

"We'll get both and anything else you'll need. It'll be good to have some chickens around again. I've missed having eggs every now and then. Sam, do you remember what Uncle Toby used to say about eggs?" William asked, laughing.

"Yes, indeed, I do. He would eat eggs every morning, but they had to be from chickens that had a rooster with them. He said that's what kept lead in his 'pistol.' He was about ninety when he told me this," Sam answered.

"Maybe we should think about what he was saying," Colonel Byrd said with a chuckle.

"He also smoked a pipe and chewed tobacco till he was ninety-five, and he drank spirits all his life," William added.

After the good meal, delicious gingerbread, and the hearty ale, Kelly was feeling much more like herself.

"Can I join you gentlemen at your camp tonight?" her father asked Captain Sam and Bear.

"Indeed, you are most welcome, Sir," Sam answered.

"Did ye bring a good wool blanket with ye?" Bear asked. "I fear ye will need it tonight."

"No, I'll need to buy one before we leave for your camp," McGuffin answered.

"We'll take our leave and visit the general store then," Sam told William. "But first, may I have a word with your lovely bride?"

"Of course," William answered. "Why don't the rest of us get a breath of fresh air? Bear, you can smoke your pipe."

The men all stood and then promptly left, leaving her and Sam at the table. She eyed him quizzically. What did he need to say to her?

"Kelly, I just wanted you to know how pleased I am that William has married you. As his oldest brother, I look out for him and I want to be sure he remains happy. I think marrying you is the best thing he's ever done."

Kelly lost her breath at the compliment. She tucked his words away in her memory, wanting to remember them forever.

She started to say something and he said, "Please. I have more I need to tell you."

She became instantly alert, wondering what exactly was on Sam's mind.

"Kelly, I also believe your marriage to my brother William is the best thing you will ever do. He is a man of honor and principle. A man of high virtue who will do everything in his power to keep you safe. He is nothing, nothing, at all like the men who attacked you. And nothing like that Harpes bastard. It's like night and day. Darkness and light. Goodness and wickedness. Let William share his goodness with you. You'll be safe, I promise you. He would never do anything to hurt you."

Tears welled up in her eyes. But they were tears of joy. She was so happy she could barely speak. Kelly appreciated Sam's brotherly advice, especially now that he really was her brother. She made herself say what was on her heart. She had to admit the truth graciously and honestly. "I love him very much. More than I thought a person could love another. I admit I harbored some misgivings about a physical relationship and that made me behave strangely for a while. But I'm no longer afraid. I realized, just as you say, that William is nothing like those men who attacked me. And he is not anything like that slick Harpes. William loves me and treats me with kindness and respect. Almost from the day we met, I found myself strongly drawn to him. Pardon me if I'm being too bold or inappropriate. I don't want to appear brazen."

"No, we're family now. And after what you went through, your fear was perfectly understandable."

"Perhaps, but I don't feel fear anymore. I just don't know much about…I just want to be able to show William how much I love him."

"Do you trust him?"

"Yes, completely."

"Then focus on your trust. On your love for him. Keep trust and love in your mind and your concerns will disappear like the setting sun."

Kelly straightened her shoulders and stood. As Sam paid for their dinner, she strode out of the inn to her husband, then with

William's arm wrapped around her shoulder, watched as the sun set in the west beneath a cloud-free rose and amber sky.

CHAPTER 20

Their horses laden with the bare essentials they'd picked up at the general store before leaving town, Kelly and William arrived at the cabin in the soft, almost black, purple of twilight. Before dismounting, Kelly once again admired the view of the rolling hills spread out before her. Thousands of majestic trees, silhouetted against the sky, joined together in a dark curling ribbon that stretched across the horizon. It was too late to see much of it now, but the many splendors of nature she'd seen yesterday—a canopy of trees flashing brilliant fall foliage, late blooming wild flowers, the brisk creek, and the wide open landscape—made her think she would never tire of being here.

And living here with William would make her life a dream come true.

As soon as her feet touched the ground, she felt at home. But her boots had barely landed before William swept her up into the cradle of his arms. "Welcome to our home," he said with a gentle softness in his voice and eyes.

"I can hardly believe it's true," she whispered. She laid a hand against her chest. "It is our home." She placed an arm across his broad back. As he held her close, she could feel his uneven warm breaths on her cheek.

Jauntily, William inclined his blonde head to one side. “Are you ready?”

Her heartbeat raced, but she gave firm a nod of consent.

He bounded up onto the porch, somehow managed to open the door without dropping her, and stepped across the threshold. After shutting the door with the heel of his boot, he looked down and caressed her with his eyes.

She buried her hands in his thick hair and drew his mouth to hers. His kiss was slow and so gentle it was soul soothing. She quivered at the sweet tenderness of it. When he pulled his lips away, she dropped her cheek to his chest, and with a sigh of pleasure, relaxed, sinking into his cushioning embrace.

For a moment, he just stood there quietly. He seemed to be savoring the moment. Then, he lowered her feet to the floor, took her hand above her head, and spun her around in a small circle. “Our first dance, my lady,” he said gallantly. “As husband and wife,” he added.

She had to chuckle, remembering how they’d enjoyed dancing together when Sam and Catherine married. At the wedding, William held her for the first time as they’d danced. It was also the first time desire stirred within her. Now, after twirling her around a time or two, her need for him swelled within her. And, as he pressed her body to him, her heart called out to his.

He gazed down at her, his eyes brimming with tenderness. “We’re home,” he said, his voice somewhat husky. “We should get settled. I’ll go tend to the horses and bring in our supplies.”

“And I’ll get a fire going in the hearth,” she offered. “I see kindling in that bucket and some wood was stacked on the front porch."

As Kelly worked on getting the fire going, a blaze of love already burned brightly in her heart. Feeling as though she'd entered a safe sanctuary, her mind filled with a calm peace. William's presence, the cozy haven of the cabin, and their mutual love surrounded her.

At this point, she was beyond the burdensome chains of fear. She had no more worries. She envisioned her future here with William with confidence and clarity.

William made several quick trips into the cabin with their packages, his rifle and other items. On his last trip, his arms full of their food supplies, new blankets, and linens, he nearly dropped it all. Kelly knelt before the hearth, coaxing the small flames to a larger life. The flickering fire made her long hair sparkle like strands of gold and cast her face and form in a warm becoming light. Her figure had more curves than the surrounding hills.

She turned her head toward him and stared intently. Was that longing he saw in her eyes? How he wished he were right. He hoped he could be sensitive enough to her feelings tonight.

He tossed everything down on the table and went to her. He offered her a hand and tugged her to her feet. "Do you realize how beautiful you looked just now? I never want to forget that image—the first time I saw you in the light of our hearth."

Something intense flared within him. How could he show her how much he loved her? Then he had an idea. He unsheathed his knife. "Come here," he said as he moved toward the bed.

She followed, curiosity filling her sweet face.

He started carving a heart into the wall beside the bed. When he finished, he etched their initials into it—W.W. and K.W.

"Good thing my name's not Wilma," she said.

Despite her jest, he could tell she was pleased because, while he carved, she never stopped smiling.

A deep contentment settled within him. He liked pleasing Kelly and he wanted to go on making her happy the rest of their lives.

When he finished carving their initials into the heart, he turned to her. "Now, whenever you're in our bed, you can look up and see that our hearts are one."

"I know," she said, "I can already feel yours beating within me."

Her loving words called for another kiss. But this time he deepened it, letting her feel his passion. After thoroughly kissing her, he said, "We've already eaten dinner. Would you like some wine? I told the store owner it was our wedding night and managed to talk him into selling me the only bottle he had."

"I've never had wine before. What's it like?"

"We used to enjoy it quite often back home. Our brother Edward, the only one of my siblings who remained in New Hampshire, sells quite a lot in his store. It's made from grapes grown in vineyards, but it's not sweet like grapes. Sometimes you can taste a bit of walnut, cinnamon, vanilla, or dried fruit. A good wine, like this one from France, will make your mouth pucker a little. But it has the effect of relaxing most people, including me," William said, "and after the day we've had, I would enjoy relaxing a bit."

"Wine sounds delightful, but let's put everything away first and we'll need some water from the creek," Kelly said. "And you'll need to bring in a few more logs."

"Already you're a bossy wife?" William teased, affectionately, while he removed one of his pistols, lead pouch, and items from his pockets. He set them all on a small table by the door. "But you're right. Once we start drinking that wine, the only thing I'll want to do is wrap my arms around you and never let go."

"That sounds delightful too," Kelly said coyly.

He took his new coat off, not wanting to get firewood chips all over it, and hung it on a deerhorn attached to the wall by the door. He went to her and ran his hands up her arms, bringing her closer. Her soft curves molded to the contours of his body and she was just tall enough that he could rest his chin against the top of her head. They fit together as if God had made them for each other. Maybe He did, he thought, as he hugged her one more time before attending to his tasks.

He'd always thought he could never be happy with just one woman in his life. Now he realized just how wrong he'd been. Never had any of the, admittedly far too numerous, women in his past made him feel anywhere close to what he felt for Kelly. It wasn't just his undeniable physical attraction to her. He was pulled to her by a far greater force—love.

Not wanting to appear too eager, he took his time as he brought the logs in and then strolled to the creek, a bucket in each hand. The drenching rain earlier in the day caused the peaceful brook to spread out of its banks for a few hours before receding, leaving behind a boggy and muddy bank. Through the moonlight, he could see the still somewhat swollen stream flowing swiftly by. He scanned up and down the creek, looking for a place to access the water easily. But it looked muddy every direction. Intent on getting the water quickly for Kelly, but not wanting to bring mud into their new home, he tried hopping from rock to rock to reach the creek. But in the darkness, his boot skated across a particularly slippery rock and he plunged face first into the mud. His entire body mired in the deep sludge, William lifted his face, and spit out dirty rain water and bits of grass.

"Bloody hell," he swore. His wedding night was not starting off well. He rubbed his face, trying to get the mud off, but his hands were equally dirty. Raising himself up on his palms, he realized his best white shirt and cravat were no longer the least bit white. And his brand new silk waistcoat appeared ruined. "Damn."

He stood, teetering, his boots clutched by the thick mud. He pulled one out and heard a whoosh. He stepped back with that foot and then pulled his other boot clear. His best boots would never be the same. Oh well, it was time for a new pair anyway.

There was only thing to do—immerse himself in the creek completely and let the rushing rainwater rinse all the mud off his clothes and body.

"Wait. I have a much better idea," he said aloud and turned around.

Kelly quickly dusted off the bed and then put the fresh linens and blankets on it. Making sure no wrinkles were apparent, she smoothed the blanket again and fluffed the pillows. She studied the bed for a few moments. Her stomach fluttered and something pleasurable rippled through her. She moistened her lips and grinned in anticipation.

She found two pewter cups, in a cabinet, for the wine. When William got back with the water, she would rinse them out thoroughly and wipe the table down. Her immediate priorities taken care of, she wondered where he was. He should be back by now. Something pulled her outside.

She opened the door and gasped. "Good heavens. What on earth?" William, covered head to toe in thick mud, was approaching the porch.

"I was thinking, my bride, perhaps a dip in the creek might be in order for both of us. I seem to require your assistance with getting clean," William said, smiling, his white teeth shining through his mud-covered face.

She glanced at him playfully. "William Wyllie, did you deliberately fall in the mud to lure me into that stream?"

The thought of a bath, even if it would be in the chilly stream, appealed to her immensely. At least the wind mercifully died down and the temperature had come back up a little.

"No, my dear, I am innocent of any premeditation. Attempting to be a dutiful husband, I was simply rushing to get your water in an area not favorable to moving swiftly."

She could tell he was trying to sound dignified to make up for how perfectly ridiculous he looked. Even covered in mud, though, there was something warm and enchanting in his manner.

She tried to suppress a giggle. Amusement flickered in his pale blue eyes, and then she laughed. Soon he was laughing too and before long, their merriment had her sitting on the porch, in hysterics, holding her sides. Their tears of hilarity felt good. How long had it been since she'd laughed this hard? She couldn't even remember. And it had helped her forget all the terrible events of the last day. That was all behind her now, shed with her tears of laughter.

Half laughing, half crying, she stood and took a long look at her husband. He was so handsome, even covered in mud, her breath caught in her throat. His beckoning eyes, still sparkling with tears of laughter, now also smoldered.

"Shall we attempt to get you clean?" she asked, her heart racing.

"Are you prepared for the challenge?" The question in his eyes probed deep into her.

"Yes, husband, I believe I am."

William was amazed at the thrill her answer gave him. She not only appeared unafraid, she openly admired him.

"Bring that bar of soap we bought," William said, "and you'd better leave your boots and gown. It's awfully muddy down there."

"That, I could have guessed."

William watched Kelly shamelessly tuck the bar of soap between her breasts and then stared spellbound as she removed her gown, stomacher, and petticoat. Her body silhouetted against the light coming from the open cabin door, her every movement sent a thrill racing through him.

Her eyes seemed to beckon to him and he swallowed, finding it increasingly difficult to just stand there and watch her. Soon, she wore only a shift, stays, and stockings. Her burning eyes held him motionless for a moment before she lowered her thick lashes. She reached down, removed the garters above her knees and rolled her stockings off. When she glanced up, her eyes sparkled impishly as though she were playing a game.

He liked this game very much.

In two strides, he was beside her. He lifted her into his arms, spun around, and marched toward the stream. He held her out in front of him, away from the mud, as much as possible.

Her eyes narrowed suspiciously. "Just what do you think you're doing?"

"Doing?" he asked, with false innocence.

"You'd better not be planning to toss me into that stream!" The warning was gentle, but firm. "I prefer to ease in."

A twinkle of moonlight lit her blonde hair, making it gleam with shadows of deep gold.

"Sometimes, it's better to just take the plunge," he answered. "The water's cleaner out in the middle." He trudged straight into the swollen creek, and tossed her in.

Her outcry was shrill and sharp. She found her footing and stood, the water only a little more than waist deep. With her hands on her hips and glaring at him, she said, "That was not easing in!"

Mockingly, he placed his hands on his hips, and then moved toward her. "Oh this is going to be fun."

"William Wyllie, you're a muddy mess. At least let me get you cleaned off before you touch me again."

"If you insist." He just stood there at attention, his hands clasped behind him.

She cautiously moved toward him, and removed his cravat. "I'm going to use this to wipe you down. I think it's pretty much ruined anyway."

"I wholeheartedly agree with your assessment," he declared.

"We need to hurry. This water is chilly," she said, shivering, as she sponged water onto his face and neck.

"Then I will attempt to warm you," he said. Taking her small waist in his hands, he started to lower his mouth to hers.

She quickly moved away. "Oh no you don't. Not until your face is spotless."

William instantly ducked his head into the water and vigorously scrubbed his neck, face, and hair. His face close to the water, with one eye open, but pretending he couldn't see, he groped for the bar of soap. He started patting her chest until his hand found one of her breasts and he cupped it. "I know that soap is in there somewhere," he said, his hair dripping water into his eyes and mouth. Then he palmed her entire chest. She was laughing gently and his mouth turned up with amusement. He loved making her laugh. "I can't seem to find it," he said.

"Keep looking," she said, shocking him.

His head still bent to the water and his eyes closed, he moved his hand lower and rubbed her stomach before lowering his fingertips to the mound of her womanhood. He pressed his palm between her legs and she gasped.

"It's not there!"

"Oh, yes it is," he teased and stood up. "And I'll prove it to you later."

Her eyes bright with desire, Kelly rubbed soap onto the now somewhat clean cravat and then put the bar into his outstretched hand. While she washed her own body, he rubbed the bar over his clothing and scrubbed until the last traces of mud were gone.

"William this is such a beautiful place," she said, scanning around them.

He gazed about too. She was right. In the soft light of the moon, the picturesque view was so serene and peaceful he could almost feel it restoring his soul as he beheld it. And her presence here made the place all the more extraordinary. “Some people look for a beautiful place to make their home. Others, like you, make a place beautiful.”

She shivered at the compliment, or maybe she was chilled? “Are you cold?” he asked.

“No, not any more. It’s actually kind of nice, don’t you think?”

“Yes, it is,” he said, never taking his eyes off of hers. He rubbed the soap in his hands until they were slick and then tucked the bar into a pocket. He began to rub her neck, letting his fingers gently glide up and down, up and down, each time descending a little further. When they finally reached her breast, he let his fingers explore, slowly, lightly. The soft mounds and their hard peaks made a hot ache grow inside him.

He felt her quiver and he gazed deep into her glimmering eyes as he rinsed the soap off of her. When he’d finished, she reached up and hauled his head down to her lips with a sense of urgency. He was equally eager to kiss her, and he did, as his hands explored the curves of her back. “I love you,” he whispered into her ear.

She drew a deep breath. “And I love you,” she said and then kissed him again and locked her arms around his waist.

“Are you clean enough? More importantly, am I clean enough?” he asked.

Standing tall, with her hands clasped behind her, just as he had done earlier, she looked him over. Then she circled around him. “I believe you’ll do,” she said and started sprinting toward the cabin. “Don’t forget to fill those buckets with water,” she called over her shoulder.

She ran like a deer, light and springy on her feet. He wanted to chase after her, but carefully retrieved the buckets instead and then filled them with water from the middle of the stream. He returned to the cabin and, leaving his wet boots outside, brought the water inside. “Do we have any towels?” he asked.

“Yes, I added two to our linens order at the store,” she said. She was already digging around in the bag containing their purchases. “Here they are. They’re small, but they’ll do.” She handed him one of the linen towels.

He took it and started drying her dripping hair. “We can wipe off a little with these and then move over to the fire to finish drying.”

Kelly took her towel and, standing on her tip toes, tried to reach his hair, but soon gave up. “You’re too tall,” she complained.

“We need to get out of these wet clothes,” he said.

Her lids slipped down over her eyes before she said, “I guess you’re right.” She went over to her bag, resting on the floor by the bed, and yanked out a long shift. She turned her back to him and began removing her stays.

“Do you need help?” he volunteered, hoping she did.

“No, I can manage. Go on now. Get out of those wet clothes too.”

William tried not to watch her, but he couldn’t help himself, stealing glances her way as often as he dared. As he was taking off his breeches, he caught a brief glimpse of her bare back side. His eyes widened and his mouth dropped open. Sweet heavens, she was magnificent. The thought of his eyes feasting on her front side too was nearly overwhelming. He quickly changed into a long dry shirt.

He needed to distract himself and do it quickly or he would risk embarrassing himself or scaring her. He found the wine bottle, unwrapped it, and used his new corkscrew to open it. The shopkeeper had suggested he buy one and while the man wrapped the bottle well for William, explained that the first corkscrews were patterned after a gun worme, a tool with a spiral end used to clean musket barrels or to extract an unspent charge from a gun's barrel. Now, local blacksmiths made corkscrews because using a cork to stopper a bottle was becoming commonplace.

"I found two cups. They're on the table, but need to be cleaned," Kelly called to him. She was now sitting near the fire, combing her hair.

He rinsed the cups well and then wiped them out with one of the towels. After placing another chair beside her, he brought the wine bottle and cups and sat them on the floor in front of the hearth. He poured a cup for Kelly and then gave it to her.

She took the cup with both hands, and studied the wine. "It's a beautiful color, such a deep rich red," she said. "If it tastes as good as it looks, it will be a delight."

"Wine is indeed a luxury, especially on the frontier. I was lucky he had a bottle. Otherwise, we'd be drinking rain water. I did encourage him to procure more."

After he poured himself some of the wine, he held his cup up. "A toast to our marriage, our new home, and our future."

"And to your health," she added.

"And yours."

She took a tentative sip and with widened eyes said, "That's heaven in a bottle."

He chuckled and took a taste himself. "I would have to agree with you. Perhaps that's why Christ's first miracle was making wine for a wedding feast." In his opinion, fine wine was one of the many ways to experience heaven here on earth.

Tonight she would experience another.

"William, we will be so happy and content here. I know there will be both happy days and bad days, but they will always be good days as long as we're together. And, I guess they will even be good days when one of us finally passes, because we will have all our happy memories to remember."

"I look forward to all the memories I haven't lived yet with you," he said. "The past is yesterday, our future is tomorrow, but this moment is today. That's what's most important."

She regarded him enigmatically, over the rim of her cup, as though she were letting his words seep into her along with the wine.

They sipped their wine, comfortably enjoying each other's company, until the bottle was empty and the fire changed to burning embers.

CHAPTER 21

Her mouth dry, Kelly swallowed and clutched the sheet to her neck as William eased in next to her. Intense emotions whirled within her. But fear was not one of them. This was her hero lying next to her. The man she loved. Her husband.

He sat up, turned his head toward her, and smiled lovingly. A lock of his shiny blonde hair fell in his beautiful eyes. Deftly, he reached down and peeled his long shirt off.

Through the waning light from the hearth, she caught a glimpse of his broad muscled back. His golden skin gleamed in the dim firelight. Before he lowered himself to the bed, he drew the sheet up over both of them.

His nearness and undress was overwhelming. Her heartbeat throbbed wildly in her chest. It was difficult to breathe. Her mind raced, imagining what would happen. She bit down on her lower lip, feeling her insides vibrate. Perhaps it was the wine making her feel so peculiar.

Should she do something? If so, what? She hated being so naïve, feeling so awkward. She wanted to yield to the burning desire within her, but didn't quite know how. Her brain raced but she couldn't think. She felt confused, clouded, drugged again. Earlier that day, he had said he would teach her what she needed to know. So why should she agonize over it now? She guessed it was because she so desperately wanted to please him. Not knowing what else to do, she just smiled nervously in the darkness, anticipating.

Her newly awakened sensuality made her want more of him than those first delightful touches at the creek. Amid the swirling rushing water, he'd made her more comfortable with his antics and good humor. But he had also given her a delicious sample of just what his fingers could do to her.

William drew himself closer to her and picked up a lock of her hair. He caressed it gently and then pulled her over to him, resting her head on his chest and tucking her body against his own. She could feel the movement of his breathing against her cheek and hear his blood pounding through his heart. It beat nearly as fast as her own heart. Yet he exuded an air of calm and confidence.

For a while, he just held her and her heart began to settle down to a more even beat. He seemed to be giving her a few moments to rest. Breathing in his clean scent, she closed her eyes and reveled in the comfort and security of his strong arms. Her own muscles began to relax. The tension in her legs and arms slowly dissolved, and the ache in her lower back, from being horseback most of the day, eased. Soon she felt like she was floating on a wispy cloud. It was heaven in a bed.

He kissed the top of her head affectionately. The gesture was so simple, so pure, so reassuring. Her worries about what she should do next or what was about to happen between them faded.

William was giving her time to become accustomed to his nearness. His mouth grazed her cheek, and he pressed a kiss into her palm, sending a tingle racing up the length of her arm. Then he slipped a hand up her arm, ever so slowly.

She drank in the sweetness of his tenderness. Abruptly, her attraction to him became powerful, compelling. A delightful shiver of wanting ran through her chest and spread downward. Her body suddenly ached for his touch.

Compelled by an irresistible craving for him, she moved her hand across his broad chest and then down his shoulder to the bulge of his upper arm. She could feel the strength of his muscles and the warmth beneath his skin, and it stirred her own desire even more. He was almost hot to the touch. If he was always like this, she would never again be cold in bed. Her own body seemed be heating up too.

Extremely aware of his virile appeal, she found herself fancying a peek under the sheet to see if the rest of him was as impressive as she thought it might be. She lifted the sheet, pretending to pull it over her shoulder and let her gaze quickly swing downward. Her eyes widened and her senses reeled. The glimpse of his magnificent body sent a tremor racing through her. She bit her lip to stifle an outcry of delight.

She wanted him to find her equally desirable. She was not blind to his attraction to her, but she had no idea how she compared to other women. Would he find her equally appealing? Was she too thin? Her breasts too small? She fought against the self-doubt, refusing to succumb to it. As casually as she could manage, she asked, “William do you find me attractive.”

He whispered into her hair, “There’s only one word to describe you, my love.”

"What's that?"

"Perfect!"

Reaching deep inside of herself for the courage she needed, she sat up, tugged her shift up and over her head, and tossed it to the foot of the bed. Even in the near darkness, she couldn't miss his obvious examination of her body.

His reaction was swift and he reached for her and pulled her over on top of him.

Their breasts now pressed against one another's, skin to skin, heart to heart. And his manhood rested against her abdomen. Her self-confidence leapt.

And the growing ache inside her spoke of her own intense desire for him.

Being on top of him gave her a sense of control—she was making love to him! This fueled her courage even more. She lowered her head and kissed him, and then kissed him again, exploring his mouth and lips with her tongue, as he ran his warm hands over her bottom and then back up her back. Then she trailed her lips down to the pulsing hollow at the base of his neck, while he planted soft kisses against the side of her head.

She didn't know if she was doing this right, but she let her body lead her. She buried her face against the sinuous muscles of his chest, kissing him, while his hands explored the planes of her back and then cupped her bottom. Her skin tingled pleasantly at his touch.

Reclaiming his lips, she gave herself freely to the strange hunger inside her, and let her kisses become more insistent this time. Enjoying herself immensely, she kissed him repeatedly, releasing his lips only long enough for them both to take a few gasping breaths. Soon her chest was heaving and a sort of wild energy filled her.

"Kelly," he said and brushed a gentle kiss across her forehead. His breath was warm against her face.

She smiled at the sound of her name on his lips. His tone held both reverence and desire.

"Yes, William," she answered in the dark.

"Are you ready?" he asked.

The question sent a tremor rippling through her.

In answer, she rolled back onto her back and drew him to her.

William could hardly contain his elation. Kelly's eagerness for love-making was something he'd longed for. But he never anticipated the keen and uninhibited passion he felt from her now.

Loving him with reckless abandon, her kisses sent shock waves through his entire body and left his mouth burning for more. She'd matched the passion of his kisses with her own intensity—each kiss more urgent and exploratory than the last.

It was time to teach her, though, that there was more to love-making than just kissing, although he was thoroughly enjoying every single sweet tasting smooch. The lingering taste of the wine in her mouth made her kisses all the more delightful. And the brush of her doeskin soft lips against his set him aflame.

But now, the beauty and allure of her shapely body teased him, waiting to be explored and then cherished. Her body was so feminine, so enticing, so alluring. He was acutely aware of each place his warm flesh touched hers.

And every single pore she touched—seduced, beguiled, captivated—made him want to surrender to her budding charms.

He felt the intoxicating sensation of his lips against her neck as he placed lingering whisper soft kisses there. He continued to explore the creamy flesh at the base of her neck and then let his lips nibble on her ear lobe. Even her ears were sensuous.

"Kelly, I love you," he breathed into her ear.

He reclaimed her lips, overcome by a compelling need to kiss her again. But now her lips held a dreamy intimacy that hadn't been there before. His heart leapt as he realized they were slowly becoming one.

Soon they would be one. One body. One flesh.

Inch by inch, his fingertip slowly outlined both breasts before he fondled one, its tip already marble hard. Her back arched against the bed and he slipped one arm under her while he slid his other hand across her silky belly and then down the curve of her hip.

He continued the gentle massage over and over again, keeping his touch feather light, until he finally moved his hand to the inside of her thigh. She moaned and bent her knees and he knew the bud of desire just blossomed inside her. He would nourish that bloom patiently and tenderly until it flowered into its full glorious beauty.

Only then would he allow himself atop of her to feel the sweet caress of her entire body against his and release his ardor, unrestrained.

Reaching down, he continued to explore the inside of her thighs, reveling in how velvety her skin was there, like the downy softness of rose petals. Moving his hand up, he delicately stroked, with the merest of touches, her womanhood for the first time.

The intimate contact made her cry out in pleasure.

He reveled in the moment, appreciating the awe-inspiring significance of what that touch meant to him. She was his—his wife—his lover.

He paused to kiss her again, deep and hard, with all the love in his heart.

Then he began a sensuous path to guide her to ecstasy for the first time.

Kelly squirmed beside him, gasping, and tightened her grip on his shoulders and arms.

It made his own desire flare, yet again, strong and agonizingly urgent. But his own needs would wait. He made himself focus on the poignant beauty of her body's awakening to the power and passion of love.

She whimpered and her trembling limbs clung to him. Her body sought something she didn't yet fully understand.

Soon, though, she would.

CHAPTER 22

The morning sun gilded the horizon as Kelly strolled down to the creek for water. The bright sunshine caressed her upturned face and a slight breeze brushed kisses on her jaw. Birds chirped and sang from every tree and she thought she heard the bellow of an elk off in the distant hills. The cool air, made clean and crisp by yesterday's rain, made her pull her shawl tighter.

The stream's water, no longer as swift as it was last night, hummed peacefully as it flowed by, brushing against rocks and brush. The lovely, colorful hills around her rose gently, inviting her to wander them.

She stopped and closed her eyes for a moment reveling in her beautiful surroundings and her happiness. Her mother had often said joy comes in the early morning. And she did feel pure joy this morning. Her spirit, light, buoyant, and carefree, soared for the first time in years. Her world was perfect. Except that, William had left early to see about the prisoner in his jail and arrange for the man's trial. But she was well used to being alone and he had promised to be back soon.

She opened her eyes and surveyed the picturesque setting, wondering who had named it Whispering Hills. She couldn't wait to hear the wind speaking to her through these hills. Words whispered soak into your heart so much faster than other words. Perhaps that is why these hills whispered.

Already she loved this place and the palatable feeling of rightness it bestowed. Mostly because of the man who had loved her so completely last night. But also because she now had a home to call her own. And a life of her own. Before she had been a part of her parents' life and later only a small part of her father's. But this was her life. Whispering Hills would be the home that held her hopes and dreams.

She also felt far braver here—her dormant inner strength renewed. She sat her bucket down, stretched, and drew in a deep chest-expanding breath of cool air.

As she stood there, invigorated, a sense of belonging filled her, and it gave her comfort. She decided she would bless Colonel Boone until the end of her days for his generosity. And if she and William ever had children, she would teach them to do the same. Maybe they would even name one of their sons Daniel.

Kelly decided to take a stroll around the place before she got the water. She wandered aimlessly, with no particular purpose except to familiarize herself with her new home. After a few minutes of exploring, she stumbled upon an old forlorn cemetery at the crest of a rise. Two simple stone markers lay flat against the green grass. The names carved in the rocks were covered with grass, leaves, and dirt and difficult to read. She plucked some of the leaves away, revealing only a few of the letters. It didn't really matter to her who they were, but she promised herself she would take care of the graves. Later, she'd bring a hoe and shears and clean the burial place up.

When she'd left her home, leaving her mother's grave behind had been perhaps the hardest thing she'd ever done. No one would keep the weeds down or leave her mother flowers on her birthday. She hoped that someday, someone would find it and, like her, care for a stranger's grave.

After she'd finished her walk about, she filled the bucket and started back toward the cabin. William had taken care of her horse before he left, letting her mare out in the pen to graze, so Kelly decided to start her day with cleaning. She would give the cabin a thorough cleansing and when she finished with the inside, she would start tidying up the outside. There were bits of leaves and branches on the porch and she intended to keep it as clean as the inside of her home. In the spring, she would plant some flowers, mint, and other herbs in front of the porch and perhaps start a garden nearby.

She warmed the coffee William had made before he left and set a Dutch oven in the coals, loaded with plenty of water, beans, some salt, and the wild onion she'd found on her stroll. As she sipped her coffee, she studied the cabin's interior and decided what to tackle first. Then she started on her chores, her heart content.

After a couple of hours, she took a deep breath. It smelled cleaner and fresher now. She collected a few sprigs and twigs with fall colored leaves and made a bouquet for an old pot she found in the corner. Then she baked some corn bread in the hearth and when it finished baking, she sat it on a brick to cool. The sweet aroma made her stomach growl. William thought he would be able to make it back by noon, so she decided to wait and eat with him.

As she continued her chores, she thought about their lovemaking. The awakening experience had left her reeling.

Afterwards, he had held her in his arms, stroking her head gently as she slowly recovered.

Her own driving need shocked her to her core and, even now, made her face warm. And the way William was able to answer that need stunned her even more. She didn't know it was possible to feel those things. He was a masterful lover. She had underestimated everything about being intimate with him. It was so much more than she anticipated. Spectacular even. And she was eager to learn more.

She wondered if William could have gotten her with child. She would know in a couple of weeks, but for now, she set aside the thought.

Suddenly drowsy, she decided to lay down and rest her eyes for a few moments. But her exhausted body and the warmth of their bed soon lured her into a deep, dragon-free sleep.

A wet tongue was licking her face. William?

Kelly's eyes flew open. The face of the cutest puppy she had ever seen stared back at her, its eyes equally wide. With its puppy paws balanced precariously on the curves of her chest, the fat little ball of fur started wagging a fluffy tail and moved toward her neck.

When he licked her chin, she giggled and sat up. The long-haired golden puppy tumbled into her lap and curled into a tight ball. She glanced around, but there was no sign of William.

"Where did you come from little one?" She stroked the pup's downy back several times and then picked it up. A male. A boy with huge feet and an even bigger belly. And long velvety ears that flopped down on either side of his warm brown eyes.

William burst through the door, his arms full of more supplies and packages. A huge grin covered his face. "How do you like our new boy?"

"He's completely adorable!" she exclaimed, standing up. "Is he mine?"

"Indeed."

"I've never owned a dog. Oh William, how can I ever thank you!"

He chuckled. "I can think of some ways. Come see what else I got you."

Holding the puppy, she hurried over to the table now laden with all manner of items. She gave William a big kiss before examining the bounty. There was a new wool blanket, a block of cheese, a pound of sugar, an apron, candles, some paper and ink, a pretty blue shawl, and a few books.

"Books, you got me books!" She opened each one reverently and then gave him a peck for each one.

"I remembered how worn your tomes were back at your cabin. They were falling apart and you had to leave the books behind. I wanted to replace them for you," William explained.

"I read each of the three more times than I can count," she said.

"The shopkeeper promised me they were all good stories. And he said that one, The Art of Cookery, contained some excellent recipes and as well as perfumery guidance. Take a look at the page where I put the ribbon."

Kelly opened the book to the ribboned page and read,

Sweet Scented Bags to Lay with Linen

Eight ounces of damask rose leaves, eight ounces of coriander seeds, eight ounces of sweet orrisroot, eight ounces of calamus aromaticus, one ounce of mace, one ounce of cinnamon, half an ounce of cloves, four drachms of musk-powder, two drachms of white loaf sugar, three ounces of lavender flowers and some of Rhodium wood. Beat them well together and make them in small silk bags. A mortar, pestle and a grater are essential for creating a strong scent. Place the mixture in an 8 inch by 8 inch square piece of cloth and tie together with a ribbon.

That will be fun to try someday, she thought. This cabin could use a little sweeter scent. "How thoughtful. Thank you once again, William."

"It is my great pleasure to bring you joy."

"Being with you is my greatest joy."

"And I you. But, I have to hurry back to town. I need to finish questioning Helms and interview the witnesses to the shooting at the blacksmith's, and then later today, I have to meet up with Sam and Bear at our old campsite. I need to retrieve all my things and my law books before the two of them leave to return to Cumberland Falls. Not that anyone is likely to steal my humble possessions, but I wouldn't want to risk someone stealing my law books."

"I hate to see Sam and Bear leave," Kelly said. "It's reassuring to have both of them around."

"Indeed, but it's time they got back to the others. I'm sure Sam misses Catherine. After all, they are newlyweds."

"I think he would miss her terribly even after they'd been married for fifty years," she said.

"Sam told me something interesting at the swearing in

ceremony."

"What?" she asked, her curiosity growing.

"It seems Catherine is an extremely wealthy woman."

"Truly?"

"Not only that, her family is English nobility. And her late husband had a verified claim to ten thousand acres surrounding Cumberland Falls. That's about fifteen square miles. Now she owns it. Or rather, she and Sam own it. She insisted that they share everything."

Kelly felt her eyes widen and her mouth drop. She blew out a breath. "She never let any of us know."

"She wanted Sam to marry her for love, not her wealth, so she kept it a secret from all of us, even him. She didn't tell Sam until a few days into their honeymoon."

"I'm astounded. She always seemed elegant, almost regal, but never would I have guessed she was noble. She's so kind and humble." She stroked the pup's head as she talked.

"Well she is definitely noble. She even has a large estate in England that produces a substantial income each year," William explained.

"That explains her fine clothing and all her pretty things. And why she could buy Jane and me those gowns and under garments to wear to her wedding. She was always so generous with all of us."

"Yes. She even gave a nice chunk of land to Stephen and Jane, so they won't have to worry about filing a claim, which could take many months. Stephen has already nearly completed their new home. In fact, by now, it's probably finished."

"That's wonderful news. Their new baby will have a new home.

Can we go visit?" she asked hopefully.

"Of course, perhaps in the springtime. But for now, I need to attend to my duties here."

"Please say goodbye to Sam and Bear, and to my father, for me. I said my farewell to Papa after our wedding dinner, but I'd like you to tell him that I'll miss him. Now that I have paper and ink, perhaps I should write him a note you can take with you. I'll encourage him to stay strong and sober."

"Splendid idea. Don't let me leave without it."

The puppy started licking her fingers. "Are you hungry boy?"

"Of course he's hungry. He's a puppy," William said.

"What will I feed him?"

"I hadn't thought of that," William confessed. "Do I smell cornbread? What's in the Dutch oven?"

"I made beans and cornbread," she said, proud of herself.

"I can tell coming home to you every day is going to be delightful in so many ways," he said, and tugged her to him, hugging her. "For now, he'll just eat what we eat. When I get a chance, I'll buy some game from Lucky McGintey."

"How is the sweet old fellow?"

"His aim is still true. He brought a pack horse loaded with meat into town earlier today."

"What do you think we should call this little boy?" Kelly asked, continuing to pet the pup.

"He's yours so I'll leave that up to you."

"How about Riley?"

"Riley Wyllie. I like the sound of that," William answered and kissed her. He leaned down to kiss the pup too, but Riley licked him on the nose.

She brought a hand up to stifle her giggles.

"He can't hold his licker," William said with a wide smile. "We'll have to keep him away from the pub." He threw back his head and chuckled richly.

His jest made her laugh as well. "Here, you take him for a minute and I'll serve us up some food."

"I'd better clear our table off. Let's just set him down for a while," William suggested. "He's going to need something to chew on. All puppies like to chew on things."

"I noticed an old leather strap by the smokehouse."

"Were you out exploring today?"

"Yes, I found two graves on the rise behind us."

"Probably two of the many relatives Boone lost while settling Kentucky," William said.

"It made me think of my mother's grave. I feel badly that I've left her behind."

"We all leave love ones behind eventually. While I never met your mother, I'm sure she would want you to do what was best for you. I have no doubt she'd understand," William said. "She's not there anyway. She's with the angels in heaven."

"Of course you're right. I'll start thinking of her as being there instead of back home in Virginia."

"Kelly, when you went walking, did you take the pistol I left for you with you?"

"No, I didn't," she confessed. "I forgot. I set out to just get some water, but couldn't resist looking around for a while before I got started with my cleaning."

"The place does look remarkably better. But promise me you will always keep that pistol handy. I'll buy you a rifle too and a good long knife. And keep my ax inside with you too. Once Riley gets to be the big fellow he promises to be by those feet, he can alert you to danger. But until then, you'll have to be especially careful."

"I promise," she said.

He took her hand and led her to their bed. "Now it's time to thank you properly for all your hard work."

"But it's the middle of the day!"

"Indeed."

CHAPTER 23

The weeks flew by and her days at the cabin seemed to Kelly more like a pleasant dream than anything else she could compare them to. Her puppy grew like a spring weed, each day getting taller and heavier, until finally she could no longer easily carry him in her arms. By the season's first frost last week, he could even bark and growl like a grown-up dog. She grew more attached to Riley by the day and thought of him as her child. An exceedingly hairy child, his thick coat was a light golden color, much like William's hair. Her constant companion, she sometimes felt like she had two shadows.

But he wasn't her child. Her first child now grew inside of her. When she'd missed her monthly flow for the second month, she knew for a certainty. And joy filled her from the top of her head to the tips of her toes. She placed a hand on her belly wondering if their child would be a tall boy like William or a little girl with blonde hair like hers. She wanted to make a special dinner for William tonight and then tell him her wonderful news. After studying her new cookbook while she drank her morning coffee, she decided to make bread, a soup, sliced smoked ham with a mustard sauce, fried potatoes with garlic, and maybe William's favorite custard for desert.

It was frosty again this morning. Crystals on every tree and shrub glittered in the first rays of the sun and bespangled every object in their yard. Interlocking ice crystals hung from the branches and leaves of trees, and painted the grass blades white. Although she had never heard the term, William had called it a hoar frost, and said it wouldn't last long.

With her new blue shawl tied tightly around her and her warmest socks and clothing on, she milked the cow and started gathering eggs. Just as she had done back at her old cabin, she had named her egg chickens after the first few books of the Old Testament. "Good morning Genesis! And how are you Exodus?" Leviticus, a soft chestnut in color, was her favorite chicken. Fuzzy feathers surrounded her head, like untidy hair, giving her an unsettling, but amusing appearance. She did not name the chickens she raised solely for their meat.

Finished with the cow and eggs, she made her regular morning trip to the creek, with Riley trailing beside her, his tail wagging enthusiastically. All of a sudden, Riley stopped, his tail frozen in mid wag. His eyes focused intently on something, his lifted nose pointed toward the forest. She peered into the woods trying to determine if it was a deer or perhaps a reckless rabbit that made its presence known. It was not unusual for Riley to take notice of other animals in his area, but he rarely barked. Or growled. But he did now. A low throaty rumble tumbled down his chest. The sound made the hairs on her neck stand up.

She slipped her hand into the deep sturdy pocket she'd sewn onto her apron to hold her pistol and gripped the handle. The feel of it in her hand was reassuring. Filling her bucket with her other hand, and keeping one eye on the tree line, she watched

Riley. His guard was definitely up. "What is it boy?"

In response, Riley barked just once. But the bark was serious, a definite warning. Something wasn't right.

"All right. I understand. Let's go back now, I'll keep a watch out," she said softly, her own sense of danger beginning to needle her.

As calmly as she could manage, she started back toward the cabin. But Riley didn't follow. She looked back for him. His stance was rigid, menacing, and he hadn't moved an inch. What was he doing? He wasn't old enough yet to intimidate anything, except maybe a rabbit or squirrel.

"Riley, come boy," she urged and kept walking, more briskly now. Nervously, she took a quick glance over her shoulder when he didn't obey.

"Riley, come, now!" she yelled.

He caught up with her. But this time, his tail wasn't wagging. He whined and nudged her hand with his cold nose. Could he smell something? He raced up to the porch, as if to encourage her to hurry. And she did.

Alarm erupted fully within her as she leapt onto the porch, some the water splashing on her boots. "Riley, inside."

But, acting like a great brave watch-dog, Riley leapt off the porch and ran off, barking, toward the woods.

Her heart sank. But there was nothing she could do now.

She hurried inside, slamming and barring the door behind her. Immediately, she peered through one of the port-holes, but noticed nothing unusual. Best be ready though in case there really was trouble out there.

She grasped the rifle, opened the pan, filled it with powder, closed the pan, poured powder down the barrel, placed the ball in the barrel, drew the rammer, and rammed the powder and projectile.

The nagging in the back of her mind refused to be stilled. Something or someone was out there. It was early morning and William said he wouldn't be back until late in the day. She struggled with the uncertainty in her mind. Should she saddle her mare and try to find William? No, she would have to risk exposing herself until she got the horse saddled. Should she wait on the porch where she could see her surroundings better? No, someone could sneak up behind the cabin. Should she just stay barred up inside until William returned? Yes, that was definitely the safest plan.

She heard the nicker of a horse and the answering soft, low, breathy whinny of Ginger. She peeked through the front port-hole hoping to catch a glimpse of whoever it might be. But spotted nothing. Unfamiliar sounds, though, seeped in to haunt her.

In quick succession, she peered first through the side portal, and finding nothing crossed the cabin and looked out the other side as well. Nothing. Then she went back to the front port-hole, and put her face to the hole.

Kelly flinched and sucked in a breath. She retreated a step and then another, her heart pounding.

An Indian's dark eyes stared back at her. He gave her a narrowed glinting glance. "No Boone woman!" His tone was hostile. The rest of his words were in his native tongue. He wasn't alone. Other footsteps resounded on her porch and she could hear Riley barking and growling at the intruders to his territory.

Fear gripped her, but she mustered her courage, raised the

rifle, and advanced toward the portal. This was her home and she would defend it!

The savage stepped back as she presented the long rifle through the opening. He quite openly studied her, and she him. His long sinewy arms gripped a tomahawk. His coarse hair hung straight, and the skin of his bare hairless chest was a reddish brown. He seemed impervious to the cold. And to fear.

It was the closest she'd ever been to a native and her heart thumped wildly in her chest.

He let out a fierce high-pitched cry, clearly intended to scare her.

She found the alarming sound exceedingly unnerving, and it sent shivers up and down her spine. But she wouldn't frighten that easily. She would be safe as long as they didn't set fire to the cabin.

She was tempted to just fire the rifle, but feared that killing one of the braves would cause the others to attack. Should she shoot anyway? The flintlock rifle held one shot. Then she would only have a second shot with the pistol. She would have to make both shots count and then quickly reload, before they could break down her door with their tomahawks.

She took a deep breath to steady her nerves. She trained the rifle's sights on the brave's chest. She didn't want to kill him; she just wanted him to leave. But if she had to kill, she would.

He swiftly darted away, out of her line of sight.

Then she heard something on the side of the cabin. She instantly swiveled her head in that direction. Another Indian peered into her cabin from that porthole, his dark eyes animated and glimmering. A quick look at the other side of the cabin revealed the agitated face of yet another brave! Dear God, how many of them were there?

She remembered what Captain Sam had said about how important it was to make Indians believe you are brave, even if you are scared witless. If you display fear, they are far more likely to attack. She put her face close to the portal, the rifle protruding well out in front of her, and ignored her rapidly beating heart. "Leave my cabin. Now!" she roared, making her words a command, spoken with as much authority as she could muster.

Then a dirty hand reached over from the side and grabbed for her rifle. Fingers tightened around the long barrel. Using all her strength, she struggled to hold on to it. The brave's other hand gripped the rifle too and then both hands commenced pulling the rifle away from her. She could feel the precious weapon slipping away. "No!" she shouted, and fought to hold onto it. She put both of her legs up against the wall beneath the portal. Using her legs and weight for leverage, she wrestled the rifle back inside, but fell backwards in the process.

"You bloody beast. You'll not take my rifle," she shouted as she scampered up.

Kelly quickly traded her rifle for her already loaded pistol. She put its shorter barrel against the portal, but not beyond it. She'd learned her lesson.

She looked out again and her heart froze. A brave cruelly seized Riley by the neck and held him out at arm's length. She'd heard that natives often ate dogs. The thought made her want to retch. A sweat broke out on her face. She couldn't shoot the Indian without risking hitting Riley.

Her pup growled and wiggled trying to free himself from the Indian. Annoyed, the brave smacked Riley's face with the back of his hand.

"You forest demon, leave my dog alone," she bellowed. Powerless to stop him, her rage made her grind her teeth together.

Riley took the blow and then lips curled back, bared his teeth and growled ferociously.

At that, the Indian delivered a wallop to the dog's side. Riley yelped in pain.

Kelly screamed. "You bastard!" she yelled. She stomped her foot in frustration. She desperately wanted to help Riley, but exposing herself would mean risking her baby's life.

The despicable brave yanked out a knife and his expression grew even more malicious.

"Oh God. Oh God. No!" Now she wanted to bawl, but held a hand against her mouth, holding her horror in. She resisted the urge to throw open the door and race outside.

What should she do? She had to save Riley. Her nerves twitched madly. Her mind raced. Trade. Trade them something. Sam said Indians typically honor trades. But what? Her eyes darted around. Her new shawl? She grabbed it and put her face to the window. "Trade? Trade for dog?" She held the garment up to the port-hole for him to see and then pointed to Riley. "Trade?" Would they understand the word? She prayed they would.

Then two other braves rode up. The muscled, shiny arms of one held the three large hams from the smokehouse. Another Indian carried a sizable bag loaded with apples from their orchard and one of her egg chickens—the one named Deuteronomy. Its neck hung limp and flopped with each step of the brave's horse.

Thieves! If they were hungry, she would have given them food if they'd just asked. But stealing food, especially during winter, was wicked and the worst kind of pilfering.

Following behind the braves who'd stolen the food, another more impressive Indian, his shaven head bedecked in colorful feathers, rode into sight. But this one's plunder was far more precious. Someone's little girl. A crying blonde-haired child of about five years rode in front of the imposing Indian, her fair ivory complexion in stark contrast to his dark skin. Her tiny legs didn't even reach to his knees. Dressed poorly, the child had to be nearly frozen.

The sight stunned and sickened Kelly. Her stomach clenched as if gripped by icy fingers. "Lord have mercy," she whispered aloud. Now tears filled her eyes in earnest as her heart reached out to the bawling little girl. She desperately wanted to help her. But how? What could she possibly do? Frustration made her pound her fist against her hip.

A bitter anger rose up inside her, climbing above her fear and shock. Suddenly enraged, she banished her tears and sorrow and replaced them with determination and grit that felt like a solid rock inside of her.

Somehow, she would help this child, she vowed, clenching her jaw.

The Indian carrying the sobbing child barked some orders to the others. The one on the porch in front of her reached in and yanked her shawl out.

She jumped back, but let him take it. Would they release Riley? Would they kill him? She shuddered at the thought. If they hurt him, she would shoot the Indian that did it, she swore to herself. She couldn't shoot the one holding the child for fear of hitting the little girl, but she would sure as hell kill the brave who harmed Riley.

Then the brave dangling Riley dropped him to the ground.

Thank God.

Riley sprung up and raced to her door, then turned and started snarling at the braves, now leaving with their pickings and someone's precious daughter.

Kelly listened until she could no longer hear the little girl's wretched heartbreaking cries.

CHAPTER 24

William rubbed his forehead. Since early that morning, he had diligently tackled the official paperwork and tiresome details included in his duties. His stack of new statutes needing to be read, warrants to file, lists of tax evaders and tax payers, correspondence, and all the other administrative work his job required, seemed never ending. What he wanted to do was far different—pursue criminals and see that they received the appropriate punishment.

And what he really yearned to do was even more different—he wanted to jump on his horse, go home, sweep his wonderful new wife up into his arms, and carry her to bed. He gave a few moment's thought to doing just that. But his steadfast sense of duty held him back. He needed to put in a full morning's work before he went home again to satisfy his aching, seemingly insatiable, need for her.

He stood and went to the window to stretch his aching neck and tight shoulders. The sky remained the grey blue color of early winter. He noticed though that the occasional intrepid rays of sunshine already melted the earlier frost.

Just outside the fort's entrance, a group of men were talking excitedly, and gesturing wildly as they hurried inside the enclosure. "Looks like trouble," he told Deputy Mitchell, who sat nearby cleaning his pistol. "You're in charge 'til I get back," William said. "I have a feeling this may take a while."

He grabbed his shot flask, powder horn, and weapons. As usual, his long knife already hung from his belt. He donned his tricorne and coat and hurried outside.

"Sheriff Wyllie," one man yelled as he strode toward William. His voice sounded frantic and worried. "Please help."

"What is it?" William called, lengthening his stride in the man's direction.

"My daughter. Savages have stolen her!" the man cried.

"You're Mister Merrill, are you not?" William asked.

The man, holding the reins of his winded mount, nodded. Anxiety etched the features of his face. His dark hair hung on his forehead in clumps that got in his eyes. When he swiped them away, William could see his pleading eyes.

"How old is your daughter Mister Merrill?" William asked, laying a calming hand on the man's shoulder. William could feel the poor father trembling with worry.

"She's just five. Please, we have to hurry. They stole her away this morning while I was hunting. My wife says they headed away from my place toward Whispering Hills, where Colonel Boone used to live. We visited there once with Boone and his family," Merrill answered, his voice wavering and his expression grim.

William's stomach clenched as though bony fingers just clamped around it. "That's where my home is. My wife is there." Immediately, dread and anger knotted inside him. They would need the militia. He turned and sprinted toward Colonel Byrd, with Merrill and several other men in tow. The Colonel, standing tall and shouting orders, was training his militia on the far side of the Fort's inner courtyard. Good, the men had already been mustered. That would save valuable time. He needed to reach Kelly and the little girl before the Indians could harm them. Just thinking of the possibility threatened to shatter his nerves. Trying to keep his worry under control in front of the other men, he took several deep breaths as he hurried toward the militia.

"Colonel Byrd," William yelled as he ran up to Byrd with Merrill trailing just behind him. "Urgent news."

"What is it, Sheriff Wyllie?" Byrd asked.

"Mister Merrill, tell the Colonel what's happened, while I saddle my horse," William directed. "And don't worry, we will get her back."

He ran to the nearby stable, his own apprehension building inside him like a developing thunderstorm. After quickly saddling Smoke, he rode back out to the Colonel, and then nearly vaulted off his stallion. His chest felt like it would burst if they didn't get going soon.

"What's your plan Sheriff Wyllie?" Byrd asked immediately. "Twenty-one men await your orders. Since it's your home that may be under attack, I will defer to you."

He checked the powder in his weapons and then tightened the cinch on Smoke as he spoke. "I'll leave at once with Merrill. You and your men follow us as soon as you can. Bring plenty of lead."

"As you say," Byrd said and then starting barking orders to the militia.

William and Merrill mounted and turned to leave, but stopped when a rider stormed through the Fort's gate riding to beat the devil.

The rider brought his horse to a skidding halt in front of the Colonel, William, and the others.

"What news do you bring?" Byrd asked the man and everyone else gathered in around the fellow's lathered horse.

"The Shawnee attacked Logan's Fort in retaliation for Colonel Logan's raid," the rider answered, nearly out of breath.

The man appeared both anxious and weary. He must have ridden all night.

William was already alarmed. Stephen, Jane, and their daughters now lived not far from Fort Logan. Sam and Bear would have ridden through the settlement on their way to Stephen's new home about ten miles north of the Cumberland River. And all three brothers often went into the settlement for supplies. He didn't want to wait any longer to leave, but he had to know what else the man had to say.

"But Logan's Raid was ten years ago!" the Colonel objected.

William had been studying Kentucky history lately, as well as Kentucky law. A decade ago, Logan and his militia attacked Shawnee villages along the Mad River while their warriors were away raiding settlements here in Kentucky.

"It was, Sir, but as you know, in retaliation for native attacks on settlers, Colonel Logan's forces burned Shawnee villages and food supplies and killed a considerable number of Indians who were not warriors. One of Logan's men killed Moluntha, one of their older chiefs. So we speculate the attack is in retribution and stems from the long-held hatred of Logan by natives from the Ohio Country."

William remembered reading that the killing of Moluntha was

in retribution for the Battle of Blue Licks. A hotheaded soldier angrily felled the old chief with a hatchet, and, as he tried to regain his feet, killed him with a second blow and scalped him. The Shawnee then sought revenge by increasing their attacks on the whites.

It was the same scenario, replayed over and over, back and forth, again and again, with only the details changing. The memory of a person wronged, no matter the color of their skin, is long.

"Colonel, we must leave now!" William urged. "Mister Merrill's daughter is in grave danger and my wife may be as well."

"Please Colonel Byrd, you and your militia must depart straightaway to help the settlement at Fort Logan," the rider pleaded. "A large number of Indians attacked. The women milking the cattle had to run for their lives. The men protecting them fired back. Arrows hit two of the militiamen—killed one and wounded the other. Captain Logan knew someone had to help the wounded man or he would certainly be killed. He asked for volunteers to go rescue him. No one volunteered."

William knew right then that Sam and Bear were not at Fort Logan. If there was danger involved, Sam always volunteered and Bear would only be a step behind him.

The rider, both he and his horse still breathing hard, continued to relate his story, trying William's scant patience.

"Logan decided to go alone to rescue the man. He used a large bail of wool as a shield and rolled it in front of him to get to the man, picked him up, and ran back to the fort. Then we watched in horror as the Indians lifted the scalp of the dead man in full view of the fort, including his screaming wife. Then the natives surrounded the fort and started building fires all around us. I escaped to seek help using our hidden tunnel to the well house."

"This is disturbing," Merrill grumbled, "but I have my own Indian troubles. My daughter is stolen. Colonel Byrd, we need to be on our way now."

"I agree," William said, "let's go."

"My apologies, Sir," Byrd said quickly, as he turned to William, "but my men and I will not be able to assist you. Given the uncertainty of the situation at Fort Logan, and the number of threatened settlers there, I feel I need to take the entire militia there. I'm sure you and Mr. Merrill will be able to prevail against a small band of natives."

William didn't object to pursuing the child's kidnappers without the militia's help, but it did concern him that Colonel Byrd was leaving Fort Boonesborough and the town virtually undefended. The last thing the town needed now was a serious Indian attack like the one at Fort Logan. Boonesborough was overflowing with farmers and others ill-equipped with either experience or weapons to defend against attack.

"Colonel, do you think Boonesborough is in danger of a similar attack?" William asked.

"No. We have Colonel Boone to thank for that. He and his men fought valiantly for our fort and the local natives respect him and honor the peace accord they made with Boone," Byrd explained. "Merrill's daughter was undoubtedly kidnapped by a renegade band."

For a moment, William considered trying to enlist the help of some of the men who had come into the fort with the child's father. But, with the twenty members of the militia gone, he was concerned about leaving Boonesborough with even fewer men to defend her. Most of these men were unarmed shopkeepers anyway. No, with Merrill's help, he was certain he could take care of this himself.

"Then Mister Merrill and I will set out without delay to rescue his daughter," William said.

"We wish you God's speed," Byrd said, his expression tight with strain.

"And to you as well, Sir," William said, reaching up to press his tricorne on snugly.

William and Merrill took off at a gallop. As soon as they exited the fort and crossed the town's busy main street, he nudged Smoke to an even faster run. At this pace, they should reach the cabin in less than twenty minutes.

William felt the seconds of every one of those minutes despite their grueling pace. The muscles of his shoulders and back tightened as Smoke's strong legs pummeled the hard ground mile after mile, the hooves of both horses throwing up clumps of mud and frost moistened fall leaves.

They were riding too fast and too hard to talk and the silence between them grew tight with tension. William pitied the man. To have a daughter stolen by Indians might mean he would never see her again. But if William could do anything to prevent that, he would.

The poor girl was undoubtedly beyond terrified. He just hoped they could reach her before the Indians disappeared into the hills with the child, her life forfeited to slavery.

As concerned as he was for the little girl, his own uneasiness for Kelly's safety grew with every mile. If natives appeared while she was inside, she could bar the door, and stood a good chance of staying safe. But if they came while she was out and about, as she often was, then...he squeezed Smoke with his legs and leaned forward, encouraging the stallion to run even faster.

Why would Indians go toward Whispering Hills? Perhaps they thought Boone still lived there. What would they do when they found Kelly there instead? His face twitched at the question.

A warning cloud, filled with foreboding, settled in his mind.

CHAPTER 25

Kelly flung the door open and let Riley inside.

He jumped up on her apron, whimpered, and studied her with his big brown eyes, tail wagging again just a little.

She could tell he was checking to be sure she was all right. Except for her heart, still pounding furiously in her chest, she was fine. Relief that the Indians did not attack her home more forcefully filled her and she let out a long breath.

She fell down on her knees, hugged Riley, and patted his sides, overjoyed that he wasn't hurt. She was so thankful that they were both okay she started to weep. "Riley, Riley, you brave foolish boy," she said stroking the top of his head and sniffling. "You could have been hurt. Next time listen to me."

Tail wagging more vigorously now, he licked the salt and tears from her face and put a big golden paw reassuringly on her arm.

"I love you too," she said and kissed his wet black nose.

Kelly wanted to keep loving him, but she needed to get going.

She had to help that little girl. What if the child were her little girl? She would want someone to help her. For this child, that someone could only be her. She couldn't wait for William and risk losing the Indians' trail. She had to go now.

She swiped the remaining tears from her eyes and prepared to leave. She quickly changed into her riding habit, found her jacket, threw it on, and then retrieved her paper, ink, and goose quill.

William,

Indians came this morning. Stole our hams, apples, and a chicken. Almost killed Riley. Worse, they have a little girl captive. I am going to track them. Forgive me, but I must try to help her. Follow me. I'll leave an apple trail starting at the big Sycamore tree. The apples should be easy to spot. There are five Indians.

Don't worry, I have all my weapons, and God by my side.

Lovingly, Kelly

She stared at the first note she'd ever written William and prayed it would not be her last. She pressed her lips against the paper, wanting to leave him a little of her love, before placing it back on the table in plain view.

Kelly looked down at the note, fear gripping her for a moment. A shiver of dread swept through her. She paced back and forth beside the table. Was she doing the right thing? Could she do this? Her brows drew tighter and her face tightened. She picked up the note. Her courage started to flutter away on the wings of doubt.

No! She would not lose her nerve. She would not panic and give in to fear. She would use that fear to make her stronger. She would feel the fear and do this anyway, because that child needed her. She slapped the note down on the table again, and patted it firmly with her palm.

Marshalling every bit of courage she possessed, she filled her canteen, attached her knife to a leather band and tied it diagonally across her chest. She tossed the long straps to the powder horn and shot flask over her neck, letting one hang off each hip. She tucked her pistol securely into a wide belt and grabbed her rifle, and then decided that she needed to organize her jumbled thoughts and hastily made plans before she took another step.

She knew how to track and handle a rifle. She'd done it for years hunting her own food. And five horses would leave a distinct trail—unless the natives took steps to hide their tracks. Since they had stolen a child that was a definite possibility.

The braves probably intended to sell the girl as a slave to another tribe. Sam once said that Indians preferred those captured young because they made better slaves. They were too young to fight back and most would forget their own lives in time and adopt the ways of the tribe.

She would leave a good trail for William to follow. He would find her, she was sure of it. But if he didn't, she would find the Indians' camp, wait until late in the night, then quietly grab the girl, keeping the child's mouth covered to keep her quiet, and carry her away to safety. It could work, but it would take a great deal of luck and answered prayers. She hoped the Indians were sound sleepers.

If it didn't work, she had four weapons. Then she remembered the old Indian tomahawk Captain Sam had given her. He said a person living in the wild needed an abundance of weapons because they all served different purposes. She found the hatchet in the drawer where she'd stored it after William had sharpened it. She gripped it tightly in her hand, measuring its weight, feeling its power.

Five weapons. Five Indians. She hoped she wouldn't have to use any of them. Then, feeling the need for more than hope, she prayed in earnest.

God, please let William swiftly find me and keep that poor little girl unharmed until we reach her. But if I have to do this alone, grant me courage and the ability to use my weapons skillfully so that I may bring that sweet girl safely back to her family. And I beseech you with all my heart to keep my unborn child and me secured from danger. Amen.

As she finished the prayer, a sense of purpose filled her, and she gathered her renewed strength as well as her weapons.

She could do this!

"Riley, you must stay here and guard our home."

The dog's big brown eyes gazed up at her and then he sat down, as though readily accepting his assignment.

She patted him on the head before shutting the door behind her. She wished she could take Riley with her. But with her on horseback, the young dog would not be able to keep up and there were too many wolves, coyotes, bears, mountain cats, and other possible threats. She couldn't risk him falling behind and being attacked by something.

She grabbed her large sack of fresh fall apples from the cellar, hurried to the horse pen, and saddled Ginger. Then she tied her rifle on and hung the apple sack from the saddle. She hated to waste the good apples, they would have made excellent pies. But they would be easy for her to toss and large enough for William to readily spot.

The mare was fresh and slightly high-headed, but Kelly

managed to keep the horse under her control as she started out at a brisk pace toward the enormous Sycamore tree on the other side of the stream.

Her pulse began to beat erratically as the realization of what she was about to do fully hit her. She passed the Sycamore and urged Ginger into the dim light of the forest.

Hurry William.

CHAPTER 26

William and Merrill wrenched their lathered mounts to a stop in front of the cabin. William flew off Smoke's side and barged through the door. Riley raced out of the cabin as soon as he opened it. But Kelly was nowhere in sight.

He ran outside and yelled, "Kelly," several times. The silence following her name each time he yelled it made his heart sink lower and lower.

As he turned, he glimpsed Riley running toward the tree line but William's focus remained on finding Kelly. He quickly scanned all around the area, but found nothing unusual except that Ginger was not in her pen and the door to the smokehouse was open. He hurriedly poked his head inside to be sure she wasn't hiding in there. As he suspected, their hams weren't there.

Neither was Kelly.

Merrill's eyes searched over the ground around the cabin. "Horses. Looks like five of them. The same number of braves that came to my house. I suspect they have stolen your wife as well. I pity the poor woman." The man wisely left the reason for his pity unsaid.

William took a deep calming breath. He refused to accept the possibility that she'd been stolen again. He decided to take a closer look inside to see if he could see any indications of a struggle. Merrill followed him into the cabin. There were no signs of a scuffle, but a note lay on the table. The handwriting appeared hastily scribbled. He read the message aloud as Merrill listened.

"Your wife is incredibly brave," Merrill said, following William as he charged out the door.

A pain squeezed William's insides as he thought of the danger Kelly had put herself in. Her big heart may have led her to danger of the worst kind. At least she couldn't be too far ahead of him and she was well-armed. And, with luck, he would catch up to her before she reached the Indians. He swallowed the knot in his throat that threatened to choke him.

Before taking off, they took a minute to fill their canteens and let the horses drink at the stream.

As they remounted, Riley reappeared at the tree line, near the big Sycamore, holding an apple in his mouth. That was one smart dog.

"We're coming, Riley," William yelled. He guided Smoke across the stream to the opposite bank, remembering their first night at the cabin. "Keep your eyes open for those apples," he reminded Merrill, and took off at a gallop.

William soon noticed Riley falling behind and his tongue hanging out. He quickly dismounted and called to the big pup. Riley came running with what had to be all the energy he had left. He reached down, picked the dog up, and then remounted, laying Riley across the saddle in front of him. He kept one hand on

Riley's back to keep him from sliding off. He would keep their puppy safe.

Content lying next to him, and lulled by the trot of the horse, Riley soon drifted off to sleep.

They followed the trail Kelly wisely left for some miles. He had never heard of leaving a trail using apples, but it made a lot of sense. Easy to drop and easy to spot. Leave it to his clever wife to think of something so ingenious.

The woods became thick and dark in places. The shrewd Indians didn't seem to be following any sort of trail. Their path wove through the forest, sometimes heading due north, sometimes east, and then north again, making their route difficult for anyone to follow.

"If your wife hadn't left this trail for us, this band would have disappeared. We'd never find them," Merrill said. "Where did she learn to track like this?"

"She had to hunt her own food for many years," William said. "I think she used to track turkeys and other small game." He could usually see the tracks of the Indian's five horses himself, but now and then, their trail disappeared completely, especially when the path crossed rock covered ground. Merrill was right. The Indians would have been difficult to track without Kelly's bright red signals.

"I pray we reach your wife before she reaches those savages, and that my little darling is still safe," Merrill said, his tone strained.

William just sat in lonely silence, peering ahead, gripping Smoke's reins tightly in his clenched fist.

Kelly rode as swiftly as she could without losing sight of the trail the Indians left. Sometimes she would have to pause to study the ground carefully until she picked up the tracks again. Then she continued on, stoically, ignoring the heaviness in her chest. She recognized that she was putting herself in danger, but it couldn't be helped. It was up to her to find the little girl. She didn't know if she could rescue the child, and it would take all of the courage she could muster, but by God, she would try. Please Lord, give me the strength I'll need. Even if she couldn't manage a rescue when the time came, at least she left a trail leading to the child.

As Kelly rode, she realized the little girl reminded her of herself. Maybe it was because she was blonde. Or that the child was alone and frightened, no doubt hoping her father would come and rescue her. Or maybe it was just because she desperately needed someone to help her. As William had helped when those men attacked her.

She was glad she had thought of a way for William to follow her. How desperately she needed him. It would be noon before he left Boonesborough to come home. If only she could reach out and touch him somehow. She closed her eyes and willed her love to connect her to him. In her mind's eye, she could see him clearly. His sparkling blue eyes looked back at her with a caressing warmth. She longed for the protectiveness of his strong arms.

She opened her eyes and brushed away the sudden tears filling them. She loved William so dearly. She didn't want to risk losing his love or their unborn baby. Or leaving William alone. But what choice did she have? None. She would not leave that poor little girl at the mercy of those braves. She would help the child and God would help her. She had to stay strong.

It would all be over soon, one way or another.

Ginger suddenly pulled up and raised her head high, her ears pinned back.

Kelly took a firmer grip on the reins. What was it? Her heart thumped uncomfortably within her.

Horses have a keen sense of smell. Did the mare smell something? "Whoa, now, whoa girl," she soothed. Kelly patted the horse's shoulder and ran her hand calmingly down Ginger's neck to keep her still while she listened.

She sensed someone was behind her even before she heard a horse walking. She turned to look behind her. An Indian brave, garbed and adorned like the band she trailed, kicked his horse hard and rode toward her.

Her heart hammered against her ribs as she urged Ginger to a swift run. She wove through the trees, dangerously fast.

Nevertheless, the Indian managed to catch up with her. She couldn't miss the musky smell of him as he pressed his mount close.

She quickly glanced over her right shoulder. It was the brave who hurt Riley! Her anger at him rose up again.

She yanked the pistol from her coat, aimed as best she could on the galloping horse, and fired. The ball missed.

He reached for her, his face mean and threatening, intending to pull her off her horse.

She couldn't let him. If she fell, she would almost certainly loose her baby. She leaned away and kicked Ginger even harder.

Her entire body, but especially her exposed back, started to tremble. She had to do something and quick. With her right hand, she took a firm grip on the tomahawk she'd stuck in her belt. Simultaneously, she tugged hard on Ginger's reins and turned the mare to the right while flinging the tomahawk backwards with all her strength.

Unable to stop his mount in time, the blade slammed into the Indian's chest. He howled in pain, slid off his mount, and tumbled to the ground.

Kelly pulled her horse to a stop and cautiously rode back to the Indian. Breathing hard, she looked down at the brave, amazed, and shaken. As her nervous mare, quavered beneath her, a quiver of triumph surged through her veins. She had done it!

Then an involuntary chill swept through her and a soft gasp escaped her lips.

She had just killed a man.

CHAPTER 27

William heard a shot echoing deep in the forest. "Kelly!" he cried out.

Tucking Riley securely under his left arm, he bent forward and urged Smoke to a full out run. Merrill followed closely behind him. Keeping his head down to avoid low hanging branches, William rode hunched over the stallion's mane. The shot's report sounded as though someone fired a weapon from no more than a mile away. He would be there in a couple of minutes.

William noticed a horse's track that came from the woods and joined the trail they were following. Had someone come up behind Kelly? Caught her unawares?

His temper flared. Clenching his teeth, he shook with impotent rage, wanting to find her now. His heart ached with his fear for her. Desperately, he needed her to be all right. What would he do if she weren't?

No, he wouldn't think like that. She would be okay.

His thoughts raced. He needed to prepare. First, he would do something Sam taught him. He tied a knot in his reins in case he needed to drop them to fight with both hands. Then, holding the reins with the same arm holding Riley, he pulled his pistol. Merrill did the same.

He peered ahead trying to spot something, anything. Then he saw it. A body lying on the ground, partially obscured by the lay of the land. Was it a man or a woman? For a few moments, terror clutched his heart.

With every stride of the horse, he grew more certain. A man.

"Kelly!" he called, his heart beating wildly.

"Kelly!" Merrill tried as well.

"Yell with me," William said. Then they both yelled her name out at the same time.

They reached the body and took only a moment to look down at the brave. A hatchet protruded from the dead Indian's chest. Could Kelly have done that? It looked like the tomahawk Sam had given her. The same one he'd sharpened for her recently. But even a sharp weapon is useless without courage. And this would have taken a great deal courage.

He took off again and Smoke surged to a full run. He called her name yet once more. "Kelly." The boom of his voice traveled through the forest. This time when it did, he soon caught sight of her, racing back toward them at a thunderous pace.

Thank you, Lord.

The tight knot within him began to ease and when she was close enough for him to see her beautiful face, relief filled him. He urged his stallion up next to her and leapt down, carrying Riley with him.

She dismounted as well and threw herself into his outstretched arms.

William hugged her fiercely and then enfolded both her and Riley against his chest, kissing the top of her head and her face repeatedly.

"My boys," she breathed. She took a moment to catch her breath. Then her expression darkened with an unreadable emotion and she swallowed before she could speak. "I killed a man."

Everywhere he touched, he felt a terrible tenseness in her body. "We know. We saw the brave's body about a mile or so back. You defended yourself Kelly. There's no shame in that. You can tell us how you managed it later. Mister Merrill, this is my wife Kelly," William said. "Mister Merrill's daughter is the one taken captive."

"We have to help her William." She turned to Merrill. "I promise you, we will get her back," Kelly swore.

William was surprised at the vehemence in her voice. She could not have sounded any more determined if the child were her own daughter.

"Let's go," Merrill urged, still horseback and looking ahead anxiously.

They both remounted and took off, letting Kelly take the lead. She'd done a great job so far tracking the Indians.

William kept Riley with him and the pup settled onto the saddle in front of him again.

"Do you think the one I killed was one of the band of five?" she called toward him.

"Yes. They probably sent him back to be sure they weren't being followed," William answered.

"With him dead, that leaves four to deal with," Merrill said. "Mrs. Wyllie, your bravery is the stuff of legends. I'm so grateful for your help."

Kelly turned her head back toward Merrill. "What's your little girl's name?"

"Hannah. She's the best daughter a man could hope for." Merrill sounded on the verge of tears.

"We have to hurry!" Kelly called to them, and urged Ginger to an even faster pace.

William drew Smoke alongside Kelly and continued to peer well ahead of them, wanting to spot the Indians before the natives heard them coming.

After about a half hour, he thought he perceived movement some distance ahead. He held up his hand, motioning for them to stop and be quiet. He pointed.

"Is it them?" Kelly whispered.

"Please God, let it be so," Merrill murmured.

"I think I see smoke. They must have stopped to rest," William said.

"And eat our hams," Kelly grumbled under her breath.

"William, what's your plan?" Merrill asked in a hushed voice.

"Let's tie our mounts and Riley back a ways in case they make noise," he said. "Kelly, you'll wait with the horses and Riley."

"No," she said, her face full of defiance. "You may need my help."

William frowned, realizing she was right, but not wanting to place her in harm's way.

She boldly met his eyes and showed no sign of relenting—her courage and determination like stalwart pillars of strength that held her up.

Accepting that he stood no chance of changing her mind, he quietly turned Smoke backward.

They led the horses behind some large boulders. After tying their mounts and Riley to trees, the three retrieved their rifles from the saddles. William checked the powder in his long rifle and then Kelly's shorter barreled rifle, while she reloaded her pistol. He gave a moment's thought to making her stay behind. The thought of an arrow hitting her made his heart tremble. But, since the Indians were now stopped, with three shooters they would stand a good chance of quickly overcoming the band with a surprise attack.

"Kelly, you stay with me. Understand?" He looked directly into her eyes to be sure she consented. "You've been extraordinarily brave so far, but I don't want you taking any more chances."

She shook her head in agreement.

He glanced over at Riley. Exhausted, the pup already slept soundly. It was a fortunate thing young dogs slept so much. They didn't need him barking now.

"Okay, we have three rifle shots and both of you have pistols and I have two. That's seven shots for four Indians. We will have the advantage of surprise, but we will have to make each shot count."

"Please keep Hannah out of the line of fire," Merrill urged.

Keeping his voice low, William said, "Mister Merrill, as soon as we can get you close enough, call for your daughter. If she does what I think she will, she'll run toward you. I'll shoot the Indian closest to Hannah. Kelly, you shoot the one furthest from Hannah with your rifle, that way you can remain far back. After you fire, reload without delay and if you have another shot at a brave with your rifle, take it. But don't fire your pistol unless an Indian is coming right for you. I want you to save a shot so you'll have it if you really need it."

He turned to address the girl's father. "Sir, that will leave two braves to kill. You shoot the one nearest you and I'll take the last one. If any one of us misses, we should still have three shots left between us."

He placed his hands on Kelly's arms. "Promise me you'll be careful."

Kelly nodded and eyed him confidently. Her face intense, she pulled back her shoulders and took a firm grip on her rifle. She looked like a beautiful warrior.

For the second time, he wondered if letting her come was a mistake. But he had no right, even though he was her husband, to either let her or stop her. It was her decision. And he admired her courage.

"Excellent plan," Merrill said, his profile strong and resolute. "We're going to get my daughter back!"

"This plan hinges on them not hearing us," Kelly said softly. "So watch what you step on as we advance. And keep a tree between you and them as much as possible. Their quivers are full of arrows."

William smiled, pleased with Kelly's cool-headed thinking and bravery. In the face of danger, her strength blossomed once again.

He gave her a quick hug and took off quietly.

CHAPTER 28

Kelly didn't like leaving Riley behind. But they had no other choice. With luck, the puppy would still be asleep when they got back.

For a moment, as they advanced quietly toward the Indian camp, her determination faltered. Perhaps she should have waited with the horses. She had a baby to think of now. No, she had to help William. An extra shot from her rifle might mean the difference between success and failure. Between her child and the little girl having their fathers.

She forced her nerves to settle down. She'd proved to herself that she could muster courage when needed, and she would do it again in but a few minutes. She prayed the three of them would stay safe in the skirmish.

She followed behind William, with Mister Merrill to their right, a few tree trunks away. William took his time, keeping his footsteps as light and soundless as possible. He seemed remarkably composed. Every muscle of his body spoke of strength and confidence.

Merrill's face, on the other hand, appeared tense and drained of color. She couldn't blame him. This was a risky undertaking. But her own nerves felt steady and sure. She could do this. She had to for the little girl's sake.

They were close enough now to smell the smoke of the campfire and she thought she heard the miserable whimpers of the girl. Soon, she could hear them clearly and the woeful sobs ripped at her heart. She couldn't imagine how terrible it must sound to her father's ears.

They quickly located Hannah's position and William motioned for Merrill to head in that direction. The father, stooped low and moving stealthily, made his way toward his daughter.

Biting her lip, Kelly waited where William had mouthed for her to stay, while he silently made his way to a position where he would have a clear shot at the Indian sitting next to Hannah.

Warily, she peered around the large oak she hid behind, her cheek up against the rough bark, still cold and damp from the earlier frost. Numerous vines hung down from the tree, helping to conceal her, but she could still see the braves chewing on her hams. They seemed to be relishing the tasty smoked meat.

Their thievery made her angry all over again. They would pay dearly for taking a man's child and another's food.

Little by little, she knelt to one knee and slowly brought the rifle to her shoulder. She selected the Indian who would be her target and waited for William to take the first shot. She hoped it wouldn't be long. She could feel her palms beginning to sweat despite the chilly temperature.

"Hannah, Hannah!" Merrill shouted and exposed his body for her to see.

The Indian sitting next to Hannah grabbed his bow and

jumped up from where he sat.

William fired instantly, hitting the brave in his exposed chest as the Indian pulled an arrow from his full quiver.

As the girl's gaurd fell, Kelly carefully took her shot at another brave, his hands still holding a hunk of her ham. The Indian dropped like a felled tree to the leaf-covered ground.

"Papa! Papa!" Hannah ran toward her father as fast as her little legs could carry her.

As she scampered toward him, her tiny arms outstretched, Merrill stood and fired his long rifle at one of the braves. But his shot missed.

The Indian that was his target pulled back his bow. He aimed at the running child.

Kelly's heart stopped as she watched in horror. God no!

William fired his pistol and, his aim true, hit the brave square in the chest just as the Indian released his arrow.

The shaft flew through the air faster than Kelly's eyes could follow it, yet time seem suspended. The whole world moved in slow motion, a second divided into a thousand torturous moments. At the final instant, she saw the father jerk his daughter safely behind a tree just a breath before the arrow flew past her and slammed into another tree's trunk. The frightening sound of its impact vibrated through the forest and Kelly's heart.

Merrill snatched his child up and wrapped the girl in his arms as he spun around to take cover behind a nearby larger elm. Thank God, the child was safe.

Kelly turned her eyes and caught a glimpse of the final brave as he ran behind a boulder. It was the Indians' leader—the one with the feather adorned head—who had clutched the little girl against him on his horse. She suspected he would be the most difficult to fight. But she had faith in William.

A second later, she heard the whoosh of an arrow. It whizzed through the air in a twinkling and hit the tree closest to William with a loud thump. Involuntarily, she gasped. The sight chilled her to her core.

William still had two pistol shots. But the Indian wasn't within the weapon's range. To use his pistols, he would have to get close. Much closer than he was now. She flinched when William took a quick dash to reach a closer tree. Her breath froze in her throat and her heart clenched. This was so risky.

She was more afraid for him than she was for herself.

To her great relief, she saw William reloading his Kentucky long rifle.

That reminded her that she needed to do the same. Reluctant to take her eyes off watching for the brave, she hadn't yet reloaded her rifle. She forced herself to quickly look down and get the weapon loaded. It seemed to take her forever.

When she finished, she listened for sounds of the native, but only heard her own rapid heartbeats thrashing in her ears. The silence rattled her tensed nerves even more.

Then the brave stood. Dear God, he was much closer to her now, angled so he could see her side. Breath-robbing fear gripped her as he released an arrow in her direction. Reflexively, she whirled around to escape behind the tree, her eyes squeezed closed, her fingernails digging into the tree bark to hold her shaking body in place.

She heard William fire his rifle, but the shot, echoing through the forest, didn't sound like it hit anything.

When she opened her eyes, she glanced down, and realized the arrow pinned her skirt to the tree. Shaken, she reached down and with trembling hands broke the arrow's shaft, tossed it aside, and pulled her skirt free. The sound of the fabric ripping seemed impossibly loud. She quickly tucked her torn skirt behind her.

Another arrow whipped through the air and sunk into the tree she stood behind, just inches from her face. The arrow and her heart both quivered violently.

She heard muted sounds nearby. Should she run? Fear wavered inside her as she tried to comprehend what she'd heard, what she should do. She did not want to die here. She could not let this Indian kill her. If she died, so would her baby. William didn't even know yet.

She considered bolting out of hiding, running to William, away from this Indian closing in on her. Cringing against the tree trunk, she gasped for air, finding it hard to breathe. She placed a hand against her belly, conveying her love to her unborn child. Suddenly, she felt a fluttering feeling, like the wings of a butterfly brushing against the insides of her tummy. Remarkably, her fear vanished, and a mother's protective instinct took over.

She took her rifle in both hands and keeping the sights in front of her eyes, and her finger poised on the trigger, quickly surveyed the area around her in every direction, but spotted nothing.

She glanced up and observed William creeping nearer to where he thought the Indian still was.

But the brave wasn't there anymore. She could smell him now. He was somewhere close to her.

~

Gritting his teeth, William quickly reloaded the rifle again. He needed to reach the brave before the ruthless bastard could shoot Kelly. The Indian already shot two arrows at her, one close enough to pin her dress. Damn it, he would not let this son of a bitch release another arrow. This time he wouldn't miss.

The girl's father had wisely hunkered down, his flintlock pistol in his hand, with his daughter. William motioned to him to remain where he was. Merrill nodded in understanding.

William glanced back over toward Kelly. A crushing wave of apprehension swept through him. Oh, bloody hell!

Riley was running up behind Kelly, wagging his tail and wiggling his rear end with excitement at having found her. The dog must have slipped out of the collar he'd put around his neck.

To his dismay, he saw Kelly turn toward Riley, take a few steps, bend down, and reach for her pup.

His stomach churned with alarm and frustration. "Kelly, turn around!"

Before he got the last word out, the Indian reappeared, this time much closer to Kelly. Anger scorched the edges of his control, but he refused to let it take him entirely. He forced himself to remain deadly calm. William raised his rifle, lined up the sights down the long barrel, and took careful aim. Just as his finger started to draw back the trigger, the Indian darted out from his hiding place.

Eyes widened with the intent of butchery, the brave released a terrible screeching yelp and rushed toward her, his tomahawk upstretched above his feathered head.

The blow would be lethal.

At the sound of the native's shriek, Kelly glanced up and

screamed with stark black terror. Then she dropped Riley and fired her rifle, but missed.

He would have but one chance to save his wife. His love. He took a steadying breath, trailed the running brave's back with his sights, and gently squeezed the trigger, willing the lead ball to find its mark.

The ball whacked into the top of the Indian's back with a loud thud. He jerked and then wobbled for a moment. But to William's horror, the brave, still holding the tomahawk, took another long stride toward Kelly.

She fired her pistol.

As the second bullet struck him, the brave lurched, pitched forward, and collapsed to the ground, planting the tomahawk in the fallen leaves, mere inches from Kelly's boots.

She jumped back, grabbed Riley up with one arm, and clutched him against her breast.

William ran to her, holding his breath. By the time he reached her, he thought his chest would burst. "He almost had you!" he cried harshly and gave her a little shake. Ferocious protective emotions took over. The thought of losing her bloodied his wits. Crushed his courage. Tore at his insides. Turned his soul raw.

He could no longer control the pent up fury within him. He tossed his rifle down and clenched his fists tightly, breathing hard. "Oh God…Kelly…you nearly died!" he shouted.

She looked up at him, eyes frightened, and shriveled a little.

Terrible guilt immediately assailed him. His anger was the last thing she needed now. With difficulty, taking a deep breath or two, he made himself regain self-control. He pursed his lips in exasperation and quickly chastised himself for acting like a brute.

She still clung to the puppy. He took Riley from her, sat him down on the ground, and then stood. "I'm sorry," he said, but she didn't respond. Worried, he appraised her with a penetrating look.

She seemed pale, the color drained from her face, and her eyes appeared unnaturally bright and glassy. Her lower lip trembled as she dropped her rifle to the ground and held both of her shaking hands against her tummy. After what just happened, it was no wonder her stomach hurt.

With an overwhelming surge of affection, he hauled her into his arms, wanting to weep with sheer relief. The fierceness of his emotions was something he never experienced before. His love for her at the moment, all consuming, overriding everything. He closed his eyes and concentrated on treasuring the feel of her in his arms. He felt her trembling, and it made his own heart shake within his chest.

"You're all right, my love," he said, kissing the top of her head repeatedly, and stroking her back. "We're both just fine. You're in my arms."

Shock held her immobile for a few more minutes. She was so muddled and battered by her emotions, she couldn't speak. Finally, she glanced down at the hatchet and shuddered, then gazed up at him and whispered, "Too close."

William had to agree with her. His own distress at the near attack on her almost overcoming his self-control.

He glanced behind him. The last of the child's abductors lay dead, red blood pooling on his bare back and seeping into the ground beneath him.

Kelly was safe. The child was safe. He let out a deep breath and hugged his wife even tighter.

It was over.

CHAPTER 29

Little by little, wrapped securely in William's strong arms, Kelly recovered from the shock of her near death. With each gentle kiss he placed on her head, she felt her fear dissolve, like an oppressive grey fog yielding to the warmth of a bright sun.

Finally able to think and breathe normally, she wanted to go to Hannah to see if the little girl was all right. They weren't far off and she walked with William toward Merrill and his daughter. She would offer the distraught child whatever solace she could.

When they neared the two, they heard the father's reassuring voice as he attempted to comfort his traumatized child. Hannah sat in his lap, still sobbing. He whispered soothing words of endearment and stroked her small blonde head repeatedly.

The child's eyes were so red it hurt Kelly to look at her.

"She won't stop crying," Merrill said, his voice full of concern, as he wiped his daughter's runny nose with his handkerchief.

Hannah buried her freckled face in her father's jacket and, still bawling, clung to him with her little hands.

Kelly bent down to the little girl. "Hannah, you have such a pretty name. And you're quite a lovely girl too. You have hair the same color as mine. See, I'm blonde too," Kelly said, holding out some of her long locks.

Hannah turned her head slightly in Kelly's direction.

"But I can't see what color your eyes are. Can you show me?" Kelly coaxed.

Hannah turned around completely.

"Your eyes are a beautiful green."

"You know, I got stolen away once too, by an awfully bad man. But, you know what?"

"What?" Hannah asked. It was her first word.

"I got rescued too. Just like you," Kelly said. In a soothing voice, she probed further. "Isn't it wonderful your father came and got you? He saved you and now you're safe. Do you understand that you're safe?"

"I am?" Her small voice was fragile and tremulous.

"Yes, you are," William assured her, kneeling down next to her father. "I'm Sheriff Wyllie from Boonesborough and you are safe with us. Do you know what a sheriff is?"

Hannah shook her head no.

"It's the man in a town who helps other people when they are in trouble," William explained, keeping his tone gentle. "So I came with your Pa to help him rescue you. And this is my beautiful and brave wife Kelly."

"Do you like puppies?" Kelly asked.

"Mm-hmm," Hannah murmured.

Kelly smiled broadly. "Me too. I adore puppies. Do you want to meet my puppy? He's almost a dog now and he's far braver than he should be for his age."

When Hannah nodded she would, Kelly called for Riley who frolicked a short distance away energetically exploring the forest floor with his nose.

Riley immediately ran up and put both of his paws on the girl's little lap and began licking her tear-streaked face.

"He likes me," Hannah said, with a little giggle.

Hannah's father looked at Kelly with gratitude in his eyes.

"I'm not surprised Riley likes you. I like you too," Kelly said.

"His hair is the same color as ours," Hannah said, sniffling, but not crying now.

Good, she was thinking about something other than her horrific experience.

"Would you like to go home?" her father asked. "Your Mama is worried about you."

Kelly couldn't even imagine the worry that must be tormenting Hannah's mother. And waiting to learn of her daughter's fate would be agonizing. They needed to hurry back.

"Yes, Papa, please," Hannah said, her voice calmer and stronger now.

"I'll go pack up what's left of our hams," William said.

"Find my blue shawl too. I had to trade it to them for Riley," Kelly said.

William eyed her incredulously.

"I'll explain later," she said.

❧

William started to wrap the shawl around Kelly's shoulders, but she pulled it into her hands. She turned and handed it to Merrill. "Wrap your daughter in this," she said, "she'll need it, it's growing colder by the minute."

After Merrill wrapped Hannah up, he gave his daughter some water. The girl drank greedily. William wondered how long it had been since she had any food and water. The poor child had suffered enough. "Merrill, why don't you take the Indians' horses back with you? You can sell them and use the money to buy Hannah whatever she needs."

"Sheriff that would be a true kindness. There's so much I'd dearly love to purchase for her—books, new clothing, boots, a warm coat, and a maybe a doll."

"A doll Papa!"

"Yes child, and some candy too!" he answered with joy in his voice. "And maybe a dog like Riley to watch over you!"

William smiled. "I'll speak to my friend Lucky. He found Riley for us."

"Thank you, Sheriff Wyllie," Hannah said, looking up at him, her smile missing a couple of teeth and her face filled with childlike hope.

"It would be my pleasure Hannah," William said. "For now, we need to find a stream to water all these horses."

"I think I can put Hannah in front of me and still manage to lead two horses. Could you pull the other two behind you?" Merrill asked William.

"Indeed, it would be my pleasure, Sir. We need to hasten if

we're going to make it back before sunset," William said. He looked around for Riley and spotted him gulping a few chunks of the ham thrown down by the Indians. "That ham is salty. You'd best give him a little water too," he told Kelly. Then he picked up the hams he'd wrapped in an Indian blanket.

Lastly, William retrieved the tomahawk that nearly struck Kelly from the brave's outstretched hand. It could come in handy someday. He stared down at the Indian's back wound, still oozing dark blood. The little lead ball wedged somewhere within this brave gave Kelly enough time to draw and aim her pistol, saving Kelly from a horrific death. He would never forget the image of the brave raising his deadly weapon with the intent to slay his beloved wife. He shook his head wanting to rid himself of the chilling vision.

As he stuck the hatchet in his belt, he peered over at her, the sight of her soothing to his frayed mind. He watched as she grabbed the sack of stolen apples and then picked up a native's bow and a quiver filled with arrows. Then she found another full quiver, and put both across her back. He shook his head, not surprised at his plucky wife. Evidently, she intended to learn how to use a bow and arrow.

With the forest raining leaves down around them, Merrill carried his daughter, and they all ate apples in companionable silence as they marched side-by-side back toward the resting horses. Riley trailed behind, his tail wagging. After just a few bites from her apple, Hannah laid her head on her father's shoulder.

William suspected the child would be asleep before they even reached their mounts.

His prediction proved right. William gently took Hannah from her father and after Merrill mounted, he handed the sleeping girl up to him. "Hopefully, she'll sleep until we reach home," William said.

"She's done in, as I'm sure you both are too," Merrill said as they settled into their saddles. "I can't tell you how grateful I am for your help."

"It's Kelly you should thank," William said. "I'm just doing my job, but it was her wits that allowed us to find your daughter. And her bravery surprised even me." He turned to face Kelly. "How on earth did you manage to kill that brave that followed you?"

"That nasty fellow was the one who hurt Riley when the Indians raided our home. I was so mad at him I was beside myself. I think he intended to kill Riley and take him with them. So I traded my shawl for Riley, sticking it through the portal. When he snuck up behind me on the trail, I shot my pistol at him. But since I was horseback, my aim was off and I missed. When he reached out to pull me off my horse, I had to do something. I was desperate. I remembered I had the tomahawk Sam gave me and how he once foiled an attacker by stopping suddenly and hurling his hatchet backwards." She described what she'd done and then added boldly, "I just pretended I was Captain Sam for a moment."

William chuckled. That didn't surprise William. He'd done the same thing a time or two. His warrior brother was an admirable hero for a reason. On their long journey to Kentucky, they had all learned a lot from Sam. "I can't wait to tell Sam what you did," William said, smiling broadly. "I'm enormously proud of you wife." The strong woman he always knew she was deep down inside her had emerged fully. "But please try not to put yourself in such jeopardy again though. I swear my heart would not be up to the strain."

He nearly lost her twice. Three if you counted her father

taking her back. The events she went through would have tried the mettle of even the bravest of souls. But she had kept her head and found her courage, refusing to be defeated, no matter what obstacles she faced. And Kelly proved that strength was not limited to the men in their family.

He couldn't be more proud of her. But still, he couldn't help the scolding look he gave her.

She raised her chin and stared in his direction. "I know I took a terrible chance. But I wouldn't have gone after them if weren't for Hannah. William, if you could have heard her pitiful cries, you would understand why I did what I did. It broke my heart when they rode off with her. I just had to help her. I came up with a plan and just carried it out."

"You were very strong today Kelly," William told her.

"You never know how strong you can be until being strong is the only option you have," Kelly replied.

After riding a couple of miles, they reached the spot where the dead Indian lay with the tomahawk in his chest. William was leading two of the horses he'd given Merrill, so Kelly jumped off Ginger, put her boot up against the dead man's hip, leaned over, and retrieved her hatchet. "I might need this again," she said, looking up at William.

"Lord, I hope not," William said, shaking his head. He knew there was something special about Kelly from the very beginning. But he had no idea then just how special she was. His heart swelled with pride for his strong brave wife. She would do well on the frontier.

"Hannah's mother and I will be forever grateful for your bravery Mrs. Wyllie. And I promise you, when our daughter is older, she will learn of your courage and how much our family owes you," Merrill said, his voice cracking and filled with deep gratitude.

"Whatever strength I had today came from God," Kelly said, lifting her gaze heavenward.

"Then we will thank God as well," Merrill replied.

"I believe we all need to thank Him," William said.

CHAPTER 30

Under a canopy of glittering stars, William and Kelly—cold, hungry, and weary—finally arrived at the cabin. She looked so drowsy, he insisted she just go into the cabin and lie down while he took care of the horses. When he finished, he warmed some corn cakes and made bacon and coffee.

When the food was ready, he reluctantly woke her to eat a bite and then helped her to a chair at the table.

As they ate, his eyes searched her pale face, reaching into her thoughts. Unusually pensive, something occupied her keen mind. He understood she was too tired to talk, but something else lingered behind her eyes and weak smile. Was she reluctant now to stay at the cabin alone? He couldn't blame her.

In truth, that concerned him too. Women on the frontier often managed the homestead or fought bravely to defend their homes while their husbands worked, hunted, or served in the militia. But could he leave Kelly alone, while he tended to his duties, to fend for herself? The possibility of further threats to her safety made his stomach clench.

He decided to wait a day or so, until she was well-rested, to broach the subject.

The next morning, before leaving, he made sure Kelly's rifle and pistol were loaded and he left one of his two pistols with her as well. He would buy another and more powder and ball when he got to town. He'd been wanting one of the new Ketland brass barrel smooth bore pistols anyway.

After a lingering kiss, he reluctantly left Kelly and hurried into town, wondering how Colonel Byrd and his men fared at Fort Logan. He hoped that by now, they'd reached the fort safely and somehow averted a major battle.

With the militia gone, Boonesborough stood unprotected. He would have to do something about that. He urged Smoke to a canter and soon neared the fort. As the morning sun lit the scarred battlements and blood-stained walls of the fortress, he remembered the many brave men and women who fought for a place in the wilderness and a new future for their families. It astonished him that in a land so vast men could not seem to find a way to live together peacefully.

Opening his office door, he found Deputy Mitchell already there organizing some of their paperwork. Still a pimpled face young man, the deputy wasn't experienced enough yet to handle serious situations, but his dedication and willingness to learn made up for his lack of grit. The office smelled of wood, ink, and the grease Mitchell used on his shiny black hair.

Mitchell looked up, holding a turkey quill in his ink-stained hand. "Sheriff Wyllie," the Deputy greeted enthusiastically and stood, "you've returned safely!"

"It was an arduous, but successful mission. We all escaped harm and recovered the little girl. She's now safe at home."

"That's wonderful news. We were all hoping for such a positive outcome." Mitchell pointed to the paper sitting on his small writing desk. "I was just registering a complaint about another stolen pig."

One more stolen pig. Somewhere out there, there was a hog thief he needed to catch. Deciding to let the stolen animal wait, William asked, "How many men do we have guarding the fort?"

"Well none. As you know, they all left with the Colonel."

He thought through the men he'd grown to know well since arriving in Boonesborough. The only one he could think of who might be able to advise him was Lucky. "Deputy, go find Lucky McGintey, if he's not out hunting, and let him know I need his counsel here." As a long hunter and lifelong companion of Daniel Boone, McGintey knew more about Kentucky than just about anybody. And as William's closest friend, he could trust what Lucky had to say.

Mitchell turned to leave and William called after him. "And ask Tom Wolfe to come as well if he is able."

The land speculator had a good knowledge of the latest political developments and native issues facing Kentucky. William would just have to ignore, for the time being, how Wolfe and his heartless mother had treated Kelly. He rolled his eyes at himself, realizing he wasn't being fair. Mrs. Wolfe was just looking out for her grandchildren. He needed to forget what happened. The important thing was that Kelly was well now and, thanks be to God, safe.

While he waited for McGintey and Wolfe, William paced restlessly about the room. He thought about his brothers and the rest of their family and worried that Indians might be threatening their homes as well. He desperately wanted to go to them to be sure they were all right or to help them if they were facing trouble. But now he had Kelly to think of too. He couldn't risk taking her into an area where hostilities might be developing. They would just have to wait to visit his family in the spring.

He couldn't leave now anyway. With Colonel Byrd and the militia gone, it was up to him to ensure Boonesborough's safety. He held a sacred trust, put in his hands by the townspeople and by Daniel Boone. He peered down at his hands, feeling the weight of that trust. Even if an attack on Boonesborough was unlikely, he couldn't risk the lives of even one family. He had to get the town prepared. He would need to send runners to all the remote homesteads to warn them to be extra cautious. Fortunately, most people lived in town or close to town.

Perhaps his concerns were premature. From the rider's description, the Indians had killed and scalped only one man. Maybe the natives would withdraw once Colonel Byrd and his men reached Fort Logan. But would the Indians realize the militia's presence there meant Boonesborough stood vulnerable?

His deputy soon arrived with McGintey and Wolfe. The two were both already aware of the incident with the girl's capture and the situation at Fort Logan. In Boonesborough, good news traveled fast, but bad news traveled even faster. William filled them in on the details of the girl's rescue.

"The Shawnee don't steal white women or children anymore," McGintey said. "Big Eagle made a promise to Daniel Boone and that Chief at least keeps his word."

"I suspected as much, but I'm glad to hear it from you," William said. "So you think the child's adductors were just a small band of native outlaws?" Like white settlers, there were unprincipled men among the natives as well. Unfortunately, more often than not, their actions reflected negatively on all natives. William wondered why that wasn't the case for wicked white men.

"That would be my opinion, humble though it is," McGintey pronounced. "I could be wrong, but I don't think we have anything to fear here."

William turned to Wolfe. "What's your opinion of the situation at Fort Logan?"

"Fort Logan has never fallen in an Indian attack. They have a secret tunnel from the fort to the springhouse, which covers the nearby spring. The fort's occupants can obtain water, undetected, in time of siege. And by now, their winter stores of food would have already been laid up," Wolfe explained. "The land around the fort has been cleared of all trees and growth so Indians have no cover. Even if they are under a serious attack, with the arrival of the militia, things should be well under control soon."

William was relieved to hear that. "Lucky, how long do you think it will take the militia to get there and get back?"

"Well, Fort Logan lays quite a ways yonder. I'd say roughly 40 miles south. To get there they would go through Grant's place and then Myres Mills' place. Tell me, Deputy, were the militia all horseback when they left?"

"Yes," Mitchell replied, "although some of their mounts didn't look like they could cover more than twenty miles in a day, at best."

"Well, that means about two days there and two days back," Lucky concluded. "And if they spend a couple of days at the fort, they'll be gone at least a week."

"A week." William repeated. "I'm concerned about leaving Boonesborough undefended for so long. I suggest we gather the town men under the big elm and recruit volunteers to man the fort." He suggested the location because the area under the big tree's outstretched branches had served as Boonesborough's outdoor meeting area for years.

"Sir, I don't think that would be wise," Wolfe disagreed, his bushy brows drawn together. "You are significantly overstepping your authority. The defense of the town is a function of the militia, not the sheriff."

"I don't give a damn whose responsibility it is, just as long as it's taken care of. And I'm the man to see it done."

"But it's been years since our fort has been under attack. We have a treaty in place," Wolfe persisted.

William placed his hands on his hips and widened his stance. "I agree, Sir, but I am prone to be cautious. Better to be prepared than caught unawares. And Indians are not the only potential threat on the frontier. You saw what those six unruly murdering buffalo hunters did to this town before my brothers and I finally stopped them. And there could be natural threats too, like wildfires spreading from the forest or the Kentucky River flooding the town again if we get a big rain. We need guards stationed in each of the blockhouses with their eyes open and their weapons loaded. Spread the word, noon, under the elm."

"That should leave enough time to let everyone know," Mitchell said. "I'll get some help notifying all the outlying homesteads to be on guard." The Deputy turned on his heel and strode to the door.

"Thank you, Deputy," William said, giving Wolfe a sideways glance with narrowed eyes.

"All right sheriff, I'll defer to your judgment in the matter,"

Wolfe conceded.

William gave an impatient shrug and turned away. He picked up some of the papers on his desk.

"I heard you recently married. Congratulations and please convey my best wishes to your lovely wife. She's a fine woman," Wolfe said.

His voice was courteous but was he sincere?

"I wish she could have remained in my employ. My mother can be a mighty stubborn woman sometimes."

William shook his head in understanding. "Kelly's nightmares were traumatic. I'm pleased to say that all that is behind her now."

"Glad to hear it. I'll start spreading the word about the gathering," Wolfe said as he shut the door behind him.

Lucky stayed behind, sitting quietly and leaning on his well-worn long rifle. "He'll come around. Give him some time."

"Over-stepping my authority," William grumbled. "How dare he question my mandate to protect Boonesborough? I know I'm being overly cautious, and we have no reason to be worried, but I'll feel better if we have men in place in case they are needed, for whatever reason. If we fail to prepare, we are preparing to fail."

Lucky stood, moved closer to him, and looked at William intensely. "Boone thought much the same way. It saved us more than once. Chances are we will be just fine until the militia get back, but I admire your way of thinking. You're a good sheriff, William. The best I've seen."

He valued Lucky's opinion and the compliment made his chest swell a little. "And you're a good friend." He patted the aging hunter's shoulder affectionately.

Lucky's weathered hands reached into a pouch and he offered William his flask. "Let's celebrate your nuptials."

"My marriage was more than two months ago," William said laughing.

"You're still happy ain't you?"

"I've never known such happiness. I didn't know it was even possible to feel like this toward a woman."

"Well, that's reason enough to celebrate," Lucky said.

"After the last day and this morning, whiskey does sound like a pleasant diversion," William said, "but no. I have a hog thief to catch."

"Lucky, do you think it's safe for Kelly to stay out at Whispering Hills by herself every day?"

Lucky took a swallow and wrinkled his forehead as he considered William's question, then he answered with dignified calmness. "For some women, I'd say no. It'd be too far out. But for Kelly, I'd say she'll be just fine. I understand she's used to living alone in a remote area. She's a real smart one too. She knows how to watch out for herself. And from what you described, she proved herself in this most recent incident."

"Indeed, she more than proved herself. I couldn't believe it when I spotted her hatchet planted in that Indian's chest. And, her rifle shot struck straight through the heart of another, and she managed to fire her pistol under the worst of circumstances."

"Hell, it's thieves and unfriendly Indians who better watch out," Lucky said, his voice chuckling and hearty. "Women on the frontier learn toughness fast. It's that or perish."

"She's come a long way from the shy young lady who moved

here a few months ago," William said.

"Mostly due to you. You've been good for her—helped her become the person she was intended to be."

"I've tried to be a good friend, as well as a good husband. I won't get into why, but she needed a friend."

"It's plain to see you two are as tight as two coats of paint," Lucky said. "How's that puppy working out?"

William had asked Lucky to locate a good dog for Kelly and he'd succeeded. "We named him Riley. Kelly is completely enamored with him. He's going to make a good watch dog. In fact, Mr. Merrill wants one like him to protect his daughter."

"I'll see if I can locate another puppy for the child. Your pup's grandfather belonged to my friend Harry. Harry's passed on now. The dog was loyal to that man to the end. He was lying atop Harry's forehead when I found my comrade dead one day." Lucky took a slow deep breath, undoubtedly remembering his old friend.

"What happened to the dog?" William asked.

"I adopted him. He trailed me around these woods for years and then he finally passed on too. It's been years and I still grieve for him," Lucky said, looking down at his moccasin clad feet. "Well I'd better go help spread the word. I think I'll start at the Bear Trap. I could use a pint of ale about now. And you can put my name down at the top of your list of volunteers."

By late afternoon, William breathed a sigh of relief. That morning, he had written a letter to the sheriff of Lexington, informing him of the activities of Harpes and his partner Belle. He explained the circumstances surrounding the death of Harpes and the man's confession regarding procuring women and then drugging them until they were compliant. He urged the sheriff to identify which women wanted to return to their homes and to help them. Finally, William added that if the sheriff needed him to testify, he would gladly make a journey there to do that. He also asked that he be made aware of the outcome of the investigation as soon as possible and assured the sheriff that Judge Webb, who also presided over the court in Lexington, would inquire as to the outcome on his next visit to the city. William knew it was not out of the realm of possibility that Lexington's sheriff might be one of Belle's customers and he wanted to apply enough pressure to ensure that action would be taken to help the doomed young women Harpes had tricked with his cunning lies.

After sealing the message, he arranged for the post rider to carry the letter to Lexington. The post rider had the exclusive privilege of carrying letters, papers and packages on his route. One of William's many duties was to impose serious fines on any person who impeded the post rider or his delivery of mail, so he knew the man well and the rider promised to expedite the letter's delivery. That pleased him because he'd been concerned about all those unfortunate women deceived by Harpes. The sly man came alarmingly close to ensnaring Kelly in the same trap.

Walking swiftly, he returned to his office, and organized and scheduled the numerous men who had volunteered at the noon meeting into duty shifts. He made sure at least six well-armed men stood guard at all times, with six more waiting inside the fort in case they were needed. Deputy Mitchell helped him post the roster and schedule onto the trunk of the big elm tree, as he promised the townspeople.

With his volunteer plan in place, he and the deputy next set out to find the hog thief. After questioning a dozen or more people, a citizen on his way into town, hailed him and reported seeing a man trying to sell a hog at a bargain price to someone who was leaving Boonesborough. The concerned citizen suspected that if the pig disappeared from Boonesborough, the rightful owner would never see it again or be able to claim the animal.

Apparently, the potential sale had not been successful, because William found the thief camped east of the fort a fair distance away. The animal, fit the owner's description exactly, and stood tied nearby.

"Let's put those two swine where they belong," he told Mitchell.

At the sight of them strolling toward him, the robber started to pull out his pistol, but William was faster and he strode up purposefully aiming the weapon at the man's chest.

Smothering a groan, the thief dropped his weapon, and William tied his trembling hands behind his back. "Don't try my patience by denying your thievery," he warned.

The Deputy led the grunting, snorting, oinking pig away to return it to its rightful owner.

William followed, roughly leading the other groaning, sniveling, blubbering, swine by his collar, off to the jail at the fort. Along the way, numerous people jeered and ridiculed the robber and congratulated William.

He wondered what sentence the intolerant Judge Webb would give the hog thief. Farm animals were highly valued. The serious fines imposed on thieves could include a substantial fine, paying the rightful owner of the stolen animal a large quantity of tobacco, or even branding. The later form of punishment was William's least favorite, and so far, at least, he had not had to carry out that sentence. It required him to brand the top of the hand of the thief with a 'T'. His office held two brands—the 'T' for thieves and an

'M' for those convicted of manslaughter.

As he followed the pig and the Deputy back through town, he found himself craving some of the ham back in his smokehouse.

And, an even stronger hunger for the woman he loved filled his heart.

CHAPTER 31

As she hastily made bread, Kelly hummed a tune William often played on his fiddle. She wanted to get it to rise and then bake the loaf before William got home, hungry and tired. Last night, he made her go to bed early and let her sleep late too and, as a result, she felt well rested. But he'd gotten up early, as usual, and left for town before dawn. He was off duty tomorrow, so this would be the perfect night to tell him her big news. They could stay up as late as they wanted celebrating and planning for their child.

With her new cookbook open, step by step, she followed the directions precisely for making bread, a rare treat. She couldn't wait for the tantalizing aroma of fresh bread to fill their cabin. While the dough was rising, she would make a barley soup, put potatoes on to fry with garlic, and slice up some ham. Then she'd make a pudding of some sort. There were so many tempting pudding recipes in the book, the hardest part would be choosing which one to make. It was the special dinner she'd planned for them to enjoy two nights ago, when she was going to tell William she was with child, but the arrival of the band of Indians had changed all her plans dramatically.

Her hands covered in sticky dough, she sprinkled more flour on the table. She thought about the events of the day before, as she used her muscled arms to knead the bread dough. Her chest swelled with pride at having overcome the Indian who chased her. She hated the idea of killing another human being, but it couldn't be helped. If she hadn't, she'd be the one dead. The whole incident did make her feel far more confident in her own ability to defend herself.

Captain Sam would be proud of her. And she knew William was too. He was just equally annoyed that she had put herself in so much danger. But she would do it all over again if need be.

When she was sure the well kneaded dough felt just right, she formed it into a round ball, scraped the sticky flour off her hands, put the ball in a greased bowl to rise, and covered it with a cloth.

She couldn't wait to tell William her news. She had to figure out exactly how to do it. The names of boys and girls kept slipping through her thoughts. She felt sure if it was a boy, William would want to name him after his oldest brother Sam. And if it was a girl, she wanted to name her after her mother. Her heels bounced up and down with her excitement.

She wondered which night's lovemaking brought this child into her womb. She could recall the ecstasy of many magical nights over the last few months. But one or two of those evenings made her heart soar with the memory. A warm shiver passed through her as she remembered the mind-boggling thrill of their smoldering passion.

To think she'd once feared she would be unable to give herself completely to any man. William certainly banished all her worries. And he helped her replace her fears with an abundance of love and passion.

After several hours of cooking, Kelly was more than ready to give her body a rest. She decided the afternoon was warm enough to get some sun. She grabbed her shawl, a blanket, her pistol, and her rifle. With Riley trailing happily behind her as usual, she made up way up the hill that lay east of their cabin. Someone, probably Boone or his son, had diligently cleared a narrow footpath of undergrowth and brush and it made the trek up the hill a pleasant one. The trail passed along a narrow gorge, and spring water surged in spots and trickled in others through a rocky channel between banks clothed with a variety of small trees and a profusion of ferns. The scene's remarkable beauty made her smile broadly.

She reached the crest and after a few minutes found what she instantly knew would be her favorite spot. The sight before her could only be described as magnificent. She took in the expansive view and nearly lost her breath to its beauty. The vista displayed a living breathing pageant of nature. Splashes of showy color dotted the hills—scarlet, ginger, orange, gold, amber, and green trees—creating a stunning tapestry woven with dazzling skill. She could almost smell the rich colors.

As she spread out her blanket, she wished she'd remembered one of her new books. She would just have to remember it next time. She carefully lowered herself down, instinctively already treating her body more gently than before she learned she was carrying a child. Leaning back on her palms, she closed her eyes for a moment and let the gentle breeze blow her hair back. The day was unusually warm and the sun's rays kissed her upturned face and neck.

Opening her heart, as well as her ears, she listened to the potpourri of sounds encircling her. She heard birds calling to one another, busy squirrels hiding their winter food stores, ducks flying south for the winter, leaves tumbling to the ground and finding their place, the muffled hum of the spring's water flowing down the hill, and…the wind.

The breeze rolled and curled, full of life, and then, finally, it whispered.

And she knew it conveyed a message meant for her. She listened intently, determined to grasp what it said. Her senses alive, her perceptions vivid, her heart beating stronger, she felt more aware of her surroundings than ever before. She listened intently, sat up straighter, and cocked her head to the side.

She didn't hear anything, but she sensed it—profoundly. A soul cleansing spirit, carried on the breeze, wrapped around her heart. She let out a slow breath as every trace of shame left her heart and love filled it.

Then she did hear, clearly and distinctly, Boone's words from her marriage ceremony. 'Listen to the wind—it talks. Listen to the silence—it understands. Listen to your heart—it knows.'

They were such extraordinarily beautiful words that she had made a point to commit them to memory. She would always remember them and cherish them forever.

And now, she released those sacred words into the world around her, giving them back to the home Boone had loved so much. Back to the hills, so that they might be whispered to others who needed love.

Then she listened again, her hand resting on her belly, and plainly heard her mother's voice whisper, "Bright is thy path sweet babe."

Her heart knew love as never before.

And the heart of her child knew love as well.

❧

William rode toward home. With every lengthy stride of his stallion, he left more and more cares about Boonesborough behind and his thoughts soon grew filled solely with Kelly. He hoped she'd spent the day resting, because he planned to keep her up half the night. The thought brought a smile to his face. He mused about some of their more erotic nights and decided on a couple of things he would try tonight to ensure this too would be a memorable evening.

She was so beautiful and he reacted so powerfully to her. She was his perfect match. Even her head fit perfectly in the hollow between his shoulder and neck. And her intoxicating body was beyond perfection and made him feel like a breathless boy of eighteen.

But it was her spirit that he found most enthralling. Strength, courage, and faith ran strong in her character. And only love guided her open heart. She was truthful and guileless. If she ever managed to deceive or hurt him, it would not be intentional.

She'd come so far since he first met her—from the traumatized victim of abuse and rape to a woman whose strength was admired by not only him, but now, also by so many of the townspeople. He wanted to do everything he could to help her feel good about herself and to make her glad to be with him. She was a priceless diamond he cherished and she seemed to sparkle more with every day that passed.

He quickly unsaddled Smoke and got his feed as well as Ginger's, and then raced toward the cabin anxious to hold Kelly in his arms. Even his long legs couldn't get him there fast enough to suit him.

Before he even opened the door, intoxicating aromas assailed him. Was that fresh bread he smelled?

"My Darling," Kelly cried as she opened the door. She ran onto the porch and hugged him, dressed in her nicest gown. She'd piled her long hair on top of her head in some sort of dazzling display of curls and ribbons. She smelled of lavender, roses, and fresh air. Something else was different that he couldn't quite put his finger on. Her lips appeared pinker than normal, her eyes sparkled, and her cheeks glowed.

"My love," he said. "You look spectacular. Let me look at you!" He clutched her fingers and whirled her around in a circle. "Positively ravishing." He had a feeling he would remember how she looked just now for a very long time.

"Thank you, Sir," she said and then looked past him. "William, look, it's snowing!"

He turned around and, with the bright rays of the setting sun spilling over their hills and through the trees, he saw a sky and forest full of what looked like tiny white stars. "My mother used to say the first snow signals a coming blessing."

"Your mother was a wise woman," she said.

A wonderful aroma drifted out onto the porch. "What are all these wonderful smells? Bread? You actually made bread."

"I did!" she proclaimed, taking him by the hand and leading him inside. "I used the cookbook you gave me." Then she excitedly rattled off the rest of the items she'd prepared for their dinner.

"Is this a special occasion I forgot about?"

"It is indeed a singular occasion. But you will have to wait to learn just how special."

He bent down to pat Riley and then just decided to pick him up. Carrying the dog around cradled in his arms, like the spoiled baby that he was, he surveyed all the luscious bowls of steaming food spread out on their table. "I can see I am in for a real feast," he said. "Don't worry Riley, I'll sneak you a couple of bites."

He stood in front of the hearth for a moment to warm up and then put Riley down, removed his tricorne, weapons, powder horn, and lead pouch. As he turned back to her, she was smiling from ear to ear. Her obvious animation made him wonder just want she was up to.

"Is all well in Boonesborough?" she asked.

"Yes, I caught a hog thief today and organized some volunteers to stand guard duty at the fort, since the militia has gone to Fort Logan." Not wanting to spoil the festive mood, he left unsaid his letter to Lexington's sheriff.

Her youthful liveliness faded anyway as concern filled her face. "Is there some reason the fort needs guards?"

"No, I just believe in being prepared. Colonel Boone asked me to care for our town and I mean to do so."

"I do hope Colonel Byrd and his men will return safely."

"Indeed," he said, taking a seat at the table. "I wish I had known we were having a special dinner, I would have tried to secure us another bottle of wine."

"I made some spiced tea for us. I thought you might want something warm after your chilly ride home," she said, pouring him some.

After she sat the pot on the table, he tugged her into his lap, and then took a sip of the brew. "Hmm, delicious," he said, and then kissed her deeply. "Hmm, even more delicious." He looked her over seductively, letting his eyes linger on the creamy mounds on her chest. "Do you think our dinner would suffer if we waited to eat?" he asked, breathing into her ear, and letting a fingertip explore her cleavage.

Quickly affected by his touch and obvious desire for her, she whispered, "Perhaps if I covered it the food would not suffer too greatly." She captured his mouth with her own and chewed on his lower lip. "I warn you, though, I am ravenously hungry."

"You're not talking about food, are you?"

"No, I'm not," she answered, her voice thick and breathy.

He slipped her gown off her shoulder and started to nibble there, lingering until he felt her chest begin to rise and her breathing quicken, then he lowered his lips as far as the dress would allow to the top of her breasts. "We need to get you out of this gown," he suggested between kisses. "It's impeding progress."

"Indeed," she said, and hastily covered the food.

When she finished, he kissed her again, then they reluctantly parted to dispense with their clothing in a feverish rush. Smiling at each other, they met again in the one place in the world where they could take time for tenderness and to give each other pleasure. To make their love sparkle with life.

William's large hands began a lust-arousing exploration of Kelly's flesh.

Holding her close, he was everywhere and every touch felt like a caress. Every kiss an embrace. Every cuddle a hug. Never had their love-making made her feel so worshiped. So valued.

Enfolded in the haven of his love, her spirit soared with

happiness taking her on a glorious ride—first gliding through soft rolling hills and vales of pleasure—and then surging skyward in a wild frenzied spree of ecstasy to the tops of mountains.

Kelly wanted him to soar with her and she drew him closer to her and caressed the length of his back. Then her hands roamed freely over his firm body and she delighted in the feel of his strong muscles beneath her fingertips. Snuggling up against him, she wrapped her legs around his. As always, she felt the intense heat of his body down the entire length of hers.

She reached under William's head, wove her fingers through his thick golden hair, and kissed him, letting all her love and fervor for him flow from her lips. The tender passion he returned filled her with a desire that heated every drop of her rushing blood.

Burying her face in his neck, she deposited an ardent kiss there, while he in turn kissed her cheek and hair. The caress of his soft lips set her aflame and passion pulsated through her head, her heart, and her entire body. Then a glorious soul-reaching kiss made her wonder if a heart could burst with love. For surely hers was in danger.

She wanted to say she loved him. But the words seemed inadequate. Too little and too few to express the profound depth of what she felt now for William. Her mind searched for another way to tell him. But everything she could think of seemed insufficient and imperfect.

Then, as his hand reached down below her belly, she remembered their child. What better way to show her love. The thought elated her.

Her heart raced, passion and excitement both making her dizzy and breathless. Sparked first in her heart, then smoldering through her breasts, the blaze within her own body quickly spread out of control, like a raging wildfire that couldn't be stopped. It burned wildly, fed by her roaring desire, until a series of white-hot flashes began to explode within her, each one more powerful than the last. The final blinding flash consumed her, leaving her breathless and stunned.

❧

As they ate their dinner companionably in their nightclothes, the room lit by the bright gleam of the hearth fire and the table by the soft glow of candles, William decided he could never be happier than this. He kept smiling at her, knowing he must seem like a love-sick schoolboy, but he couldn't help it.

He also couldn't help worrying about her. He decided it was time to broach the topic. "Kelly, I've been thinking."

"Oh dear," she teased. "I don't know if I can do that again so soon."

"As delightful as that sounds, that's not what I was about to suggest."

"What is it then?"

"I'm concerned about leaving you out here all alone every day. We averted this last danger, and you were extraordinarily brave, but it could have ended far differently." He wouldn't say exactly how bad it could have been.

"William, I refuse to live in town. I hate big cities. You know that. I need the peace and solitude of the forest and hills." She threw a few more small pieces of wood on the fire and sparks fluttered off the glowing coals.

"I know how you feel about that and also know how much you love it here."

"I do, it's so incredibly picturesque. The hills are stunningly beautiful. No wonder Boone chose to settle here. And I've discovered this wonderful place at the top of the ridge. The view from there is remarkable. I went up there this afternoon and I actually heard the wind whisper."

"What did it say?"

"That you love me."

"I do Kelly. That's why I want so desperately to keep you safe. Here's my idea. Why don't we ask your father to move here as soon as he finishes helping Sam out? He and I could build a small cabin next door and he can have his own place so we can keep some privacy here."

"William, that's a marvelous idea! It would make me so happy to have him close, now that he's changed so much. I can keep an eye on him to be sure he stays strong and doesn't backslide into drinking again. And he can lend a hand around the place while you're in town every day. He would be a big help. And when he grows older, I'll be able to help him. Just as a family should. That would mean a lot to me. And to him. Oh, thank you William, thank you." She stood on her tiptoes and kissed him.

"I would do anything to make you happy and keep you safe. I love you so much my love," he said.

"I could tell that quite well earlier," she teased with a half-smile.

"It was a spectacular experience. Do you suppose we could have conceived a child? It was truly that special." They had never discussed parenthood but the possibility thrilled him.

"No," she said simply.

"No?"

"No," she repeated, her face a mysterious mask.

He couldn't understand. "Do you have some womanly problem you've never told me about?"

"No, she said again, this time with a coy look on her face.

Then her lovely eyes started to shine with moisture and her almost lustrous face blushed.

Did she not want children? "Then why?"

"Because you cannot conceive when you are already with child."

He stood and nearly knocked the table over. Dishes clattered and one of the candles tipped over. He quickly reached for it, setting it aright. His suddenly buoyant heart felt like it had jumped out of his chest. He threw his napkin down, the rest of his dinner forgotten.

Breathless, he gawked at her, letting her news sink in. For a moment or two, they just stared at each other, too overcome with emotions to do anything else. Her eyes sparkled like the sun bouncing off glassy blue water. She held her hands together, as if praying, waiting for him to respond. When he was finally able to breathe, a smile broke across his face.

Intense satisfaction shone through her eyes and her grin broadened.

Joy bubbled out of him into a laugh and then he hollered with pleasure, feeling the glory of the moment. He'd been wrong earlier. It was possible for him to be happier than he'd been just moments ago. In fact, he was so overjoyed he felt like singing, humming, whistling, playing his fiddle, all at once. Or skipping, leaping, running, shouting, bouncing on his toes—anything to express his overwhelming pleasure.

He picked Riley up by his paws and danced with the young dog, who barked joyfully.

Kelly sat back in her chair and watched with smug delight, laughing.

He tried to find his voice, to invite her to dance with them, but couldn't. Deciding a hug was more in order anyway, he held his arms out wide, and went to her. He wrapped his arms around her in an embrace so heartfelt that it heated the clothing between them.

Feeling exhilarated and light-hearted, he lifted her straight up, and twirled her in a circle.

She looked down at him with a brilliant smile.

He finally found his voice as he sat her feet on the floor. "I'm going to be a Papa!"

"He'll be calling you Papa Sheriff."

"He'll? Maybe she'll be calling me Papa Sheriff," he said, elated by either possibility, and hearing his voice crack a little.

Joyful tears filled his eyes as he held his wife and child tightly against his heart.

Life is a beautiful thing.

About the Author

Like her compelling heroes, who from the outset make it clear they will not fail despite the adversities they face, this author is likewise destined for success. Called a "deft new writer of intelligent romantic fiction," award-winning historical romance author Dorothy Wiley enjoys writing big, action-packed romantic adventures set in the American wilderness when it was still a frontier. In her exciting American Wilderness Series Romances, Wiley breaches the walls of time, bringing readers to a young America, where romance and danger are as powerful as the wilderness.

Readers describe Wiley's writing as fresh, unblinkingly gritty, and highly enjoyable with well-portrayed characters. In 2014, her first romance novel, WILDERNESS TRAIL OF LOVE, was a Central Florida Romance Writers of America Touch of Magic Finalist and her second book, NEW FRONTIER OF LOVE, was selected as an Amazon Breakthrough Novel Award Quarterfinalist. WHISPERING HILLS OF LOVE is a finalist in the 2015 BookBzz's Prize Writer Competition.

Wiley received a Bachelor of Journalism degree, with Honors, from The University of Texas. After a distinguished 35-year corporate career in marketing and public relations, she is living her dream—writing historical romances.

She would enjoy connecting with you:

Website: http://www.dorothywiley.com

Facebook: https://www.facebook.com/DoraMayWiley

Twitter: https://twitter.com/WileyDorothy

LinkedIn: https://www.linkedin.com Dorothy M. Wiley

Goodreads: https://www.goodreads.com Dorothy Wiley

Pinterest: http://www.pinterest.com/dorothymwiley

We hope you enjoyed reading
Book Three
of the American Wilderness Series Romances
WHISPERING HILLS OF LOVE

Other Titles by Dorothy Wiley
Book One
WILDERNESS TRAIL OF LOVE
The story of Stephen and Jane
Book Two
NEW FRONTIER OF LOVE
The story of Sam and Catherine
Coming soon…
Book Four
The story of Bear and ? We will just have to see what happens.

Please tell your friends…

Thank you for reading my novel. If you enjoyed reading this book, I would be honored if you would share your thoughts with your friends. Regardless of whether you are reading print or electronic versions, if you particularly liked the experience of reading William and Kelly's story, I'd be extremely grateful if you posted a review on http://www.Amazon.com. Just enter WHISPERING HILLS OF LOVE in Amazon's search box and it will take you to the correct page. Then just scroll down on the page where you can write a customer review.

Please visit www.dorothywiley.com for the release date for the fourth book in the series. Thanks for your support.

All the best,

Dorothy

ACKNOWLEDGMENTS

As I did in the first two books of the series, I would like to thank the daring and brave first-wave pioneers of early America. Their hard fought struggles for a place in the vast wilderness gave us the majestic country we enjoy today. Their stories must be remembered. Although this is a completely fictionalized and romanticized story, it still reflects some of the many challenges our ancestors faced. My husband's brave ancestors, who actually did travel through the frontier and eventually became some of Texas' earliest settlers, inspired this series of novels. There are many stories I would like to write about those amazing journeys and their life on America's frontier.

Secondly, I would like to thank my husband (also my muse) and my wonderful sister for their help in polishing this manuscript. Thanks for your continued faith in me. And my thanks to my fellow author and friend Deborah Gafford, a wonderful writer, for her suggestions and support.

Third, my thanks to my cover designer Erin Dameron-Hill whose creative talent transformed my vision for the books' covers into a beautiful reality.